Fool's Paradise

Fool's Paradise

Steve Brewer

University of New Mexico Press
Albuquerque

LIBRARY OF CONGRESS CATALOGING-IN-PUBLICATION DATA

Brewer, Steve.
Fool's paradise / Steve Brewer.—1st ed.
p. cm.
ISBN 0-8263-3124-6 (alk. paper)
1. Coronado (Calif.)—Fiction.
2. Bank robberies—Fiction. I. Title.
PS3552.R42135 F66 2003
813'.54—dc21
2003005842

Jacket deisgn: Melissa Tandysh
Book design and typography: Kathleen Sparkes
This book was set in Sabon 10.5/14
Display type is Industria and Khaki

As always, for Kelly

John Ray Mooney was dressed all wrong for a bank robber. He could see that now, as clearly as he could see the drop of sweat that tadpoled down the lens of his sunglasses. The sweat slipped off the lens and dropped onto the deposit slip where he'd been writing: "Give me all the money. I have a gu—"

Damn. The bank pen, chained to the counter as if anybody'd want to steal the cheap piece of shit, skipped across the damp spot, refusing to mix its ink with John Ray's sweat.

He looked up to see if anyone watched. The bank guard, a stout black man with a white cookie-duster mustache, glanced away.

John Ray crumpled the deposit slip and stuffed it in the pouch of his hooded sweatshirt. He took a fresh blank from the stack on the counter and, with his tongue massaging the corner of his mouth, began to compose his holdup note again.

John Ray suffered a bad case of nerves. He was no bank robber. A thief, sure, but his idea of criminal enterprise was boosting an unattended luxury car, or maybe a little harmless breaking-and-entering, quietly lifting stuff from the wealthy and well-insured. Bank robbery is different. You're the star of the show, trying to take money right out from under the noses of those enlisted to protect their assets: the uniformed guard, the smug tellers in their J. C. Penney suits, all those surveillance cameras staring down with unblinking eyes.

Small wonder the sweat streamed down John Ray's forehead, that it tickled his ribs with damp baby fingers. Georgie Zook had cautioned him it would be this way if John Ray ever tried to knock over a bank.

"It's flop sweat, like, whatchacallit, stage fright," Georgie said during one of their endless conversations at Folsom. "You think you're the big man, the boss. The suckers at the bank, they don't know what's coming. But suddenly, you're sweating and twitching and you feel like you're gonna shit out everything you've eaten in the past month. Everybody goes through it the first time. It gets easier."

A sweatsuit had seemed the perfect cover-up for a bank robbery. Easy on, easy off. Anonymous and shapeless. Cheap enough to discard once the deed was done and the cops combed Coronado.

He'd planned it so well. John Ray had checked into the Hotel Del Coronado on Sunday, two days earlier, paying cash. Each morning since, he'd gone jogging, making sure the bellmen and pool boys and maids got a good look at him stretching and running in place. Just another health nut, devoted to his morning run even while on vacation.

Hotel employees could vouch that the guest registered as Rob Petrie jogged north up the beach, his thick-soled sneakers throwing up little rooster-tails of sand. Each day, he wore clothes like a real runner—electric-blue nylon shorts and a tank top and a black fanny pack cinched tight around his trim waist. No sweatsuit in sight.

Today, out of sight of the hotel, he cut through expensive neighborhoods and green parks, finally swinging down a narrow alley to where he'd stashed the sweatsuit and the San Diego Padres cap and the .22-caliber pistol he'd use in the robbery. He'd hidden the stuff two blocks from the bank, in a concrete box with a rusty steel lid, some entry to the town's sewer system. John Ray had discovered the knee-high box his first day in Coronado, had noticed the lid sprouted a steel loop for a lock to keep kids out. He'd put a shiny new lock of his own on the box. The key stayed in the fanny pack, ready for the day when John Ray robbed the National Bank of Coronado.

Once he had the money, he planned to run out of the bank, turn the corner and cover the two blocks in a hurry. He'd strip off the sweatsuit and stash it and the gun and (hopefully) a sack full of cash in the sewer box. He'd lock it up, jog back to the fancy hotel and be having brunch poolside before the cops knew what happened.

Locals call Coronado "the island," but it's really a peninsula, a large fist on a skinny arm, separated from the rest of the metropolitan area by the boat-dotted waters of San Diego Bay. The only connections to the mainland are a high, curving bridge that spills into downtown San Diego and, farther south, a seven-mile-long spit of sand called the Silver Strand. The cops could block the bridge and the Strand highway after a bank robbery, checking every car, looking for someone in a gray sweatsuit. But they wouldn't find John Ray. He'd hole up at the Hotel Del until the search cooled, then he'd gather up his cash and mosey back to Los Angeles to pay his debt and the interest that had accumulated during his three years and five months in Folsom.

It was a good plan, solid. Georgie Zook would approve. No easy-to-identify car. No partners to rat you out later. No accurate descriptions of the robber: Just a tall man in big black sunglasses and a soggy sweatsuit.

Jesus, the sweat. John Ray pushed up the bill of his sopping Padres cap and wiped his hand across his forehead. He couldn't stand here much longer, sweating like a sinner in church, without the guard taking notice. He needed to strike fast and get the hell out of here before the glowering guard approached to see what the trouble was, see why Mr. Perspiration couldn't seem to fill out a deposit slip.

He continued writing, in big block letters: "Give me all the money. I have a gu—"

Someone brushed past him, a little too close, making him flinch. A little guy in a slouchy black suit, moving his short legs so fast he went past in a blur, leaving a cloud of hair spray and Giorgio in his wake. The squat man ignored the empty maze of red velvet ropes and went directly to the first teller window, which was manned by a horn-rimmed teller who resembled a young Woody Allen.

The customer pushed something across the counter and told the teller, in a lilting voice that filled the small bank, "I would like a cash advance of five thousand dollars, please."

Woody blanched, picked up the little guy's Platinum Card, studied it. "I'll need to get the manager's approval."

The customer tilted his head back and fired a sigh toward the ceiling. "Be quick about it, will you?"

Woody gulped and nodded and hurried away.

The customer rested his elbows on the counter, which was chest-high to him, and drummed his fingers on the marble countertop. He was young, maybe twenty-five, with an Asian cast to his features and skin the color of cashews. His thick black hair was combed straight back and lacquered lightly into place. His nose belonged on some other face, maybe on a Mayan or a Plains Indian. It angled out from between his groomed eyebrows, peaked between his eyes and then went straight down, ending in a point sharp enough to slice bread. Full lips worked against each other, as if he were ready to chew them off in impatience.

He wore a white T-shirt under the expensive suit and flat loafers woven of strips of black leather. No socks. Guys with money dressed that way, still going for that *Miami Vice* look years after Sonny Crockett had vanished from the tube. The theme music from *Miami Vice* began to play inside John Ray's head. One more distraction.

A tall, bald man with unfortunate sideburns appeared in the teller window, trailed by the worried Woody.

"Good morning, sir. I'm Gary Warren, the bank manager. How may I be of service?"

"As I told your lackey there, I want an advance of five thousand dollars on that card. I need it quickly. I'm double-parked outside."

"Yes sir. We'll need to see some identification for such a large advance, of course. I'm sure you understand—"

"Did you read the name on the card?"

"Yes sir, but we—"

"What does the card say?"

The manager looked confused, unaccustomed to brusqueness. This was a neighborhood bank in a friendly resort town. The customers were mostly local folks he could call by name or lard-ass tourists used to standing in line. He blinked rapidly, then held up the card to decipher the words.

"Prince Seri Hassan Banda—"

The name clearly gave Gary Warren problems. The customer helped him along.

"Prince Seri Hassan Bandapanang bin Mohammed."

"Yes sir."

"Do you know what a prince is?"

"Well, sure, but I—"

"Do you know who my father is?"

"No sir. But you see—"

"The Sultan of Yip. Does that mean something to you?"

Yip. That registered with John Ray. The Sultan of Yip was mentioned regularly in the magazines and newspapers he'd devoured in Folsom. Yip was a tiny island, somewhere off Southeast Asia. A few years earlier, oil had been discovered off shore, huge deposits of oil the Sultan was exploiting faster than J. R. Ewing. The Sultan of Yip was well on his way to replacing his nearest neighbor, the Sultan of Brunei, as the richest man in the world.

"Yes sir." The manager snapped to attention, practically clicking his heels in recognition of the fortune that stood before him. "Sorry I didn't recognize the name—"

"Quite all right, my good man. Just get my money and let me go about my business."

"Yes sir. I mean, Your Highness. Is that what they call you in Yip?"

The prince smiled, seeing it was all going his way now.

"My friends call me Bennie."

The manager flashed a nervous grin. He fumbled with Woody's cash drawer, then counted out hundred-dollar bills with the quick flourish of experience.

"There you are, Your Highness. I apologize for the delay."

The prince rolled the bills into a wad and stuffed them into his pocket as carelessly as he would a handkerchief.

"No problem. Good day."

The prince strolled out of the bank without a glance toward John Ray.

Five thousand dollars. Five thousand dollars would be a good start toward paying off the debt John Ray owed in L.A.

Georgie Zook flashed through his mind, the toothless con leaning back on his bunk, his hands behind his head, reeling off crime statistics. The average bank robbery nets only seven thousand dollars, Georgie had said. Most robbers only hit the teller drawers, never get at the bigger money that's kept in the vault. Quite a risk for seven thousand dollars, but an easy living if you know what you're doing.

Robbing the prince would be even easier. No cameras, no armed guards. Just a quick flash of the gun, grab the money and run. Like the old days, when John Ray was a teen-aged hoodlum, snatching purses to cover his rent.

He stuffed the deposit slip into his pocket and hurried out the door, chasing after the Prince of Yip.

2

The sight of the prince's sporty wheels made John Ray catch his breath: a red Mercedes-Benz 300SL convertible, the top down, the leather bucket seats gleaming like buttered rolls. John Ray covered the wide sidewalk in three long strides and flung open the passenger door just as the prince cranked the ignition.

"What the—"

John Ray fell into the passenger seat and slammed the door.

"Get out of my car."

"Hey, fuck you, Your Highness."

John Ray showed the prince the little pistol, keeping it low in case anyone watched.

"Drive."

"I'm not going anywhere. Get out." The foreign lilt had vanished from the prince's voice. "Get the fuck out."

A scowl crawled onto John Ray's face. He whipped off the black sunglasses to show the prince his narrow, colorless eyes, the practiced prison-yard glare that had kept the muscle boys and the Black Power types at bay for three years and five months.

The silent menace worked on the prince. His eyes widened, his tan faded a shade or two. Up close, the prince didn't look so smooth. Whiskers dotted his jawbone where he'd missed a stripe while shaving. Bleary eyes and slack skin marked the prince as someone suffering a hangover. John Ray recognized the signs, having seen them all too often in the mirror.

The prince ventured a glance up the street, but the sidewalks were empty. The tourists were still indoors, nursing hangovers or wolfing all-you-can-eat breakfasts. He was alone with a rawboned man nearly twice his size, alone to face a gun that, while tiny, could puncture holes in important places.

"Where to?"

"Straight ahead will be fine."

The prince shoved the car into gear, and it purred away from the bank.

"You'll never get away with this. My father—"

"Yeah, yeah. Your father's a big fuckin' deal. But I'm the one with the gun. Shut up and drive."

Six blocks later, the street divided at a round park, a circle of blank green grass with a single flagpole in the center. Saltbox houses in bright pastels nudged up to the street that ringed the park.

"Go right," John Ray said. "*After* you stop for the sign."

John Ray's nerve endings tingled. He could smell success. The sweat had vanished, either dried by the breeze in the convertible or evaporated by the adrenaline that rushed through him.

They covered three more blocks before he told the prince to pull over to the curb.

"Shut off the engine."

Quiet as the Mercedes had been, the silence that followed seemed abrupt and complete. Listening hard, John Ray could hear the whoosh of traffic back on Orange Avenue, or was it the surf a few blocks the other direction? The houses could be vacant for all anyone could tell. Nobody outside enjoying the morning sunshine. Nobody walking their dogs along the sidewalks. It was perfect.

The prince stared straight ahead, both hands on the steering wheel, waiting.

"You're doing fine," John Ray said. "All I want is your wallet and that bankroll in your pocket. Then I'll get out of your car and you can go enjoy your vacation."

The prince nodded and dropped one hand off the steering wheel to reach for his pocket. John Ray jabbed him in the ribs with the little pistol.

"Not yet. I'll tell you when. Make a wrong move, and I'll put a bullet through your fuckin' spleen. Are we clear?"

Again, the silent nod. John Ray looked around once more.

"Okay, now. Slow and easy."

The prince levered the wad of hundred-dollar bills out of his pocket and handed it over.

"Good. Now your wallet."

The prince stiffened slightly. "I don't carry a wallet."

John Ray jabbed him in the ribs again, harder this time.

"Is that your final answer?"

A muscle twitched in the prince's jaw while he thought it over. He sighed, and pulled a fat wallet from his hip pocket. The wallet was pieced together from shiny strips of leather, smooth and lightweight.

"Nice," John Ray said as he weighed the wallet in his hand. "Eelskin?"

The prince didn't reply. Just stared straight ahead like he was waiting for traffic.

John Ray stuffed the bankroll and the wallet into his pouch. Keeping the gun pointed at the prince, he popped open the door and climbed out of the car. He held the pistol by his thigh, practically invisible there if anyone watched from the houses.

"I want you to drive away like nothing happened." he said. "I don't care where the fuck you go. Report it to the cops if you want. But I better never see you again, or you're a dead man. You got that?"

"Got it."

"Good. Now drive."

The prince started the fine car and shifted it into gear.

"Oh, and Your Highness?" The prince finally shot John Ray a look. "Have a nice day."

Tires squealed as the prince hit the gas. John Ray waited until the Mercedes took a right turn, then he slipped the loot and his pistol into his fanny pack and hurried away, humming under his breath. The theme to *Rawhide*.

3

Twenty minutes later, John Ray used a cardkey to open the door to his room at the Hotel Del. He'd stashed the accursed sweatsuit and his Padres cap in the alley and made it back to the hotel right on schedule.

He hung the "Do Not Disturb" sign on the outside doorknob and locked the deadbolt. He didn't need a maid wandering in while he counted the prince's money.

John Ray lit a Marlboro, felt it tight between his lips. He couldn't stop grinning. He'd pulled off the robbery without a hitch. Told the prince, "I'll put a bullet through your fuckin' spleen." He wondered which tough-guy actor had spouted that line. All the TV dialogue he'd consumed over the years loitered somewhere in his brain. John Ray felt sometimes that he'd never said or thought anything original in his life. The threat had worked on the prince, though. Now John Ray was back in his well-appointed room with its antique furnishings and its lazy ceiling fan. The last place anybody would look for a robber.

He'd made at least five grand without knocking over the bank and getting the FBI sniffing after his trail. The prince probably wouldn't even report the crime. The money wasn't that much of a loss, not to a guy whose old man was worth billions.

To John Ray, on the other hand, the fistful of big-headed Ben Franklins could mean the difference between life and death.

He dropped the bankroll on the bed without bothering to thumb through it. He knew how much was there; he'd seen the bank manager count it out. The wallet was a different story. He opened it slowly, savoring the moment, better than Christmas.

The wallet was stuffed full of lovely greenbacks with their staring presidents. He carefully arranged them on the bed by denomination. Three thousand in hundreds, another six hundred in fifties and twenties and a handful of smaller bills. With the bankroll, nearly nine grand. The prince clearly was a man accustomed to carrying a lot of folding money. And now it all belonged to John Ray Mooney.

But not for long. He'd soon hand over most of it to Big Odie, as payment toward the debt he left behind when he was swallowed up by the California penal system. It wouldn't cover the whole debt, but it might buy John Ray some time, give him a little breathing room before Big Odie tried to make him stop breathing altogether.

That John Ray had done business with someone as vile as Big Odie showed just how screwed up he'd been before he was busted and sent off to Folsom. Anyone in his right mind would avoid Big Odie and his biker gang, the Sons of Satan. But John Ray hadn't been in his right mind. He'd been in love.

Hell, he might never have been totally sane. Insanity ran in his family, and he'd spent his childhood in Needles, California, the Back Door to Hell, where the desert sun baked away any sense you might've had at the start.

His mother, LaWanda, was a local character well-known to all, a hugely fat woman with greasy gray hair. She always felt cold, even when the temperature outside was well over what TV weathermen liked to call "the century mark." LaWanda prowled the streets of Needles wearing wool sweaters and heavy socks, even gloves, in a place where a swimsuit felt hot and oppressive. As if LaWanda hadn't been enough of an embarrassment, John Ray's father, Floyd, operated the Come to Jesus Dairy Barn, a drive-up ice cream stand decorated on all sides with excerpts from the Scriptures.

Floyd Mooney had wanted his only son to take over the family business, to continue the Lord's work in the Hell-on-Earth that was Needles. But John Ray focused only on escape from the time he was a boy, sitting too close to the fuzzy family TV, watching the Flintstones and munching Cocoa Puffs.

He'd waited impatiently, measuring his growth, until his legs were long enough to reach the gas pedal of a faded pink Cadillac that Floyd kept locked away in a garage behind their ramshackle home. When the day finally came, John Ray was fourteen years old and headed for Los Angeles, weaving down the road in the huge car, his pockets full of saved-up allowance and money filched from the collection plate.

La-La-Land couldn't compare to the insanity in Needles, but it was crazy enough. Street people wandering around muttering to themselves. Hookers coming on to the oversized kid from the desert. People who seemed to spend their whole lives on roller skates. And all of them trying to break into show business.

He'd chosen L.A. as his destination because he'd seen so much of it on TV. People living glamorous lives in their Beverly Hills mansions. Swimming pools. Movie stars. The reality was altogether different, especially for a kid with no skills trying to scrape by. The celebrities lived behind the safety of high walls and hulking doormen. The streets belong to the poor, the criminal, the crazy.

After his savings ran out, John Ray sold the Caddie to a street thug named Whitey Moran. It wasn't long before he was hungry and homeless, picking through garbage cans behind restaurants just to survive. Stealing went against everything Floyd Mooney had ever taught him, but hunger's the most urgent commandment of all, and John Ray soon found himself shoplifting snacks in grocery stores and snatching purses for cash.

Whitey Moran could always use more hot cars for his chop shop, so John Ray took to prowling the streets, peering in car windows for dangling keys. Boosting cars was easy and lucrative, and it beat the hell out a day job.

It wasn't long before he was caught and sent away for two years to a youth detention home. A tough, watchful kid like John Ray could pick up a lot of the ins and outs of crime at the detention home. He'd come out a different person, more focused, determined to break as many commandments as it took to live the good life.

He resumed business with Whitey Moran, boosting enough cars to rent an apartment and keep himself in food. Then he pulled a couple of easy burglaries to help him furnish the place with a TV, a stereo, a phone, some new clothes. He'd settled comfortably into a life of crime, living under fake identities, names he lifted from old TV shows.

John Ray got a wake-up call several months later when Whitey Moran was found with a fire ax protruding from his bald head. Seemed Whitey had crossed the wrong people, maybe chopped up some made guy's car for parts. Whitey wouldn't be making any such mistakes again, but John Ray learned from his example. He decided to pursue the straight life, find a real job, settle down. Crime became a sideline, not his main career.

Over the next decade, John Ray worked as a dishwasher, a house painter, a used car salesman, a bowling alley attendant, a motel clerk, and a bartender, never sticking with one job very long. Some asswipe boss would make him mad, or he'd get bored and decide to move on. Between jobs, or to supplement his straight income, he'd boost a few cars or maybe hire on with a crew hijacking truckloads of cigarettes or microwave ovens. Mostly, though, John Ray lived a settled life, centered on Budweiser and television, workdays and solitude.

Then Angel Flesch moved into John Ray's apartment building. Angel worked as an exotic dancer at the Pulchritude Gentlemen's Club in Van Nuys. John Ray knew when he saw her unloading her U-Haul that she was exactly what he'd been looking for all these years.

He'd volunteered his muscle to help her move in, and it wasn't long before they were sharing an apartment. Looking back on it, John Ray knew Angel's dreamy body had stirred some sort of insanity within him. He'd never been in love before, and he walked around giddy and grinning stupidly at what he'd been missing all these years.

Angel made it clear from the beginning that she was in search of the high life, much as John Ray had been when he first came to L.A. She wanted to lunch at the Brown Derby and have dinner at the Ivy and dance the night away at dark, nameless clubs where flavor-of-the-month acting brats held court. Most of all, she wanted the centerfold in *Playboy*. She regularly sent nude photos to Hugh Hefner, trying to get his attention and lever her way into his magazine's slick pages. No *Penthouse* or *Hustler* for her. She would crack the big time.

Every rejection or fruitless casting call sent Angel on a voracious spending spree. If she couldn't *be* exactly who she wanted, she at least could *have* what she wanted. John Ray could pay for these luxuries as easily as the next guy.

Keeping Angel's interest was a full-time job, and when his meager savings were depleted, John Ray went back to his old stand-by: boosting cars.

Big Odie and his biker gang, the Sons of Satan, were branching out around that time. They'd made and spent small fortunes dealing methamphetamine to Hollywood types who thrilled at the danger of doing business with leathery, bearded bikers. But Big Odie had decided it was time to step up in class, and the Sons of Satan had gone into the auto recovery business. You felt a loss in your life because you needed a particular car, and Big Odie would have it *recovered* from someone's garage and delivered to you for a reasonable price. No dickering allowed.

Stealing Porsches and Mercedes was more challenging than boosting random cars, but John Ray soon found it to his liking. Hanging out with Angel had given him ideas, had shown him the cool nightclubs and trendy diners that formed the stars' celestial world. It was amazing how many otherwise intelligent people would drunkenly hand over their keys to the first person who looked like a parking valet.

It had to end, of course. John Ray could've seen it coming if he hadn't been so gaga over waking up next to Angel every day.

He boosted a black Porsche Targa from outside the Viper Club, and was making good time, headed for Big Odie's garage, when the flashing blue lights bounced in his mirrors. Seemed the car belonged to Dirk Brande, who played a surgeon on an Emmy-winning TV drama and who was, as the cops knew in a town where even the busboys read *Variety*, a hot property because he was starring in the next Spielberg movie. The All-Points Bulletin had gone out with Hollywood attached, and John Ray never had a chance.

He thought it was a storm he could weather, at least during the first few minutes of the bust, when the cops were patting him down and nonchalantly slamming his head into the fender. But when the cops found a pistol and a bag of cocaine in the glove compartment, John Ray knew his heavenly life with Angel was over. No way Dirk Brande was going to step forward and lay claim to drugs and a gun. As far as the cops were concerned, the goods belonged to John Ray.

He hired a hotshot attorney and contested the charges through one court appearance after another, staying out on bail so he could keep Angel from becoming a regular fixture at the Playboy Mansion. The courtroom battle was expensive, and John Ray couldn't take the chance of stealing any revenue while the charges were pending. By the time he finally went to trial, he'd gone deeply in debt and found himself borrowing from Big Odie the final five grand the attorney demanded.

The lawyer, Dana Hastings, wore an expensive toupee and had tiny, pointed teeth that always made John Ray think of steak knives. He guaranteed he could quash the coke and firearm charges, though John Ray might have to do a short stint in the slammer for car theft, which seemed only fair since he'd been caught red-handed.

Angel showed up for all three days of the trial, sitting in the front row in her revealing clothes, keeping the elderly judge distracted. On the trial's second day, John Ray noticed that Angel took to sitting in the chair behind Hastings rather than closer to the defendant, who could've used some support, thank you very much. By the time the judge whacked his gavel down on a five-year sentence, Angel was as firmly attached to Hastings as a lamprey eel.

The last time John Ray saw her, she'd been giving Hastings a consolatory pat on the cheek as the deputies hauled his client away. John Ray was so discouraged by then, he couldn't even hate her. All he could think was this: That's no way to pet a lawyer. That's the end where the teeth are.

His past record meant John Ray skipped the penal system's minimum-security country clubs and went straight to Folsom. Which probably was just as well. If he'd had an opportunity to escape, he might've headed for Mullholland Drive to send Dana Hastings to meet the real angels. Instead, he got three years and five months to get his head back together before the parole board set him free.

He'd barely settled into the cheap Torrance residential motel selected by his parole officer before the Sons of Satan grabbed him off the street, threw him in the back of a van and roared off to see Big Odie.

To Big Odie's credit, he hadn't let the boys slap John Ray around too much. A man can't raise money if he has broken bones or a face so battered that he scares people. Big Odie just let them soften John Ray up, get his attention after they took him to Hell House, the rambling stucco ruin in the desert east of L.A. that served as the gang's headquarters. When they were done stomping John Ray, they yanked him into a kneeling position and poured a bucket of water over his head to make sure he was awake.

Big Odie was a whiskered Jabba of a man, his rolls of fat oozing oil. He wore dusty biker leathers that might've fit properly a hundred pounds ago. Somebody had hit him with a machete years before, leaving a deep scar that puckered his eyebrow and dented his cheekbone. The ruined eye was sightless and white. It was painful to look at Big Odie.

While John Ray waited, Big Odie poured Schlitz down his gullet like a man dying of thirst. In his other hand, he held a king-size bag of Krunchskins pork rinds, the top open so he could chuck them directly into his mouth without using his filthy fingers. Big Odie munched and swallowed and belched and farted, all the while studying John Ray.

"You don't look none the worse for wear," he finally said. "Folsom might've done you some good."

John Ray said nothing. For one thing, he didn't know what might set off Big Odie. For another, he still had trouble breathing from the beating.

"I been hearing things about you," Big Odie said. "Heard you handled yourself all right in the cooler. Didn't become nobody's fuck towel. That's good. I'd hate to see an old friend come outta the joint with an asshole like a railroad tunnel."

The Sons of Satan, who'd melted into the shadows of the room, chuckled appreciatively.

"You remember that you owed me some money when you went to Folsom?"

John Ray nodded, his dripping head hanging in misery.

"Believe it was five thousand we fronted you. Now, of course, we collect interest on our debts. So let's call it an even twenty grand now."

That snapped John Ray's head up. Twenty thousand dollars? Where the hell would he come up with money like that? No straight job paid that well, especially jobs available to a high school dropout with a felony record.

"I know you just got out of the cooler and you probably got nothing in your pockets but lint. And I'm a reasonable man. I know you'll need some time to raise the money. But I'll get every dime, or we won't be friends no more."

"How much time?" John Ray croaked.

Big Odie crumpled the pork rind bag and tossed it backward over his shoulder, where it landed in a midden of pizza boxes and cigar butts and shattered beer bottles.

"Let's say a week. That sound fair to you boys?"

Murmurs of assent rumbled from the bikers strewn around the dusty room.

It didn't sound the least bit fair to John Ray, whose dream of starting over was evaporating like piss in a campfire. But he nodded. He'd think of something, even if it meant running to Mexico until he raised the money. Anywhere but Needles would be fine.

Over the next few days, John Ray tried to collect a few debts of his own, but the losers he tracked down were either dead or broke or just flat-ass disappeared. For all his running around L.A., looking up old contacts, he'd gathered only a little over seven hundred dollars, enough for a grub stake for him, but not nearly enough to appease Big Odie.

Then he'd gotten the idea of robbing a bank.

Okay, so he'd never knocked over a bank before, but Lord knows he'd listened to so many of Georgie Zook's lies and strategies and statistics that he could've earned college credit in Bank Robbery 101.

At one time, Georgie had been the best bank man in the business. But some idiot security guard in Bakersfield tried to play hero, and Georgie wouldn't be seeing the outside world anymore. He shared his knowledge with anyone who'd listen, vicariously thrilled at the robberies they might someday commit. Once a man got to thinking about robbing a bank, the act was only a desperate twitch away.

Big Odie had pressed the issue. The more John Ray thought about it, the more a bank robbery seemed his only way out. He didn't want to rob a bank in L.A., where he was more likely to be recognized. And he couldn't afford to go far. Then he remembered driving through Coronado with Angel Flesch a year before he got sent off to Folsom. He remembered thinking how the town's main street looked like the set of *American Graffiti*, as if it had been lifted intact from the early 1960s. He remembered the stately old hotel, the palm trees, the beaches. The last place anyone would expect a heist, and the perfect place to hide from Big Odie. The plan clicked into place in his mind, and the next day he was on a Greyhound, headed south.

Now John Ray stared at the prince's money stacked on the bright bedspread, separating with his eyes the eight thousand he'd give Big Odie, the smaller bills he'd keep for himself. Eight grand wasn't enough to satisfy Odie, maybe not even enough to buy more time. John Ray sighed. He might be robbing that bank yet.

He slumped onto a corner of the bed and lay back, the prince's wallet still in his hands. His thumb riffled the gold and platinum credit cards listlessly. He'd never tried to pass plastic. Stores were too careful now, with all those fancy computers. He knew there were people who bought hot cards for the numbers and used computers to make purchases all over the world before the cardholder made his emergency lost-card calls. But the only guy he'd ever met in that line of work was still in Folsom.

He pulled one of the cards from its leather slot, studied the prince's absurdly long name, then tossed it aside. He pulled out others and flicked them around the bedspread. The prince's California driver's license had "DIPLOMAT" stamped across the top of it. The prince looked hung over in the photo. Behind the driver's license was another, older license. John Ray started to toss it aside, but froze when the name registered. "Ho,

Guillermo." Not Prince Seri Hassan Rama-lama-ding-dong, but "Ho." What the hell kinda name was that? Guillermo Ho.

John Ray sat up and went through the wallet more thoroughly. Tucked away in an inside pocket was a whole set of IDs for this Ho: Social Security, couple of bank cards, membership card for some fancy spa in Rancho Santa Fe.

Why would a rich prince have fake IDs? Maybe he doesn't want to be recognized when he goes places, but then why the fancy clothes and the look-at-me car? Besides, wouldn't it always be easier to be a prince? Red-carpet treatment all the time.

John Ray Mooney slapped himself on the forehead. The prince wouldn't pose as somebody else, idiot. But a con man could pass himself off as the Prince of Yip. What a beautiful scam.

Suddenly, the credit cards tossed around the bed were like scattered gold. Guillermo Ho, whoever the hell he really was, had gone to a lot of trouble to set himself up as the prince. Wouldn't he pay to get the credit cards back? Say twelve thousand bucks, enough to get Big Odie off John Ray's back?

And then maybe John Ray wouldn't need to rob the National Bank of Coronado.

4

Guillermo "Billy" Ho lay on a chaise near the Hotel Del pool, his eyes closed behind dark sunglasses. If he opened his eyes, he would see swaying palms and white gulls wheeling in a clear blue sky. He'd see the four-story wedding cake that was the Hotel Del. He could look out across the Olympic-sized swimming pool where tourists splashed with their children and women strolled in the merest of bikinis.

But he didn't open his eyes. He preferred the scents to the sights, the sounds to the sun in his eyes. All around him, the hubbub of Paradise, failing to drown out the tumult inside his own head.

If had been hours since the sweaty stick-up man boosted Billy's bankroll, but Billy couldn't let it go, couldn't apply his mind to what to do next or how long to ride the con without the credit cards. He was too busy being mad.

The big redneck with his tiny gun had ruined everything. Billy finally assumes the Prince of Yip's identity, gets rolling with a new wardrobe and a fat wallet full of future, and some desert rat screws it all up in an instant with an impulse robbery. And what had the son of a bitch been doing in the bank with a gun anyway? Just waiting for some *pendejo* like Billy with his wad of cash?

He exhaled loudly and shifted on the sweat-wet lounge chair. His body felt baked hard by the sun. He knew he should take a break from the warm rays, maybe plunge into the pool for some quick laps, but the sun relaxed him and he needed relaxation right now.

"Your Highness?" A girl's voice, young and tentative. Billy nearly opened his eyes, but he knew the imagined girl would be better than whatever actually stood there.

"Yes?"

"Can I get you anything? A phone? A new drink?"

Billy smiled without showing any teeth. "Another drink perhaps. A screwdriver. I feel in need of Vitamin C."

"Yes sir, Your Highness. I'll be right back with it."

He bestowed the smile again, but never opened his eyes. He listened to her heels click rapidly away. Service was good when you were a prince. Everything was.

Billy had first seen the Hotel Del when he was nine years old. He'd come up the coast with his father, bringing a load of old furniture to relatives who were struggling to make it in El Norte. Billy's family could afford to share. His father ran a *bodega*, and the Hos were firmly entrenched in Tijuana's middle class.

Billy hated the dusty store, hated everything about his life in Tijuana. He was constantly picked on by bullies from poorer families, bullies who felt he was fair game because the Chinese portion of his heritage meant he was less of a Mexican. Billy spent his school days in sullen silence, his afternoons either fighting or running for his life through the backstreets and alleys of Tijuana.

The boy rode into the United States in big-eyed wonder, taking in the freeways crowded with shiny cars, the taffy-colored houses, the smooth green lawns. The air smelled like money.

"I want to show you something," the old man had said as he steered his wheezing pickup truck off the freeway.

Billy rode in silence as his father drove up a road that split a strand of sand between bay and sea. The land was empty beach and wind-weary grass, and Billy couldn't imagine what his father wanted him to see.

After several miles, buildings appeared in the distance, high-rises looking out over the Pacific. The old truck rounded a curve and there before them stood a rambling white castle with a red roof and peaked towers.

"It is called the Hotel Del Coronado," his father said. "Marilyn Monroe stayed there when she filmed a movie. Have you ever seen it, *Some Like It Hot*? No? Sometime we must watch it on television."

Billy knew his father had an abiding crush on Señorita Monroe, though she'd been dead for years. No surprise he would drive miles out of his way to see a place she'd once graced with her beauty.

For Billy, it wasn't stardust that made the Del special. It was the promise of wealth. Someday, he told himself, I will be a guest there. Someday, I will have everything that beautiful hotel promises.

When Billy decided to become the Prince of Yip, that long-ago pledge resurfaced. The Del was the perfect place to try out his new scam. No one knew him there, and the real prince had never stayed there, either. An old hotel, accustomed to catering to presidents and princes, would know how to take care of his needs without a lot of questions that might trip him up. Plus, if things went wrong, escape was easy. Tijuana was only thirty miles away.

It had gone swimmingly until today's robbery. Billy had the hotel staff completely in thrall. Coronado and San Diego were flush with exclusive shops and expensive indulgences, all available to the man with the prince's credit cards.

Now it was ruined. The cards were gone. And Billy couldn't decide what to do next.

He could take a hike. The prince gets in his new Mercedes for a spin up the coast and nobody here ever sees him again. But he'd have to leave the closetful of Armani, and he couldn't bear that. He might be able to sign off at the front desk on his earlier credit card imprint, march out the door, luggage in hand, and hope they didn't want to double-check his card. But he didn't want to walk away, not yet. He'd have to leave Liza West behind and he wasn't ready for that.

Billy was hooked on Liza. The romance would be intense and fiery and brief. Once it was over, he could move on, as he'd planned all along. To the next resort in the next warm clime, the next hot woman. A party for Billy Ho, twenty-four hours a day.

Tonight, he and Liza could dine in the hotel. He'd sign all expenses to his room until he could replace those credit cards. They could eat at the Prince of Wales Room and drink in the Ocean Terrace Lounge. Then back up to his room for some rodeo sex.

Enjoy it while it lasts. Even if he recovered the prince's credit cards somehow or got new ones, it wouldn't last forever. The Sultan of Yip eventually would question the bills pouring in, question why he hadn't heard from his son. Billy had to stay just ahead, riding the wave until it played out on a warm beach somewhere. Or sent him crashing into the rocks.

"Here's your drink, Your Highness." The girl's voice again. He imagined she had freckles and pigtails. He held out his hand, let her slip the chilled glass into it. Their hands brushed, and hers felt blushingly hot.

"Thank you, my dear."

"Can I ask you to sign this?"

Billy kept his eyes closed, his voice soft and warm.

"Sign it for me, you lovely girl. And give yourself a ten-dollar tip."

"Oh! Thank you!"

"You're welcome."

Billy made the slightest gesture with his hand, a pleasant suggestion of a wave of dismissal. Her heels clicked away.

The sun needled Billy's belly. Five more minutes, then he really must plunge into the pool.

A shadow fell across his face, a sudden cloud blocking the sun from his closed eyes. The girl again. Billy imagined her in a gingham blouse, a frilly Daisy Mae thing. And no pants.

"Back so soon, my dear?"

"Glad to hear you're so fond of me, Your Highness."

That twang. The desert rat, the thief. Here, invading the sanctity of the Hotel Del, standing in Billy's sun.

He opened his eyes and winced at the man towering over him, framed by a postcard background of palm trees and sky and the hotel's dunce-cap turrets. The man had the slitted eyes, sun-creased cheeks, hard muscles and Brylcreemed ducktail of that exotic predator, the Mojave Desert redneck. Billy had seen the type all his life, cunning brutes who ran last-chance saloons or wore the badge of the U.S. Border Patrol.

"Mind if I sit down?"

The grinning redneck scraped a chair across the concrete to within inches of Billy, then perched on it, his feet flat on the ground, leaning over Billy, breathing cigarette smoke on him. He clutched Billy's hand in an inescapable handshake.

"I'd like to introduce myself. My name's John Ray Mooney, and I'm your new partner."

5

Earl Shambley sat in his threadbare armchair, the phone book in his lap and his feet in a tub of warm water. Earl had old feet for a man in his fifties. They were twisted and horny, like big prunes. Every night when he got home from the bank, he stripped out of his uniform, sat down in front of the TV in his boxer shorts, and soaked his feet. Every day at the bank, they still hurt like hell.

Twenty-five years of wearing a badge and toting a gun on the hot asphalt streets of Dallas, Texas, and what does Earl have to show for it? Bad feet, a crappy little apartment, a dwindling retirement fund and the world's most boring job at the National Bank of Coronado. Sure ain't the way a cop expects to live out his days.

Earl knew Coronado because he'd been stationed at North Island Naval Air Station when he was a young man, right out of Horace Mann High School in Tyler, Texas. The eight-year hitch in the military helped him get on the police force when he mustered out, saved him from going to college or learning a trade. The Dallas Police Department was desperate to hire blacks back then to meet long-neglected quotas and Earl waltzed right into the police academy, exchanging his Navy uniform for the dark blues of a cop.

All these years later, Coronado had seemed the perfect place to retire. A quiet little town full of safe, happy white people. The danger always existed that Earl's old adversaries might pop up and try to settle a score. But they weren't likely to find him in Coronado. And, if they did, they most assuredly would stand out from the crowd.

A man makes enemies during twenty-five years on the force. Earl collected more than his share because he always kept his eyes open for ways to supplement his piss-poor salary. He'd shake down drug dealers and pimps in exchange for their freedom. He'd engineer raids on gambling dens in which everyone escaped the dragnet, so long as they left the winnings on the table. Anyone who complained was in danger of being shot while trying to flee. Earl had the law on his side. Lot of crooks in Dallas had sworn to get even. And one apeshit guy in the department's Internal Affairs Unit had pledged to shoot Earl on sight.

Earl hit his twenty-fifth anniversary as a cop—and, therefore, retirement—hours before Internal Affairs swooped down on him, ready to bust him off the force for a string of misdeeds and abuses that read like the

Texas Criminal Code. The police chief, an old friend of Earl's with a history of immoral personal conduct, let Earl retire instead. In exchange, the chief got an envelope full of embarrassing photographs of himself in a local motel room. And the negatives.

Earl knew enough to disappear. Nobody lives in more danger than a dirty cop. If the bad guys don't get you, the good guys will.

He'd arranged the job with the National Bank of Coronado before he even knew about the Internal Affairs investigation. Just as well, too, considering that the bank checked his references. What the bank manager got was: twenty-five years as a uniformed officer, a steady guy, no flashy arrests, no awards, no major disciplinary problems. If he'd checked again a few weeks later, his questions would've been referred to the vipers in Internal Affairs.

Earl's thinning hair had gone white when he was still in his forties, but vanity and street savvy had led him to color it for the past decade. Soon as he retired, he washed out the dye and started growing a thick mustache. Within a few weeks, he looked like a different man. Older, wiser, serene. The sweeping mustache made his face look as if he was smiling, though he rarely was. Tourists automatically smiled back, thinking, What a friendly old gent!

Christ, he was bored. Sleepy little whitebread towns might be safe, but they were hell on a fellow's nerves. Earl liked to get out on the town, scout the skirts, roll some dice, pop into bars where everybody knew his name. At least, he used to like that. Been so long, who could tell? Maybe he was becoming what he pretended to be, a mild-mannered old bachelor who goes home at night to soak his feet.

The phone book open in his lap had the potential to change things. He had before him the Yellow Pages listings for the fifteen hotels jammed into Coronado. It was just a matter of time before he found the one where Prince Seri Hassan Bandapanang bin Mohammed stayed. Not likely to be more than one guest around with a name like that.

He'd started with Le Meridien and Loews, guessing a high-roller like a prince would stay in one of the newer resorts. Guessed wrong, apparently. He dialed the number for the Hotel Del Coronado.

When a woman answered, Earl asked for the prince.

"Yes sir, the prince is registered, but he's not taking calls. Would you like to leave a message?"

"No, ma'am, I need to talk to him directly. I work in security at the National Bank of Coronado. I have an urgent matter for the prince."

Earl held his breath.

"Hold on a second," she said. "Let me get my manager."

Earl needed to make his pitch to the prince straight on, without all this interference. He'd say he was concerned about the prince's safety. He saw the man in the sweatsuit jump into the prince's car that morning and just couldn't get it out of his head. Did the prince need some protection in Coronado? Or maybe just a jaded sidekick who could show him the sights in San Diego? Anybody who could go into a bank and walk out with five large in cash using nothing but a piece of plastic could be Earl's friend.

"This is Keith, the night manager. How may I help you?"

Keith's voice was prissy and self-contained, sounded like he could blow smoke rings with his asshole.

Earl fed him the spiel, even went so far as to tell him he'd seen a stranger climb into the prince's car. But Keith was a rock. The prince had left orders. No calls. Take a message.

Desperation leaked into Earl's voice: "What if the prince has been kidnapped? What if he's in the trunk of a car somewhere, and you're not even letting me try to reach him?"

Keith let the pregnant pause reach full term before he said, "If the prince is in a car trunk, I doubt I could connect you to him anyway. May I please take your message?"

"Never mind. I'll come see him in person."

Earl hung up. Damn. He needed to talk to this prince, size the man up. At least he'd found out where the prince was staying. He could get dressed, head over to the Hotel Del for a few drinks, see what he could see.

He sighed and reached for a towel. Time to get off his dead ass and onto his dying feet.

6

Liza West narrowly missed the neighbor's cat as she sped up the alley behind her Coronado home. Damn fat tabby, always scratching around in the trash. Better not wait until the last second to scamper out of the way when it's Liza behind the wheel.

She drove a deceptively sedate-looking Volvo four-door that was built like a tank. Her ex-husband had insisted on the heavy car because Consumer Reports rated it safest in a crash. With the wild way Liza drove, he'd said, she'd better have the best.

Fooled you, Sam. Not only have I avoided any accident, but I ended up with the car you bought. After the divorce, she'd considered trading the beige Volvo for something sportier, but she'd grown accustomed to its nimble bulk. Instead, she added a personal touch that claimed it as her own: A bumper sticker that said, "NO ILLUSIONS."

The Volvo's roof barely cleared the slow-moving garage door as it squealed to a stop. Then Liza was out of the car in a bustle of purse and shopping bags and clacking heels. Into the echoes of her big, empty house.

The house was another little gift from Sam, courtesy of Liza's razor-tongued divorce lawyer. It was a two-story barn with a Dutch roof and slate-blue clapboard walls. It sat on a pie-wedge lot two blocks from the Pacific, overlooking a perfectly round green park with a flagpole in its middle.

The car, the house, and its furnishings had seemed a pretty decent payoff for six years of marriage to a surgeon with cold hands. Sam West was well-groomed and meticulous, hard-working and responsible. About as exciting as boiled beef, but he spent so much time at the hospital that Liza had thought she'd be able to stand it. Turned out she was wrong about that, but what the hell, sometimes you fool yourself.

The house was big enough to handle Junior League of Coronado teas or out-of-town guests, but Liza had closed off upstairs rooms as she sold off the antiques and art that furnished them. She'd whittled the drafty house down to a more manageable nest, and she didn't want to lose it now.

She often marveled at the way she'd turned a luxury home into a double-mortgaged, half-furnished white elephant. It left her breathless, like a magic trick performed so well it defies the imagination.

It could all be explained in one word: Flabric.

Liza had gone into business for herself after the divorce, taking a second mortgage on the house and using all her savings to lease and redecorate a storefront on Coronado's charming main street, Orange Avenue. She had the perfect product in the perfect niche market. Tourists came to Coronado for the noonday sun, but they forgot about the fog that blanketed the beaches morning and night. They suddenly found themselves in need of warmer clothing and Liza provided it with quality souvenir sweatshirts.

She'd thought up the name *Flabric* herself. She wanted something that indicated weighty and warm, but cute and catchy, too. She'd had the name sketched across the storefront in expensive blue neon. Now, it seemed to mock her. Flabric. What had she been thinking? Nobody wants to be seen shopping in a store associated with "flab."

Liza thought she could change the name, remodel the place and start over with the same stock. But she needed a quick infusion of money first.

Forty-seven thousand dollars to get the store out of debt, maybe another fifteen thousand to remodel and erase *Flabric* from the public consciousness. Sixty-two grand to save her store, to save the life she'd built among Coronado's yuppie elite. Might as well be a million for all the good the calculations did her.

With debt crashing all around her, Liza had fallen back on old habits. A few days earlier, she strapped on her thong bikini and went to the swimming pool at the Hotel Del Coronado. Lots of rich men around that pool, and if she had to shake something in their faces to land a backer for Flabric, then so be it.

Liza had a friend on the pool staff who recognized it was good marketing to have lithe locals lounging among the guests. When boredom was eroding her marriage, Liza had become a regular at the pool. Sam had said her public flirtations there were the last straw. He'd actually said "the last straw," as if he were in some black-and-white melodrama.

Sam took it too seriously, as he did everything. She wasn't down at the hotel humping business toads for free drinks. She'd had enough of that kind of behavior before she met Sam. The flirtations were innocent. Little smiles and winks, the turning of heads when she passed. It was fun, and God knows Liza had little enough of that in her life. Even Sam, thick as he was, recognized the marriage wasn't fun anymore. She waited him out, not making the first move toward a separation. And when Sam finally found the balls to file for divorce himself, she took him for everything. A girl has to look out for herself.

When she reached her bedroom, Liza threw her packages on the bed and stripped off her sundress. She watched herself in the tall mirrors that covered the closet doors as she popped the clasp on her bra and slipped out of her lace panties. Her body was tan and lean, with none of the minor sag that usually accompanies reaching thirty. Lord knows she worked hard enough to keep it that way. Aerobics classes three days a week, weight-lifting at home, swimming in the hotel pool. Liza was a creature in constant motion.

As she wriggled into the red thong, she caught herself smiling in the mirror. It had been a long time since she'd played the vixen.

Her hair still surprised her. Liza had thought a change would do her good, make her feel disguised when the men approached. It was time for a look-at-me do, and her stylist, Roberto, had been happy to accommodate. He'd been after her to change for years, always saying her old style looked as if it belonged to an astronaut's wife. Roberto had clipped her hair short as a man's and bleached it bone white.

The look, along with the red bikini, had men at the pool twisting their heads off their necks. Most importantly, it had caught the attention of Prince Seri Hassan Bandapanang bin Mohammed of the island nation of Yip.

Such luck. Better than she could've hoped. Not only did the prince have millions at his disposal, but he seemed a generous sort. At a minimum, she could squeeze the prince for sixty-two thousand dollars. And what would it cost her? A week or two of willing laughter and accommodating sex.

She'd spotted Bennie, as the prince liked to be called, her second day of prowling the pool. A blushing waitress had been all too pleased to whisper to Liza that the gentleman at the far end of the pool was indeed a prince.

After Bennie plunged into the water and began to swim laps, Liza stationed herself above the spot where he flip-kicked to change directions. Sooner or later, he'd pause there. She stretched out on a lounge, arched her back, seemingly gave herself up to the sun. But behind her black sunglasses, she watched the diminutive prince bobbing through the water like a well-fed otter.

When he finally stopped and spoke to her, she didn't move. Just a smile, a casual word. She watched him run his eyes up and down her body, and she knew she had him hooked.

The next four days had been a whirlwind of meals and drinks and sex and talk. Bennie was a fun-loving, free-spending sort, nothing at all like Sam. A good reminder that men could be entertaining.

Bennie also possessed the gentle patience Liza imagined was a gift given only to royalty. Look at last night, the way he'd treated that funny ape-like man, Lowell Huganut. Bennie had met Lowell in the hotel's gym and thought nothing of inviting him along on his date with Liza. Lowell, with his huge arms and quiet manner, had been goggle-eyed over Liza and over his dinner with a real prince. Lowell was from out of town, somewhere in New Mexico, and he sported a backwoods charm Bennie found amusing.

Liza liked Lowell, too, as long as he didn't get in her way. She'd been ready the night before to talk to Bennie about Flabric, about how she needed his help. But with Lowell there all evening, she'd never had the chance. Once she was in Bennie's room, she was too busy. And it seemed in bad taste to talk about money in bed.

She tore the tags off the cover-up she'd bought on the way home, a white toga with gold braids around the shoulders. She slipped it over her head and smoothed it into place. Very nice. She looked as if she belonged on a Grecian urn.

Liza glanced at her gold watch. Late, and she still needed to freshen her make-up and pack her evening clothes and stick on the false eyelashes she'd be batting at the prince. Christ, what a girl had to go through.

She drove the six blocks from her house to the Del, terrorizing a romping Irish setter and two carloads of pasty tourists before screeching into a parking lot behind the hotel. She slung her beach bag over her shoulder and hurried past the tennis courts and the bustling outdoor bar, aware of the hungry male eyes that followed her.

She'd told Bennie she'd meet him by the pool, and she followed the promenade around to the ocean side of the hotel. A breeze rippled the flags and palm trees that decorated the grounds, but the big pool was set inside a protected rectangle created by the newer wings of the hotel. Down there, out of the gull-streaked wind, it would be ten degrees warmer. Just right for sunning and sipping something with a paper umbrella in it.

Liza spotted Bennie on the far side of the pool, in the best available sun, sweat-soaked in a red Speedo. They wore matching suits. How karmic.

Bennie clearly was engaged in conversation with the man next to him, though he remained supine in the lounge chair. The man sat upright one lounge over, looking out of place in his long-sleeved shirt and faded jeans and cowboy boots. He had a weathered face, a high forehead and slicked-back brown hair. He gestured emphatically with thick hands, as though trying to persuade the prince of something.

Bennie wouldn't look at the man, and the way he avoided eye contact made Liza think the redneck might be a panhandler. But how would a panhandler get into the Hotel Del? Finally, Bennie's roaming eyes settled on Liza and he waved. She waved back and bounced on her toes to show him how excited she was to see him. It made him smile. Points for Liza, who just kept racking them up.

The stranger followed the prince's gaze. His eyes were narrow slits, but they widened measurably when he got a look at her. She turned away, twitching her hips just enough as she trotted down the stairs to the pool.

They'd be talking about her now. Who she was. How the prince had met her. Wow, she must be something in bed. Men were so easy to predict.

She vamped up to them on the pool's concrete apron, passing a foursome of fat businessmen who gazed in reverential silence at her legs.

"Hi, Your Highness," she said. "Who's your friend?"

7

Lowell Huganut tried to get Liza West out of his mind. He was wearing a wrestling cup while he lifted weights and he feared he'd get a boner so sudden and strong that it would shoot the cup across the gym. Someone could get hurt.

Lowell had nearly embarrassed himself the night before when she sauntered into the hotel bar where he was drinking with the prince. He stopped talking in the middle of a sentence, his mouth hanging open, his heavy lower lip drooping. He gawked at the tall Ice Princess as she paused in the doorway, looking around. Then, she'd walked right over to him and the prince, sat right down. Oh, man.

Lowell flushed, then counted three more bench presses. Two hundred and thirty pounds. Ten times. Set it back on the rack. Rest. Do it again. Think about the weight, man, not the woman.

But that was precisely Lowell's problem. He'd been thinking about the weight, not women, forever. His life revolved around exercise and weight control, habits he acquired while wrestling in high school. The memories of making weight back then still pained him. Running laps in a hot gym, wearing plastic garbage bags to sweat off water weight. Puking his guts out after a thousand sit-ups. Lowell had been state heavyweight champion, but it had come at a price.

Keeping in shape, working out only five or six days a week, seemed like a light load after all that. Kept him busy, made him happy. Everybody needs a hobby. But it ate up a lot of his spare time. Between his job and caring for his ailing mom and pumping iron, Lowell hadn't taken time to settle down and get married. He feared sometimes that he'd waited too long. He was thirty-two years old. Still a fine catch, but starting to look a little suspicious. Some women, they see you're past thirty and never married and they figure you must be some sort of kook, destined to be the neighborhood crazy bachelor, cursing at passers-by and pissing on the lawn. Women had good imaginations that way.

He hoisted the bar again, lowered it to his chest, pushed it smoothly toward the ceiling. One. He liked bench presses because he could watch the muscles work in his long arms. They were like divine machinery, pistons and gears, well-oiled and pumping. Two. He was a fine physical specimen, even if he was past thirty. Women looked at him, he knew that. He felt their eyes. But they looked at his arms and legs and butt. When they got to his face, they tended to lose interest. Three. Too bad there weren't exercises you could do to change the shape of your head. He had a face like a chimp. Long upper lip, big proud ears, a forehead like a bench, a resting place for the elbows of taller men. Four. His body cast a certain simian shadow, too. He had broad, sloping shoulders and thick arms that hung nearly to his knees. His legs seemed to belong to a shorter man and were slightly bowed. All in all, he was a perfect argument for evolution. Five. Women liked him if they got to know him. He had a frank, naive manner and a quick, hooty laugh. But he was shy and stammery at first, and it took people a while to warm up to him. He was trying to be more confident. Six. A big, shy monkey who wore thick glasses. He looked like those ceramic statues you used to find in tourist traps, a Hamlet-like ape pondering a human skull. And all the bench presses in the world wouldn't change that. Aw, hell. Seven, eight, nine, ten.

He grunted to his feet and wiped his face with a towel. Think about the weight, Lowell. He lumbered over to a leg press machine, set it on two-fifty and saddled up. He could do so many of these that he didn't even bother to count anymore. If you count, then you think and Lowell didn't want to think. His brain was full. He just kept pumping until his wind gave out. His legs never would.

Lowell's life had changed one month ago, when he bought a raffle ticket from a Girl Scout who stopped by the firehouse where he worked in Truth or Consequences, New Mexico. Nice kid, only two bucks. Lowell stowed the ticket in his wallet, didn't give it another thought. Two weeks later, he saw the winning number in The Herald and damned if it wasn't his. He was surprised and almost too embarrassed to claim it, but the guys at the firehouse pestered him until he went to the travel agency downtown and collected his prize: Four days and three nights of vacation luxury at the historic Hotel Del Coronado.

Lowell hadn't taken a vacation in years. Not a real vacation. He spent some of his accumulated time off taking his mother on long, comfortably dull car trips to visit relatives in Texas or Arizona. They'd roll across the prairie between knife-edged mesas, listening to country radio stations. His mother would pause in her knitting occasionally to nag him to stick to the speed limit. He kept meaning to go someplace after she died, but he was busy with work and weightlifting and his vacation time at the fire department piled up.

Then he wins a free trip to San Diego, a place he'd never visited, put up at some hotshit hotel, doesn't cost him a dime. Next thing you know, he's met a prince and the prince's truly awesome babe and they're partying together. It was incredible. He'd been awake half the night, reveling in the richness of his new life. Because an event like this, it had to change your life, right? You become friends with a prince, you travel in whole different circles.

Even if he never saw the prince again after tonight, he had a story to tell the guys back at the firehouse, a story to tell for the rest of his life. He imagined himself as an old man, little kids around his knees, saying, "Tell us again about the prince, Grandpa." And all his imaginary grandkids had the white hair and wide green eyes of Liza West.

Lowell let the weights clang. He stretched his legs, felt the hot blood coursing through them. Enough for today. He checked the clock on the wall. He needed to shower and spruce up for his dinner with Bennie. His second dinner with a prince. Oh, man.

8

Billy Ho was blessed with the grace and timing of the perfect host. Entertaining meant a quiet watchfulness, an effortless mastery of food and drink and temperaments and conversation. They called it "playing" host for a reason; it was a performance. Billy was a star.

His talents had been rewarded. He'd never worked a single day at an honest job. Big shots needed people with Billy's oily skills and gracious manners to hang around, give their mansions some class. Call them what you will—houseboys, butlers, chauffeurs, guests—Southern California was full of Kato Kaelins.

Billy thought he was stepping up to the big-time, tapping into that vast pool of Yip wealth. But every con has its complications, and in this case, the problem sat across the table from him at the Ocean Terrace Lounge. John Ray Mooney tried to fit into the prince's party, but he was awkward and tentative, suspicious of everything someone else said.

Billy smiled and prodded when necessary, but mostly he watched and managed. He signaled the waiter whenever a drink looked less than half-full, which he believed made him an optimist. He made little jokes at his own expense. After dinner downstairs, he'd ordered every dessert on the menu, and insisted that everybody, even the hesitant Lowell, sample each one.

All the while, he worried and strategized about this new problem in their midst, this John Ray Mooney with his slick hair and coarse ways. John Ray seemed to be loosening up now that he had a few whiskeys in him, and Billy watched him carefully to make sure the big galoot didn't blurt out about the prince's pretenses. Billy needed to continue to be the prince in everyone's eyes, at least for a few more days, until he could get his credit cards back.

Liza gave Billy a little pat where her warm hand rested high on his thigh.

"So, Bennie, tell me again, what will John Ray be doing for you?"

Billy had waited all evening for this question, and it figured it would come from Liza. She'd played the Bambi with him, but he'd known all along that somewhere under the willing smile was a hardened businesswoman, twice divorced. She sat very erect now, very close to Billy, her eyes the vivid green of grass snakes.

Billy gave her the prince's gentle grin. "John Ray will be my aide, my right-hand man."

"Like a bodyguard?"

"An associate."

"Some guy who follows you around and carries your wallet?"

"An assistant."

"Okay." Liza flashed the high beams at him. "Whatever you say. I just don't want to worry that your body needs guarding."

"Ah. Well, there was a little incident today . . ."

John Ray shifted in his chair and coughed, but Billy ignored him, kept smiling at Liza, waiting for the question. It came from Lowell, who'd sat silent as a stump for the past hour.

"What happened?"

Poor Lowell. He's the junior executive whose job is to second the motion.

"Nothing worth mentioning, really. A robbery."

Liza sat forward, her face only inches away from Billy's. "You were robbed?"

"Yes, my dear. But it was nothing, I assure you."

"Did you call the police? I know the police chief in this town. Maybe I could—"

"No police. It's not necessary. John Ray here—" Billy turned to find John Ray staring at him with prison-yard eyes. "—recovered my wallet and returned it to me. Thanks to him, it was resolved quickly and peacefully."

Liza, too, let her gaze settle on John Ray, who cut loose a transparent sigh of relief.

"He got your wallet back? How'd he do that?"

"Maybe we should let him tell that story himself."

Billy smiled broadly at John Ray's sudden discomfort. The ex-con cleared his throat, checked his watch, moved his drink to the exact center of his cocktail napkin.

"I thought we agreed we weren't gonna talk about that?" John Ray looked away when he said it, but Billy still could see the fire in his eyes. I keep stepping over the line, he thought, but I can't help myself. He almost giggled.

"I understand your modesty," he said, "but it won't hurt anything to tell them about your heroics."

"Heroics, huh?" Liza sounded unconvinced.

"Oh, my, yes." Billy loved that expression. Bennie used to say it all the time.

"I wouldn't go so far as to say 'heroics,'" John Ray said. He was looking around the table now, and the anger was gone. Instead, Billy could see the scam in his eyes. John Ray had found his rhythm. "It was more like a reaction, you know?"

John Ray didn't need any prompting now, but Billy couldn't resist planting a princely: "A noble reaction."

"I saw this guy running away from the prince here with a wallet in his hand. And I'm like: 'Whoa. What's wrong with *this* picture?' The guy was looking back over his shoulder to see if the prince was coming after him, so I just stuck out my arm and clotheslined him."

John Ray held out a sinewy arm to demonstrate, nearly slapping Lowell upside the head. Billy found himself wondering: The guy gets out of Folsom two weeks ago, how'd he get so tan? He must've spent every moment in the sun since he walked out the gates in that cheap suit. Or, maybe, after a lifetime in the desert, your tan never fades.

"I picked up the wallet where the guy dropped it. He jumped up and ran off."

"You didn't chase him?" Liza still seemed skeptical.

"Why would I do that? I had the wallet."

Good answer, John Ray, old boy.

"I didn't want to press charges anyway," Billy added. "I don't need the media attention. I'm on vacation."

Lowell, who seemed annoyed at having to duck John Ray's clothesline demonstration, straightened and flexed the muscles that ran across his shoulders like dimpled steel.

"If I'd been there, I woulda caught the guy and turned him over to the cops," he said.

John Ray sized Lowell up, like maybe he was deciding which parts to carve into chops and steaks.

"Well, I've got ten years on you, Opie, and I gotta tell you, that makes a big difference. At my age, I can't think of anything I want bad enough to run after it."

Billy snorted.

"I didn't even get a good look at the guy," John Ray said, and he let his eyes settle on Billy in his level Clint Eastwood way. "All I know is, he was a Mexican."

Oh, ho! So John Ray's feeling cocky, thinks he can play with Billy Ho now. Billy smiled. Guess that's what I deserve for springing the robbery thing on him. I told him by the pool I wouldn't talk about it, but I couldn't help myself.

"Yes, well, it doesn't matter now," Billy said. "Just a little adventure, something to recount over drinks. But it did remind me I could be vulnerable to kidnapping or attack. I shouldn't take such chances, for the sake of Yip. The longer I talked to John Ray, the more I liked him. I think he will make splendid employee."

Catty, Billy. Leave it alone.

"Let's change the subject," he suggested. "I want to know more about this exotic Western town where Lowell lives."

Lowell looked like Billy had smacked him. "Me?"

"Yes, Lowell. You're awfully quiet tonight. Is something wrong?"

"No, no, nothing. You're just all so . . . interesting."

"How charming. But, really, we'd like to hear from you. Your hometown isn't really named after a TV show, is it?"

Billy distinctly remembered this stretch of conversation from the day before, when he'd found himself drinking for hours with this simian fireman. At least it was something that could keep Lowell going for a few minutes. Billy needed that drone, so he could concentrate on exchanging meaningful looks and loaded grins with John Ray Mooney.

"T-or-C? I thought I told you about that."

"Liza hasn't heard it."

"True." Lowell swung his Planet of the Apes profile toward Liza. "I come from Truth or Consequences, New Mexico. It used to be called Hot Springs, 'cause there's these mineral springs there and people come there to soak and all. But back in 1950, this game show called Truth or Consequences offered a prize to any town that would change its name. We won."

"Is it a real small town?" Liza asked.

"Not that small. About six thousand people. And we get a lot of tourists there. There's this lake called Elephant Butte—"

"Called what?"

"Let me back up. There's this mountain, this butte, outside of town that kinda, in the right light, looks like a sleepy elephant. And next to that's a manmade lake called Elephant Butte Lake. See? Anyway, the lake's real popular with boaters and all, so we get a lot of people coming through, especially on summer holidays."

Billy knew the answer, but he wanted to keep Lowell going: "I suppose that creates a lot of work for the firefighters."

"Yessir. Lotta campfire problems and stuff. Lotta people getting in trouble in their boats."

"Do you work out on the lake?" The perfect question, Liza, really.

Lowell's lower lip waggled when he shook his head. "They won't let me do any water work. Can't swim."

"You can't swim?" Clearly, to a native Californian like Liza, that was sacrilege.

"I can paddle around a little. I like the water. But it's hard because I can't float. I got too much muscle density and too little fat. Sink like a stone."

"Get outta here."

"No, really. I'd have trouble making it from one side of the hotel pool to the other. It's not that I'm not strong enough to swim. It's like no matter what I do, I can't make enough headway to counterbalance the pull of the water. Next thing you know, I'm on the bottom."

"I thought everybody could float."

"Not me. Oh, I suppose I'd float to the surface eventually, but it would be too late to do me any good."

Liza made a face. Billy smiled. Lowell had used the same line the day before. So nice to know you can count on people.

"What do you say, everyone? One more round of drinks before we call it a night?"

9

Earl Shambley shook the ice cubes in his whiskey glass. If he had another drink, they might have to scrape him out of this damned hard chair with a spatula. Maybe he could nurse the cubes a little longer, while the prince and his entourage downed their final round. Then he could follow the prince out of the bar, finally get him alone.

Earl sat in the farthest corner of the Ocean Terrace Lounge, counting on the dimness and his natural camouflage for invisibility. He'd come in through the outside doors, off the pool area, and slipped quietly into the corner so he'd be behind the only one in the prince's party likely to recognize him: the redneck who'd been in the bank earlier.

The prince might have seen Earl in the bank, too, but Earl figured royalty took no notice of uniformed types. So far, it appeared he'd guessed right. The prince had looked right at him a time or two, and had shown no flicker of recognition.

Earl was exhausted. His feet hurt. The Muzak was making him crazy. He'd spied on this bunch for hours now, and hadn't once gotten a chance to talk to the prince. The redneck never let the prince out of his sight. The man never even went to the bathroom.

And who was this other guy, looked like a frigging ape? Earl had made some easy assumptions about the blonde and he had several theories on the redneck, but he had no idea whether the muscle boy had his hooks into the prince or how.

If he were still a cop, Earl would go to the front desk and order the night manager to cough up IDs on the whole crew. Then he'd run them through the national crime computers, looking for prior convictions. Maybe get a computer run on their credit cards and their telephone bills while he was at it. Maybe toss their rooms. Get some idea who he might be dealing with here. But he wasn't a cop anymore. Over the years, he'd taken for granted all the handy resources. It was tougher now that he had no computers, no contacts, no clout. Nobody volunteered information to a snoopy old bank guard.

Earl still had his ways. Like the way he'd called Washington, just before closing time at the Yip embassy. Earl had asked for a media contact and had been switched to a man with the raspy voice of a heavy smoker.

"Howdy, my name is Earl Shambley, and I'm a reporter for the Coronado *Eagle*, out in California?"

"Yes?"

"We understand the Sultan's son is vacationing here in Coronado, and we'd like to do a story about him."

"You should take that up with him," the Rasper said.

"We don't want to bother him. That's not our style. This is a resort town, see? The newspaper cooperates fully with the hotels. They're our biggest advertisers."

"Then I do not see what—"

"What we like to do is run little items on special guests, just a paragraph or two. That way, we get it covered without disturbing them."

The Rasper grunted the verbal equivalent of a shrug. Earl talked faster.

"What I need, see, is a standard bio. I'm sure you have them on file."

"I would need permission from my superior to release it. And he has gone for the day."

"That's too bad. I really need it tomorrow. We're on deadline."

"Perhaps it would be permissible . . . "

"You could sent it to me Federal Express."

The Rasper grudgingly agreed.

"Oh, and one more thing. Could you include a photo of the prince?"

So, right now, while Earl sat in the the hotel bar, trying to stay awake, the press packet was winging its way west. It would give him some information, though nothing on the prince's entourage. Too bad these others didn't have their own press agents.

The blonde, one fine-looking woman, clearly was the prince's squeeze. Barely an inch between her chair and his. Her hands danced over him like spiders. The woman was nothing less than what Earl would expect of a fun-loving prince. She'd been wearing a bikini when Earl first saw her at the pool, and he thought his heart would stop. Then she'd changed for the evening, into come-fuck-me heels and a black halter dress with a short flared skirt. Whew.

The ape-man wore a standard blue blazer, khakis and a plaid sportshirt with open collar. He mostly sat silent, grinning at the prince, occasionally taking a slug from a Coors Light. Man had an underbite. When he tipped up that bottle, looked like it might slide right down his throat.

Monkey Boy seemed oblivious to the tension that sat among them like a centerpiece, but Earl could see it crackling around the table. The blonde didn't like the redneck, maybe thought he was cutting in on her action. The prince and the redneck were in some dance of wills, testing each other with their eyes and their words. Earl read fatigue in the way the redneck held his shoulders, the way he leaned his chin on the hand that held his cigarette.

Earl wished the man would give it up and turn in for the night. He didn't worry about outflanking the woman or the biped. He could persuade the prince to ease them out of the picture. But the redneck was another story. Earl saw experience in his face, worldliness in his posture. He had some scam going, and he wouldn't take kindly to any interference.

Earl had been tempted to walk right up to the prince, hold out his hand, make nice so they'd invite him to join them. But he'd reined himself in. The only card he had to play was his concern about the prince's welfare, and he couldn't broach that with the redneck sitting right there. He needed the prince alone, just for a minute. His pitch would work or it wouldn't. If it didn't, what had it cost? A few hours he otherwise would've spend moldering in front of the TV.

The worst possibility—and it seemed more likely with every passing minute—was that Earl wouldn't get a chance to talk to the prince. Then he'd never know whether rubbing elbows with him could've added some excitement to his life.

The prince and the others rose from the table and left as a unit, the prince waving at the bartender as they moved toward the door. The redneck looked a little unsteady, whether from fatigue or liquor Earl couldn't tell. In her heels, the blonde was head-and-shoulders taller than the prince, but she still managed to hang on his arm as they teetered toward the lobby.

Earl followed half-heartedly. He could shadow the prince forever without getting any closer than this, not with that redneck within arm's reach all the time. Maybe he needed a new plan, some way to cut the prince out of the herd that followed him everywhere.

But for now, he should go home, get some rest. Tomorrow would be another long day on his feet.

10

John Ray Mooney's snakeskin boots dragged on the lobby carpet as he trailed Billy and Liza. The lobby's high ceiling was paneled in dark wood to match the front desk. A huge, bottom-heavy chandelier dominated the room like a giant's teardrop. But what caught John Ray's attention most was the furniture—plump sofas and overstuffed chairs just begging him to join them for a nap.

His reserves were just about spent. Add to that the first hard liquor he'd touched in years, and you've got a recipe for the Sleep of the Dead.

But not yet. He must be vigilant. If Billy Ho was going to try something, it probably would be now. Look at the little fucker up there, swinging along on Liza's arm, laughing and cracking wise. Cool as a cucumber. And nowhere near as drunk as John Ray. Billy clearly was accustomed to pouring martinis down his throat like it was a goddamned funnel, but John Ray was out of practice. Tasted good, though. Felt good for a while. Now he just felt woozy. No happy buzz left, no warm glow. Just a sick dizziness and the first tentative drumbeats of a headache.

He crowded into the birdcage elevator with Billy, Liza, and Lowell. The ancient machine was operated by a pudgy Asian who wore black-framed eyeglasses and a spacious smile. Like the army of bellmen who patrolled the lobby, he wore a short green jacket trimmed in gold braid and brass buttons, matching pants and shiny black shoes. He jabbered something friendly at them, and Billy said, "Lowell's on the second floor. We're on three."

The sudden movement of the elevator made John Ray blink furiously. Lowell bid them a chipper good-night and ambled off down a corridor. John Ray still wondered whether Lowell was an obstacle. He seemed to believe the story about John Ray coming to Billy's rescue. And he sure as hell still believed Billy was a real prince. He'd watched him all evening in admiration and big-eyed wonder, like the prince was a bunch of fresh bananas.

Third floor. John Ray followed Billy and Liza down the hall toward the ocean side of the hotel. Because the Hotel Del is made entirely of wood, it's warped and twisted over a century of sea damp. All the hallways tilt slightly, one direction or the other. John Ray noticed it more now because of the booze. This must be what it's like, he mused, walking on a cruise ship.

Liza's hips swished under the short skirt, and John Ray had to force himself to watch Billy rather than her. Liquor wasn't the only thing he'd gone without for years.

She kept glancing back at him, probably wondering when he was going to leave them alone and go to his own room. Nothing would make him happier, but first he had to make sure they were bedded down for the night. He didn't want to wake up and find Billy standing over him with a gun.

They reached their rooms, and Liza pulled up short.

"You're right next door?"

"Sure. Gotta be within earshot. The prince pulled some strings and got me this room."

Liza turned a flinty look on Billy Ho. "Is there a connecting door?"

Billy shrugged, smiled her off.

"I don't like this, Bennie."

"No problem, my dear. Nice old hotel. Thick walls. It's not like John Ray's going to come bursting in."

John Ray gave them a grin. "Not unless there's trouble. Then I'll be right there on top of it."

Liza beamed up the Junior League smile. "Don't worry. I'll keep an eye on Bennie."

She clutched the prince's bicep as he opened the door for her.

John Ray stayed in the hall, his own cardkey in his hand, until their door clicked shut. Then he hustled into his room and headed straight for the bathroom. By his estimate, it had been eight hours since he last took a piss.

He could hear nothing but his own firehose splatter for a few minutes, then he stood silently, listening for the sounds he expected from Billy's room. A squeak of bedsprings. A giggle. And then, finally, the thump of a headboard against the wall. The thumping got faster, found its rhythm, almost matched the steady pounding inside John Ray's head.

John Ray drank two glasses of water and checked his bleary eyes in the mirror. A strand of slick hair had fought its way free near his widow's peak and fallen down to his eyebrows. He grasped the lock, tried to twist it into a Superman curl, but it fell lank again and he gave it up.

The hair was history anyway, as of tomorrow. Billy Ho had made it clear John Ray would be getting a whole new look if he expected to keep company with royalty. Tomorrow would be a day filled with shopping and haircuts and manicures, all paid for by the Sultanate of Yip by way of the credit cards that fattened the wallet in John Ray's hip pocket.

For three years and five months, John Ray had carried no wallet at all, nothing between his ass and the chair but the thin cotton coveralls issued by the State of California. To suddenly be carrying two billfolds, his own and Billy Ho's, wasn't comfortable. He felt like he'd been sitting on somebody's hands all night.

He put the wallets in the nightstand drawer, along with the pistol that had rubbed a raw place on his back where it had been tucked into his belt-line all day. Little pistol was too square to make a good belt gun. Maybe he'd make Billy Ho buy him a holster while they were shopping.

He double-checked all the locks, then crossed to the bed, shedding clothes, and climbed naked between the smooth sheets.

Next door, the headboard still thumped the wall. John Ray was beginning to think Billy was showing off. The thought of Liza West's lithe body wowing little Billy just the other side of the wall had its effect on John Ray. Drunk and tired as he was, he felt an old familiar tingle in his belly, a warming of the groin.

Funny how it turned out she owned Flabric, that store with the stupid name where he'd bought his bank-robber sweatsuit. Too bad he hadn't seen her when he was shopping there. Things might be different. If he'd seen Liza first, maybe he would've . . .

Jesus. Give it a rest. He didn't allow himself to lust anymore, not after what had happened with Angel Flesch. Besides, he needed to focus. He needed to size up his crazy day. He needed to study his every move, make sure he'd made no mistakes.

What a day. First, the bank heist that didn't happen. Then, the quick, smooth robbery of the prince. John Ray hadn't wasted any time making use of the dual identities he'd discovered in the wallet. Of course, part of that was dumb luck. He'd been walking along the promenade, whistling the theme to *Green Acres*, when he just happened to look down to see the Prince of Yip sunning beside the pool.

He hadn't taken time to work out a plan. Boldly walked right up to the man, told him, "I'm your new partner." Smooth, baby, smooth.

Then had come the conversational equivalent of a rodeo ride, a bucking bronco, trying to negotiate a deal with the slick con man who'd persuaded a whole town he was royalty. John Ray hung on for dear life, knowing he held the all-valuable bits of plastic that made the scam work. He'd get what he wanted, or it's snip, snip, snip and they're gone.

And what was it he wanted? Most immediately, he wanted twelve thousand dollars to keep Big Odie at bay. Then John Ray had surprised himself. He'd blurted out that he wanted some new clothes, some good times, a taste of the high life. He wanted to ride the scam with Billy Ho for a while.

Until it fell out of his mouth, John Ray hadn't known that's what he'd ask for. It's like that game kids play: If you found Aladdin's lamp, what would be your three wishes? John Ray always had a ready answer when he was a kid: Number one, get the hell out of Needles. Number two, no more crazy people in my life. Number three, a big pile of money.

Here he was, fresh out of Folsom, presented with a little genie in a Speedo, and what does he wish for? Dress me up and take me to a party. Shit. Well, that, and a big pile of money. He'd figure a way to get both before he departed Billy's life. And he might be driving that red Mercedes as well.

He yawned and stretched beneath the cool sheets. Enough light filtered through the drapes that he could see the ceiling fan turning weary circles. The thumping had stopped next door, and John Ray could hear the merest murmur of sleepy conversation through the wall. Didn't sound like Billy would try to ambush him tonight. Sounded like Billy had worn himself out with Liza.

John Ray let his eyes slowly close, enjoying the luxury of it.

11

Liza West gingerly lifted the prince's hand off her hip so she could roll over without waking him. Bennie snorted, but didn't move. Poor guy. Fucked himself into a coma.

She propped against her pillows and pulled the covers over her breasts. Wide awake. In bed with a prince. If it was anybody else and she felt this antsy, she'd be up and into her clothes, out into the sleepy town in her Volvo. But Bennie might like to wake up next to her, maybe put on another bang-the-wall show for his new friend next door.

Light spilled into the bedroom from the bathroom light she'd left on earlier. Bennie looked like a little boy asleep, curled up into a ball against her. She felt a genuine fondness for Bennie. His courtly manners and lilting accent and quick smile made him fun to be around. But it wasn't love she felt. Not even close.

She'd married for love the first time, and she was determined never to make that mistake again. She'd wed Bobby Veck three days after she graduated from high school up the coast in Del Mar. The two poorest kids in the whole school, getting hitched at City Hall without a plan for the future or a nickel to their names. As blind and stupid as the pop songs Bobby played around the clock on their scratchy AM radio.

It lasted a year, about as long as everyone had predicted. It takes about a year before pinchgut poverty and despair outweigh love and great sex. After that, a couple needs something more, something deeper, to hold them together. Last she heard, Bobby was living in a trailer in a canyon up the coast, shacked up with some other sucker who thought love could take the place of ambition or persistence or hope.

Liza, of course, had moved on to better things. It had taken years, longer than she'd expected, but the waiting and working had paid off.

She'd learned early that men could be used to further her goals. By the time she reached puberty, she regularly went out on dates, often with much older boys. Dates sometimes provided the only decent meals she'd get all week. Her mother collected food stamps and welfare payments, but she'd trade them in a second for a bottle of gin. Liza tried to watch her, tried to make sure she ate and bathed and took care of herself. But nobody looked after Liza.

Fortunately, she'd been blessed with the slim symmetry of beauty. Her mother had been a looker when she was younger, before hardship and booze eroded her curves and stole the spark from her eyes. Liza had seen photos of her mom, happily clinging to the arm of a dark-eyed man who supposedly was Liza's father. They smiled and laughed in the photos, two lovers on a lark.

Liza sometimes thought those happy, tattered photos led her to cast her lot with Bobby Veck. She'd had other, more suitable, suitors, boys who came from families with money. But only Bobby made her laugh.

Once she'd seen that wasn't enough, Liza had moved south to San Diego, ready to reinvent herself. She worked in shops and bars, the sort of meaningless jobs relegated to college students. Unlike her co-workers, Liza didn't go to school. She got another kind of education. She studied men.

Society is stacked against women, she'd figured. All the good jobs and secure futures are given to males. Things had changed, sure, but the glass ceiling was for real. Why kill yourself butting against it? Liza bounced from one man to another for five years, looking for the right one, the one who could solve all her problems. Some paid her bills. Some wined her and dined her and showed her good times she could never afford on her own. More than she could count had proposed marriage, living together, a commitment of some kind. Liza saw through such overtures, knowing they were expressions of territoriality or, worse, the palpitations of true love. She kept her distance, kept her cool. Fun was fine, sex was okay, but commitment was something Liza would enter only on her own terms.

Then she'd met Sam West. Calm, serious Sam. Two years out of his residency, Sam already had built a clientele of grateful patients for whom his magic scalpel meant the difference between life and death. Tumors and clogged arteries and damaged hearts were just so much business to Sam. Open 'em up, clean 'em out, stitch 'em back together. Give the patients a few more years to smoke and drink and eat rich foods.

The men in Sam's family had been surgeons for three generations, which meant he exited medical training free of the student loans that burdened his classmates. His hard work meant a growing fortune that Liza had sized up by their second date.

She'd reinvented herself for Sam. Gone was her past and the many men who'd trooped through it. Gone was Del Mar and her drunken mother and Bobby Veck. Six months after their first date, Sam married a woman who was chaste and responsible and mature. The perfect mate to establish their place in Coronado's elite.

Liza worked hard at it. She read home-decorating books and stuffy treatises by Miss Manners and histories of the snobbish little town. She wore clothes by Anne Klein and Carole Little and makeup from Estee Lauder and just a touch of perfume. She hosted teas and attended gallery openings and learned to enjoy opera.

Through it all, she felt like a fraud. She was getting what she wanted: wealth and security and social standing. But acceptance was something else. She felt the chill at the Junior League meetings. Her past was a blank, and that didn't sit well with those who thought new money was tainted in some way. Her peers had lived in Coronado for generations. They'd gone to the same private schools and the same elite colleges. They'd married men from the exact same social stratum. They played tennis together, ate lunch together, went sailing together, toured Europe together. Liza gradually encroached on their sacred territory, and she was more beautiful than any of them, which made them bitter and picky and mean.

The harridans thought they'd finally get rid of her when news of her divorce spread through town like summer fog. But Liza was determined to go on fighting. She reinvented herself again, thanks to Flabric, setting herself up as a striving businesswoman, a success story, a member of the Chamber of Commerce. Even the snootiest of Coronado's women began to admit a grudging admiration for her, perhaps because they knew they'd never fare so well if Hubby tossed them in the dumper.

Liza, too, became more comfortable with the pecking order and with herself, despite the loss of Sam's backing. Sam might be gone, living in a dump of an apartment near his precious hospital, but Liza still had a future all her own.

Then Flabric's misfortunes began to weigh her down. Every setback, every trip to San Diego pawn shops with a trunkload of Sam's heirlooms, made her scramble all the more to keep her place in the closed society of Coronado.

Maybe it was time to reinvent herself again—as a princess. Given time and fewer distractions, she could persuade Bennie that he couldn't live without her. She smiled at the thought of Junior Leaguers chirping over their tea about how they'd known Liza long before she became royalty, back when she was one of them, a commoner.

Of course, she'd like to get a look at Yip first. Bennie had described

Yip as a thickly jungled rock rising up from the South China Sea between Borneo and Vietnam. A pleasant climate. A small, happy population getting richer by the minute. Liza knew Bennie was Muslim, though clearly not a rigid one. He ate pork, drank liquor, enjoyed all the forbidden luxuries. He seemed to have a deep appreciation for miniskirts. But who knew what it would be like when he someday ascended the Yip throne? Liza had heard about Muslim countries where the women were forced to remain covered from head to toe, only their unadorned eyes peeking out from all that modesty. And such countries often had strict Islamic laws that banned much of what made life worth living. What would be the point of being royalty if you couldn't enjoy every minute?

At least it would be warm there. Liza couldn't stand cold weather. With a nice climate like that, surely they didn't make the women wear the Arab-style robes. Not on an island, where any direction you could point, there was a beach.

Liza imagined herself at the royal beach, frolicking in her bikini, shaking up the locals. The Sultan's eyes bulging out of his wealthy head. Bennie would love it. She would be the perfect symbol for Bennie's plans to modernize life in Yip.

All such fantasies presumed her fling with Bennie developed into anything more. Bennie seemed smitten, sure, but she'd seen that before. Sometimes you can't count on men's urges. Sometimes their heads overrule their hearts and other anatomical advocates.

Liza shifted restlessly, then glanced over to see whether she'd disturbed Bennie. Not a twitch. She sighed, turned her pillow over so she could lie against the cool side.

Fantasies did her no good. She needed to focus on her immediate problem: getting the money to resuscitate Flabric. As tempting as eloping with Bennie might be, the odds were just too long. Liza needed to get sixty-two-thousand dollars out of Bennie's pocket and into hers.

Of course, that's part of the problem. The money's not in Bennie's pocket anymore. John Ray Mooney protected the money now, and she was certain he'd try to argue Bennie out of giving any to Liza for her store.

John Ray, with his hard squint and those ropy muscles and his Mickey Rourke hair. That brash way of talking, where everything's a pronouncement, spoken with blind certainty. White trash, through and through.

Where had he come from anyway? Liza didn't believe the story about John Ray's rescue of the prince's wallet. She'd seen the uncertainty in John Ray's eyes when he began to tell it. He'd covered well, but she caught that initial hesitation, and she knew better. He worried her.

She didn't worry about Lowell. He was exactly as he appeared: sweet, naive, earnest, simple. He wanted nothing more from the prince than a good time—a few beers and some exotic conversation. And, apparently, everything seemed exotic when you were from Truth or Consequences, New Mexico.

Liza liked soft, sophisticated men who spoke so quietly you had to really listen. Mild-mannered men were more malleable. Bennie, with his money and his elegant calm, fit the bill exactly. So why, when little Bennie had been on top of her, pumping away earnestly, had she been thinking about the bulging biceps of Lowell Huganut?

12

Lowell Huganut stopped running when he saw a woman materialize in the morning fog. He walked with his hands on his hips, his lungs huffing the damp air, his eyes on her.

She was tall and well-muscled, with short brown hair held out of her eyes by a white sweatband. She wore a snug blue top and white shorts that clung to her as she spread her legs and shifted her weight ever so slowly from one foot to the other.

T'ai chi. Lowell had seen people do the slow-motion martial art before, stretching and strengthening their muscles. Not something you saw every day, though, and certainly not as performed by this beautiful woman on the beach. She raised her arms slowly, performed a delicate turn with her hands, then lowered them as gently as the wings of a swan.

She didn't look at Lowell. She stared straight out at the choppy gray water, the tumbling surf, lost in the breathing and the movement. Just as well, Lowell figured. One look at the big monkey walking down the beach would ruin her concentration.

Lowell kept his white sneakers moving. He tried not to stare at her, but his eyes were round and his big lip drooped. This, he thought, is everything I want in a woman. Skilled, calm, knows how to treat her body. And, oh, man, what a body. He forced himself to look away, just so he could stand it. Otherwise, he'd need to plunge into the cold surf to get himself under control.

He tried to work up the nerve to stop walking and strike up a conversation, or at least say hi. But look at her, lost in her t'ai chi. It would be a shame to interrupt. Maybe, he thought, if she's still working out when I jog back down this stretch of beach, I'll make myself think of something to say. Lowell rarely spoke first, and it wasn't just shyness. He lived by the words his Mama always told him: Better to keep your mouth shut and have people think you a fool than to speak up and prove it.

Lowell took up his earlier unflagging pace, remembering to keep his back straight, his hands high, his elbows close to his body.

He didn't run much. He preferred the weight room, with its familiar clanks and odors. But this morning he'd awakened smelling of beer and feeling cloudy, and he'd decided a jog was just what he needed to sweat out the hangover.

He glanced back at the woman in the fog. She leaned forward, bending one knee, stretching her tawny arms before her, as if she could push back the sea. Lowell stumbled in the sand, set his eyes straight ahead, and ran.

The beach was nearly empty this early on a Wednesday morning. Too foggy and cold for most people. It felt good to Lowell, so different from the perpetual dry heat of T-or-C.

He tried to imagine the t'ai chi woman back at his ranch-style home, wearing an apron, humming her way around the kitchen. The image didn't work. The woman had the natural grace of a dancer, the determined eyes of a professional of some sort. How would she ever fit in, living with a fireman in T-or-C? Sure, his place had a view of the distant lake, but this woman needed the ocean nearby, a quiet stretch of beach where she could practice pushing back the sea.

Lowell often played this game, using his imagination to put a prospective wife into the warm home he'd built. Rarely did one fit his *Ozzie and Harriet* view of family and home. He tried not to let it bother him. Life rarely fit your expectations. You just roll with it, and learn to adjust. Maybe he'd find the perfect wife. Or maybe he'd just find someone, anyone, willing to spend her life with King Kong.

He was ready. Over the years, he'd created the perfect love nest. His mother, Agnes, had helped with the decorator touches, but Lowell had picked out most of the furniture himself. It cost plenty, because he always insisted on the best Montgomery Ward had to offer. But the end result was flawless. Shiny appliances in the kitchen waiting to be plugged in and used. A lovely living room suite stitched from a tapestry showing fox-hunting scenes. Very classy. The fox hunters moved Lowell to cover the sofa in clear plastic to keep it from fading until a wife showed up to use it everyday. Pretty soon, everything in the house was wrapped in tightly taped plastic, perfectly preserved gifts awaiting his bride.

He lived in two rooms of the house, in the back, off the carport. In one room, he kept a TV, a weight machine, an armchair, a hot plate and a half-size fridge. In the other, a bed and a bookshelf full of bodybuilding magazines. It was all he needed. The rest of the house stayed pristine if he never used it. Once a week, he went through the place with a vacuum cleaner and feather duster, keeping everything as fresh as the day he bought it.

He spent most of his time at the firehouse. Three days on, around the clock, and two days off. Even on his days off, he'd often hang out there, lifting weights, shooting basketballs, joshing with the guys. The chief liked having him around. Lowell, who knew no pain and who was as strong as two oxen, was the man you wanted at a fire with an ax in his hands. More than once, Lowell had emerged from a fire, his slicker smoking, carrying out an unconscious homeowner. He wouldn't even know he was on fire unless somebody pointed it out and hosed him down.

Such single-mindedness served him well, whether it was at work or in the weight room. Now that his mom was gone, Lowell intended to pour that same intensity into finding a wife to share his life.

He'd fallen asleep the night before thinking of Liza West, trying to imagine someone that glamorous living among the snowbirds in T-or-C. She had said at dinner that she loved warm climates, and T-or-C was nothing if not warm. But what else did he have to offer? Liza was the type who took up with a prince, not a firefighter.

Daydreaming about Liza made Lowell feel guilty. The prince was his friend, and Liza was firmly in love with him. A baboon could see that. Lowell never would say or do anything to interfere with the prince's romance, but he couldn't help thinking about Liza West. What was it Jimmy Carter had said that time, about lusting in his heart? Lowell knew exactly what old Jimmy meant.

He also had been occupied, in a very different way, by thoughts of John Ray Mooney. He'd watched the man the night before, had seen the rough edges and the proprietary way John Ray looked at the prince.

Lowell hated to think anyone a liar, but he felt certain that whole tale about the stolen wallet was so much wind. John Ray clearly had some hold on the prince, but it didn't come from being a hero. Lowell had been a hero before, plenty of times, pulling people out of fires, and he thought he knew how one acted. A real hero stays quiet about his accomplishments. A real hero has manners and modesty and style. John Ray forgot to close his mouth when he chewed. He talked too loud. He might be the kind of man who reacts, a reflex that would knock a mugger off his feet. But he also seemed the type who'd snatch up the wallet and dash away with it.

Lowell couldn't tolerate bullies. If he thought John Ray was threatening his new friend, he might have to put a stop to it. It wasn't a thought he savored. Getting rid of John Ray might be an all-day job. Lowell knew he could take John Ray in the wrestling ring, using his bulk and his strength and his knowledge of leverage. But life is not a wrestling ring and fights are rarely fair. John Ray seemed the sort who'd hit you with a chair.

Lowell certainly wouldn't make the first move, not unless Bennie told him he needed help. He'd never trust that he had the situation sized up accurately. He often was fooled by the mysteries of people's relationships, so fickle and perverse.

He worried he might just be jealous. If the prince needed a bodyguard, why didn't he ask me? If anyone fit the standard model for a bodyguard, it's me. Bennie seems to enjoy my company. Why not me?

He slowed at the thought, kicking up sand as he drifted onto part of the beach not packed down by the tides. He had a good life in T-or-C, one filled with familiar routines and trustworthy friends. He'd assumed all along that all he needed was a woman to make it complete. But now he'd seen how the other half lives. Bennie had a terrific time, living in luxury's lap. Lowell supposed a bodyguard like John Ray would get a lot of spillover—booze and food and, oh yes, women. Royalty attracted females like no amount of body-building could. Someone who spent every day with Bennie could get his pick of the castoffs and near-misses. Women, my Lord, like Liza West.

Lowell stretched a few times, then started jogging back toward the Hotel Del. He slowed when he reached the spot where he'd seen the t'ai chi woman, but she was gone.

13

Billy Ho was awakened by John Ray banging on his door at first light. John Ray hustled him out of bed, not even allowing him another tumble with Liza, and insisted they immediately begin his makeover. Billy grumbled and stumbled along, his hangover playing havoc with his equilibrium, but John Ray didn't seem to notice.

First, to the hotel's hair salon. John Ray had called the concierge and—no doubt after dropping the prince's name—had persuaded him to open the salon an hour early so John Ray could be first in line. The hairstylist wasn't happy about the early appointment. Billy wondered how long it would take her to realize she'd put mascara on only one of her sleepy eyes.

Billy was amazed at the amount of hair on John Ray's head. Once all the grease and gunk was washed out of it, the wet hair fell to his chin. At Billy's instructions, the stylist clipped off nearly all the length, leaving John Ray with the short, side-parted haircut of a businessman. Billy was surprised to find that John Ray's hair was fine and soft and *fluffy*, and it lay down perfectly.

John Ray seemed to think the haircut was enough, but Billy insisted he get a facial and a manicure, too. By the time the salon workers were done, John Ray fairly glowed.

After a quick brunch in a cafe off the lobby, they went shopping in some of the thirty stores that lined the downstairs corridor of the Hotel Del's on-premises mall. John Ray picked up some casual stuff from the Nautica shop, including a green-and-blue windproof jacket. And he bought a couple of loud neckties at a souvenir store, including one with little Tabasco bottles all over it. Billy didn't argue. Dressing up this ruffian was like putting a ballgown on a pig anyway.

When it came time to buy suits, they saddled up the Mercedes and headed for San Diego. Billy knew of shops there that sold tailor-made suits costing thousands of dollars each. But he was taking John Ray to the mall. The man was playing the bodyguard, by God, not the prince, and he could make do with off-the-rack. John Ray didn't seem to know the difference. He seemed perfectly happy riding around, spending the prince's money, jabbering like a kid.

"What the hell kinda name is 'Guillermo Ho' anyhow?" John Ray shouted over the wind that tousled his new hairdo in the convertible.

They were climbing the arc of the high bridge connecting Coronado to San Diego, on their way to the cotton-candy architecture of Horton Plaza mall. Billy didn't want to talk now. He wanted to enjoy the breeze and the sunlight dancing on the bay. Ah, the white triangles of the sailboats. How he wished he were on one, instead of trapped doing the Eliza Doolittle number on John Ray Mooney.

"Billy," he yelled back. "I really prefer Billy."

"Yeah, yeah, but what's a 'Ho?'"

Billy sighed. So much to explain. It was easier being the prince, letting "Bandapanang" trip off one's tongue.

"My father's family is Chinese," he shouted. If he'd known they were going to be yakking the whole time, he would've left up the top on the Mercedes. "They're merchants in Tijuana, three generations. Every generation marries a Mexican girl, every generation is a little less Chinese. But we're still named Ho."

"Where's Guillermo come from?"

"My mother had a brother by that name. She thought 'Guillermo Ho' sounded musical."

"Sounds like a rap song. About a hooker."

Billy sighed again.

"It could be worse. My sister's named Heidi."

"Heidi Ho?"

Billy nodded. Let John Ray chew on that one for a while.

"You grew up in Tijuana?"

"Till I was sixteen. Then I came north."

"Legally?"

"What kinda question is that? You calling me a wetback?"

"Take it easy. Just askin'"

That's what Billy needed. One more thing for John Ray to hold over him. They don't give green cards to professional house guests.

"I'm a citizen of the United States, as you should know from prowling through my wallet," Billy huffed.

"Your wallet also says you're a citizen of Yip."

"Maybe you should remember that. Just think of me as the prince at all times, and there's less chance of a slip-up."

"Don't worry about me. I don't slip."

"Then what were you doing in Folsom?"

"A minor miscalculation."

Billy smiled. Sounded like something he would say. Maybe John Ray was learning a few things after all.

"What about you?" John Ray asked. "Do any time?"

"A night or two in Mexican jail. Kid stuff. I left before they could make me do real time."

"For what?"

"Auto theft."

"In Mexico? I thought was practically legal there."

"The car belonged to the chief of police."

"Oh."

"A minor miscalculation."

Billy swung the Mercedes off the freeway at the Fourth Avenue exit and entered the traffic crawl among the funky skyscrapers that make up Downtown. John Ray leaned his head back, gawking at the cylinders and peaks and sleek black faces. Billy thinking, wait until he gets a load of Horton Plaza.

Horton Plaza is two square blocks of shops and restaurants and theaters, stacked four stories high. The place looks like it was assembled from the plans of architects from around the world, architects who'd never met each other or seen the others' blueprints. Palladian windows and Corinthian columns and Arabian arches and kitschy Deco diners, all packed around an open-air spiral of balconies and ramps and neon-lit storefronts.

John Ray was whistling as they entered from the parking garage, some tune sounded like the theme from that old Tony Randall show, *The Odd Couple*. Billy noted that John Ray swallowed the whistle as soon as they entered the mall from its sterile parking garage, too busy gaping at the Disneyland of shopping. Guy's been in the slammer, where you can't even pick your brand of cigarettes, Horton Plaza should be sensory overload. Billy was counting on it. John Ray turns his back for a second while Billy's holding the wallet and, poof, Billy's gone. One advantage of being small is being able to disappear into a crowd.

John Ray must've scented his plan because he stuck close, walking one step behind and just to one side, the perfect position for a bodyguard. Also, the perfect position to nab Billy if he tried to make a run for it.

They marched through the crowd, stepping around baby strollers and outflanking the plodders. Billy steered John Ray directly to Nordstrom's, hurried him past a jewelry counter when he slowed, and turned him over to a golden boy named Michael who wore a tape measure draped around his neck. Billy slumped into a chair, moping, waiting for John Ray to make up his tiny mind.

Fortunately, John Ray was a perfect forty-two long and Michael was smoother than eelskin and it didn't take long to load John Ray down with three new suits and a double-breasted blue blazer. Billy perfunctorily picked out some dress shirts with spread collars and a fine feel, and threw in a black cashmere T-shirt for good measure.

"There," he said. "That gonna do it for you?"

"I don't know. I was thinking shoes."

They both looked down at his battered cowboy boots.

"You definitely need shoes," Billy said. "Let's pay for this stuff before we go shoe shopping. We can stash it in the car."

"Good idea."

Michael waited patiently at the inobtrusive cash register. For customers buying in this kind of volume, Michael had all day.

John Ray slipped the prince's fat wallet out of his pocket, deftly removed the Platinum Card and handed it to Billy, who in turn handed it to Michael.

Michael gave the card a glance, then paused, looked at it more closely, reading the prince's long name. He looked up at Billy, who smiled, then over at John Ray, who didn't.

Michael opened his mouth. Billy held a finger up to his lips and winked.

The salesman blinked twice, then nodded once. Slowly. Then he rang up the sale with brisk efficiency, smiling to himself.

"Here you are, Your Highness," he said, as he handed the slip and the card to Billy.

Billy signed the slip with a flourish and palmed the credit card, but John Ray tapped him on the shoulder and he handed it over. John Ray slipped the card back into the wallet and the wallet back into his pocket. His new chinos had a flap on the pocket, and he carefully buttoned it shut.

Fine, thought Billy. Take care of that wallet. Because sooner or later you're going to screw up, and I'll have it back. All of it. And then, maybe I'll do to you what I did to the Prince of Yip.

Once they were out of Michael's sight, John Ray made Billy carry the heavy purchases to the car.

"Bodyguards gotta keep their hands free," he said as he strolled along, scoping out the store windows while Billy lugged the clothes like a freaking pack mule.

All right, he told himself, we'll buy some stupid shoes, quick as we can, and then maybe we'll head back to the hotel for a late lunch. I could use some pool time. But first, we need to stop at a bank. John Ray wants twelve-thousand dollars. Who knew where he came up with that figure? But Billy could get it. In fact, he could get a little more. Maybe get a cash advance of fifteen thousand. Then he could pocket three grand before he handed the rest over to John Ray. A little spending money would be a good idea, in case he had to run for it.

Hey. Billy would need to carry the whole wallet for the identification check. Maybe he could sneak out one of the credit cards. The Visa, the MasterCard. There were so many, would John Ray even notice if one was missing? Wouldn't work if John Ray was standing right next to him. The man had hawk's eyes. But what if he made him wait outside?

Then Billy got a glimmer, one of those quick, bright moments when the cherries line up and the jackpot is on the way. He'd go to the National Bank of Coronado. That was one place where John Ray would willingly wait in the car. And Billy could argue that they knew him there now, that the mutton-chopped manager would do anything he asked.

Billy wouldn't mention it yet. He'd wait until they were in the car, the trunk full of John Ray's new clothes. Then he'd just say it matter-of-factly. It would seem so logical. Scam him, Billy, that's what you're best at doing.

"Hey, Your Highness?" John Ray's voice came from just behind Billy's shoulder. "You wanta step on it a little? We haven't got all day."

"Fuck you."

A passing fat woman gasped at the obscenity.

"You're welcome!" John Ray said.

14

Earl Shambley's heart skipped when the Prince of Yip sauntered through the bank doors Wednesday afternoon. He'd spent the whole day puzzling over his failure of the night before, trying not to let the customers see him yawn. A very late night, and not once had he been able to get the prince alone. Then here the little fucker comes, walking right in the door of the one place Earl couldn't be seen talking with him.

The prince passed within arm's reach, and it took a second for Earl to remember to breathe.

The prince didn't bother with the teller this time. He walked straight to the desk of the manager, who clambered to his feet when he saw royalty approaching.

"Mr. Warren, I believe?"

Warren smiled nervously, bowed stiffly and didn't know what to do with his hands.

"I have some quick business to transact."

The prince seated himself in a chair next to Warren's desk, pulled out his wallet and spoke to the manager in low tones. The manager went to his feet, a credit card in his hand, headed toward the vault.

The prince needed another cash advance? So soon? The man just picked up five grand yesterday. Even expensive habits don't consume it that fast.

Somebody was milking the prince for money. Earl would bet his mustache on it. He strolled over to the smoked-glass doors and saw exactly what he'd expected. Across the street, sitting in the passenger seat of the red Mercedes convertible, was the rangy redneck. Man looked different today. As Earl watched, the man turned the rear-view mirror, studied his new haircut. That was it. That, and that windbreaker, looks like he just stepped off a fucking yacht.

So, the man's got himself a new look. Probably the prince's idea, try to make him more presentable. But why keep him around at all? And why the cash? What did that redneck have on the prince that he could make him walk into a bank for more dough?

Earl moved away from the doors. The prince still cooled in his chair, waiting for the manager to call the powers-that-be. Studying his fingernails and humming to himself. He didn't look like a man who was being forced to pick up money.

The manager returned, carrying a fat zippered bag with the bank's name emblazoned on the side.

"So sorry for the delay, Your Highness."

Warren's face was flushed bright red at the thought of handing over so much cash. Earl knew Warren would rather keep all the cash money in the vault, so he could go in and sniff it whenever he felt like it. Man was strange that way.

The prince unzipped the bag, counted out a fistful of bills and put them in the pocket inside his jacket. Warren looked like he wanted to kiss him.

The prince thanked the manager, offered him a limp hand. Then he was up, strutting toward the door, the bag under his elbow. Casual, like he was carrying his lunch.

Earl chewed on the inside of his cheek to keep from shouting after the prince.

Damn.

15

So far, Omar's first day at A-1 Auto Rental was a snap. Everything was on the computer. Just a matter of punching the right buttons. Give Omar a mouse and some decent software, he could *draw* you a fucking rent-a-car. This shit was easy. Customers come up to the counter, all loaded down with their bags, gasp out their names. You maybe make them say it two or three times, pretend the airplanes overhead drown out all business here at Lindbergh Field. Then type the name into the appropriate slot, hit "enter" and, faster than you can say boom-shaka-laka, you got everything you need to put them into a nice shiny car so they can drive around lost in San Diego.

Omar couldn't help giving them faulty directions. Tourists should get out more, see how the real people live. All of 'em want directions to the beach. Omar wants to yell, "Go west, my man!" But he also wants to keep his new job.

He had no trouble talking his way into jobs. Keeping them, though, was another story. His mind was too quick for the menial jobs he landed. He'd get bored, start jiving on customers or slipping off to flirt with some honey. Next thing you know, Omar was back at the unemployment office.

This time would be different. He liked being at the airport, everybody bustling around. So far, he'd stayed just busy enough renting cars to tourists that he hadn't been too tempted to goof on them. 'Course, he'd only been at the new job five hours. Give it a week, see how he'd feel then.

Already, Omar knew he didn't like the uniform. All A-1 agents wore purple blazers with black pants. Hertz had gold blazers, Budget had green, Avis had red, but A-1 had purple. Shit. Guess they were last in line when it came time to pick. Plus, the blazers didn't come in extra-longs. To get one with sleeves that came to his knobby wrists, Omar had to go up a few sizes in the chest. Looked like he was wearing a purple barrel.

So Omar's standing there, wearing his purple blazer and his black knit pants and his black-and-white Nike Air Street Dekes, fighting the temptation to shout "Fire!" to the crowd around the counter, when these little matching Asian fuckers come marching right up like they own the damn airport. Five of 'em. Talking in some singsong language, sounds like wind chimes. They're all wearing black suits and white shirts and narrow ties, like they're in "Reservoir Dogs," but not one of them goes over five-foot-three, and Omar just has to laugh. "Reservoir Dwarves."

The five little men frown at him in unison, and Omar stifles the laugh and says to the nearest one, looks like the boss, "How may I help you gentlemen today?"

The leader hands a business card to Omar, whose eyes widen when he sees the name: "Subi Kamal bin Mohammed." No wonder the man just hands over a card. He tries to spell that out, we'd be here all day.

"Yo, your name's Mohammed?" Omar said brightly. "Mine, too. Say hello to a brother."

Omar reached across the counter and shook the bewildered man's hand.

"Omar Medulla Muhammad's my name. Muhammad with a 'u,' not an 'o.' You a Muslim? Yeah? Me, too. I mean, my parents are. Not no Nation of Islam Muslims, either. We're talking the real thing. But Omar don't really practice the religion no more himself. Where you from?"

"Yip."

"Say what?"

"Yip. It is in Asia."

"That a fact? Hey, you remind me of somebody. That guy who does the kung fu movies? You know who I mean."

Omar formed his big hands into blades, whipped them through the air at various angles, like he was chopping down a cornfield.

"You know that dude. Whatsisname. Jackie Chan. That's it. You guys watch Jackie Chan over in this place Yip? Biggest movie star in the world, man, but most people in this country never even heard of him. But Omar knows, because Omar is in tune with the mystic influences of the East."

Kamal thought the black giant would never stop talking. Just get the car. We have business to do.

The others tried not to smile, but Kamal could see the merriment in their eyes. The Jackie Chan thing again. Everywhere he went, people noticed the resemblance. Kamal had Jackie's smile, his haircut, his lumpy nose that had been broken so many times. It had become a joke with the other members of the Sultan's Royal Guard. Kamal, with his muscles and his black belt in tae kwon do, thinks he's Jackie Chan. But, they guffawed, Kamal shouldn't do his own stunts like the Great Jackie. He might fall over.

Ridicule, Kamal knew, is the price of command. The price was especially high when the one in charge is younger than the rest. Fat Kulu had been in the Royal Guard nearly as long as Kamal had been alive. The others on this journey to America—Fong, Lombok and Serang—all had been in the Sultan's service longer than Kamal.

Kamal's work in the Royal Guard had been exemplary, despite the inner ear imbalances that had plagued him all his life. Occasionally, something went out of whack in there and Kamal lost all sense of equilibrium. One minute he's walking along normally; the next, the sidewalk comes up and hits him in the face. The Sultan had been most generous over the years, sending Kamal to specialists in Manila and Singapore and Tokyo, but none of the doctors had found a cure. Kamal had learned to live with his condition, how to sense the onset of the dizzy spells. But it still made his men laugh when he went tumbling.

Right now, after seventeen hours in the pressurized cabin of the Royal Learjet, Kamal's inner ears were abuzz. His head ached and he felt the first traces of vertigo. If this Omar would just shut up and get their Cadillac, Kamal would be fine. He needed to sit still a while, ride in a car to the hotel.

Then, he'd be ready to accomplish his mission: find Prince Seri Hassan Bandapanang bin Mohammed and take him home to Yip.

Seri. Kamal's best boyhood friend. If Kamal closed his eyes, he could picture Seri and himself as boys, racing around the palace, ducking behind trees, throwing ripe fruit at each other like monkeys. Usually, such rough play ended with Kamal falling over somewhere and scraping his chin. He always took such accidents without complaint.

His stoicism was one reason the Sultan picked him to head the Royal Guard. But the main reasons were his family ties—Kamal's parents were lifelong servants in the Sultan's household—and his friendship with Seri.

Kamal stayed behind when Seri went off to the United States for college. He moped around the palace, doing whatever tasks were given him. But the all-knowing Sultan had seen his loneliness and had placed him in the Royal Academy, where he could be trained as a security man. The oil boom was peaking then, and the Sultan felt he needed an army of security men to keep the populace from complaining while he stuffed the royal treasury with profits. It took a while for the riches to trickle down, as the Sultan explained so many times over the island's one radio station. Armed guards around the palace served as a reminder to be patient.

At first, Kamal had assumed he'd be trained as Seri's bodyguard, maybe even be sent to mythical California to keep an eye on the prince. But it was not to be. The Sultan instead promoted him to head the Royal Guard, though he was only twenty-four years old at the time. Now, a year later, Kamal felt like he'd earned some respect from his men. If he could just stop tipping over.

Kamal hadn't seen Seri in three years, and his heart pounded with excitement. How Seri must've changed, thriving in the hustle-bustle of America! He could hardly wait to see him.

His men were excited, too, though they tried not to show it in the airport. They'd chattered like cockatoos during the flight, speculating about what they'd see in the U.S.A. The Sultan rarely traveled—he had everything he needed brought to him in Yip—and none of the men had been to the States before. But, like Third World people around the globe, they had visions of what life was like in America, all based on rock 'n' roll songs and old movies and syndicated television shows. Much of the in-flight conversation had centered on *Baywatch*.

Kamal had ignored the banter. It was fine for the men to keep themselves amused, but his thoughts were on Seri.

The Sultan clearly was worried about his son. No one had heard from Seri in weeks, and that wasn't like the young prince. If nothing else, Seri usually called home so the Sultan would order the embassy to send him a pouch full of cash. But no calls had come for nearly a month. Nothing, except a steady stream of credit cards bills from all over Southern California. The Sultan didn't mind the bills, but he didn't want Seri to get out of control. He wanted his son to learn restraint. That was one reason he'd sent him to California.

The Sultan had ordered the Royal Guard to track down his son and bring him home for a visit. Sending Kamal was supposed to make it easier if Seri balked. They could recount old times and renew acquaintances during the long flight home.

Finally, the giant in the purple coat handed over the keys, along with a form for Kamal to sign. Kamal threw the keys over his shoulder without looking, knowing Fong would catch them. Fong always drove, no matter where in the world they might be working.

Kamal carefully printed his name in English on the rental forms, handed the papers back to Omar, and led Fong and the others toward the nearest door. He had no doubt he could find the rental cars. And Fong had studied maps of San Diego on the flight over from Yip. He could drive from the airport to Coronado with his eyes closed.

The Royal Guardsmen's rooms were reserved at La Avenida Inn, the only place where the embassy could find vacancies on short notice. The inn was one block from the Hotel Del Coronado, the last place from which credit card charges had originated. The embassy, across the continent in Washington, had also seen to the rental car reservation. All Kamal and his men had to do was pick up the car and check into the hotel. Awaiting them there would be a diplomatic pouch containing further instructions and five pistols—fifteen-shot Glocks with extra clips, as specified by Kamal. Given that hardware and these men, Kamal felt he could take on any force in the world, a whole battalion of Jackie Chans, if it meant helping Seri.

Omar Medulla Muhammad watched the five black-suited men march off, ugly ducklings all in a row. He'd wanted to help them with some directions, maybe send them east to Miramar or south toward Tijuana, but they didn't wait around to hear his patter. That's okay. Plenty of other tourists to come.

I'm gonna like this job, Omar thought. You see some strange shit at the airport.

16

As soon as he got back to his hotel room, John Ray Mooney dialed the phone number Big Odie had given him.

"Yeah?"

"Odie?"

"Jus' a second."

John Ray wiped beads of sweat off his forehead.

"What?"

"Odie?"

"Yeah. Who's this?"

"John Ray."

"You motherfucker. I been lookin' for you."

"Hold on a second, Odie. I've got your money. I'm looking at it right now."

"That's good, boy. That's mighty good. But your week was up yesterday."

"I ran into a few problems coming up with the cash. But I've got it now."

"Too late."

"Come on, Odie. It's only one day late. I could've called you last night, but I figured you'd be out somewhere anyway."

"I was right here. Waiting for you."

"Well, I've got it now. How do you want it delivered?"

"In person. With more interest for every day you're late."

"More? Jesus, I'm already giving you fifteen large for the time I was in the pen. How much more?"

"Not money. We have to teach you a lesson. One finger for every day you're late."

John Ray looked down at his free hand, spread the fingers. The sight made him wince. He liked having all ten just where they were.

"That seems a little harsh, Odie."

"You don't deliver that money today, you're gonna find out what harsh really is."

"I can't come to you in person," John Ray said, flexing his fingers. "But I can have the money delivered by tomorrow."

"Better enclose two fingers then. That'd be two days late."

"Aw, come on."

"You think I don't mean it?"

John Ray had never been more certain of anything.

"I'll send you the money, Odie. But I'm keeping my fingers. I need 'em."

Big Odie breathed heavily into the phone. "Where are you anyway?"

John Ray hung up.

17

Earl Shambley stood at parade rest, trying not to look at the clock. It was a round schoolhouse clock with a red second hand that ever so slowly clicked its way around the face. Whenever Earl let himself register the time, he felt insulted that so little had passed. He wanted to pull his pistol and blow the clock off the wall.

Normally, four o'clock came as a relief, the end in sight. Only one more hour on his aching feet. But today, Earl wanted the workday finished. He had so much to do. He needed to go home, change clothes and pick up his Fed Ex package of press materials. He needed to check out the hotel, see if he could learn the prince's whereabouts.

He'd entertained the motion of faking illness so he could go pursue the prince. But he didn't want to call attention to himself. Who knew where this would lead? He wanted the bank employees to be able to vouch for him later.

"Earl seemed fine," they'd say. "Just the same as always. Good old Earl."

It was important to keep up appearances. When Earl was a cop in Dallas, he kept two friends on a monthly stipend. In exchange, they kept a story prepared. Whenever Earl's fellow officers had any question about where he'd been at a particular time, his friends would swear he was with them. Earl rarely used this diversion, but it was a good fallback position. If he could keep things normal around the bank, the other bank employees would provide his alibi for free.

Earl knew the tellers liked him. His secret was the mustache. In a frowning world, Earl's face set him apart, made him seem pleasant. Usually. Today, he couldn't stop scowling at the clock.

Then the door swung open and Monkey Boy strolled into the bank.

Earl recognized him immediately, though the prince's drinking buddy was dressed very differently from his Land's End look of the night before.

He wore a sweatshirt pulled tight over his sloping shoulders, shorts and big white sneakers. His thick glasses were smeared with what looked like dried sweat. Probably been working out and never cleaned his glasses afterward. Man must spend all his time at the gym. Look at the arms on the fucker. Like two railroad ties suspended from his shoulders, swinging down to his knees.

Monkey Boy picked his way through the maze of velvet ropes and took his turn with a freckled teller named Carol. Earl watched closely as he produced a blue vinyl packet of traveler's checks and set them on the counter. The ape-man leaned over the checks, his face stricken with concentration, and began signing them, one after another.

Traveler's checks? Who uses those anymore? Everybody's got credit cards these days. There's an automatic teller machine on every street corner in America. You had to be pretty cautious to fool around with traveler's checks, had to be a little old lady or a mama's boy.

Monkey Boy stepped back while Carol totaled up the checks. He looked all around the bank, and then Earl got it. The checks are part of the act. Monkey Boy was casing the bank.

Tumblers clicked in Earl's mind. He'd suspected all along the redneck was up to no good. All that sweat. Now comes Monkey Boy, clearly scoping out the bank. Maybe the two of them were planning a heist.

Monkey Boy got his cash from Carol, tucked it into a pocket. He gave Carol a hearty smile and, flushing, tucked his head into his big shoulders and loped out the door.

Earl waited until the man disappeared down the street before he approached Carol. Her carroty hair brushed the countertop as she leaned over the traveler's checks.

"Hey, Carol."

She looked up, registered Earl, smiled. "Yeah?"

"Who was that guy with the traveler's checks? I think I know him from someplace."

"The guy with the muscles?"

"You noticed those?"

Carol blushed. Earl chuckled. Damn, it was easy to read white people.

"His name is Lowell Huganut."

"Say who?"

Carol giggled. She turned the checks around on the counter for Earl to read.

"Lowell Huganut. No, I don't know him. I'd never forget a name like that."

Another giggle.

"He must just look like somebody I used to know. That's the problem with being an old, retired cop. Everybody looks like a wanted poster."

"Everybody?"

"Well, not you, Carol. Not you."

Earl went back to his position by the door, turned to find Carol still smiling. He gave her a wink.

Yeah, they like Earl here at the bank. Big guy, looks like Uncle Ben, makes you feel secure. If they only knew the dark thoughts that churned behind his pleasant face.

He glanced at the clock. Ten minutes had passed. Time enough to change everything.

18

Billy Ho changed into his red Speedo, ready to relax by the pool after the exhausting day of shopping. He stood before the tall mirror in his hotel room, flexing his short muscles, sucking in his vodka-bloated belly. Definitely need to swim some laps today. All the sitting and drinking took its toll. A life of ease can be hard on a man.

Billy wished John Ray would hurry into his own new swim trunks, so they could get down to the pool before all the sun disappeared. Billy smirked at the thought of those trunks, with their pattern of hot-pink orchids, looked like a Hawaiian shirt. He'd tried to talk John Ray into buying Speedos, but John Ray would have none of it. The package, he'd said, is too small for the contents.

Then the phone rang.

John Ray appeared in the doorway that connected their rooms, frowning at the ringing phone. His expression said it all: The prince had left instructions not to be bothered. Who could that be? Billy shrugged. John Ray gave him a quick nod, followed by the Eastwood squint. Billy cleared his throat and scooped up the receiver.

"Yes?"

He was answered by a jumble of sounds, a language he couldn't understand.

"Hello?"

"Seri?"

"This is Prince Seri Hassan Bandapanang bin Mohammed. Who is this?"

Probably, he thought, it's a hotel employee. A new immigrant working in maintenance. A bellman offering to carry Billy down to the pool on his back.

"Who is this?" asked the accented voice.

"I told you, this is the Prince of Yip. Who are you trying to reach?"

Billy waited a full minute for an answer. Nothing but silence. He glanced at John Ray, who was scowling so fiercely at the phone that Billy feared it might melt.

He eased the phone from his ear, ready to hang up. Before he could, he heard a clank, as if somebody had dropped the phone. Billy put the receiver back to his ear just in time to hear a click and a humming dial tone.

"What was that all about?"

"I'm not sure. Some foreigner. Kept asking for 'Seri.' I told him I'm Seri, but he didn't seem to believe me."

"What the fuck?"

"I don't know. Maybe there was some mix-up. But he kept asking for Seri."

John Ray's eyes widened more than Billy had seen before, more even than when he first spotted Liza in her bikini.

"It's somebody who knows the real prince," John Ray said.

"No, that's not possible."

"Why not? You two knew everybody in L.A., according to those stories you told me. Why couldn't someone have heard the prince was staying here? Maybe they decided to look him up, find a party."

"But nobody called the prince Seri. He liked being called Bennie. It was part of acting like an American."

A chill ran over Billy, so sudden and profound that he reached for his thick Hotel Del bathrobe for warmth. If it wasn't one of Bennie's American friends looking him up, then it had to be an old friend, someone who still called him by his old name. And that meant somebody from Yip.

"Oh shit."

"What?"

"The caller was from Yip."

"How do you know?"

"That language. It sounded like the stuff Bennie would blather when he was drunk. His native tongue. And, back in Yip, everybody calls him Prince Seri."

John dragged a thick hand over his face. Billy noticed for the first time that John Ray indeed had changed. The Hawaiian trunks didn't look half-bad on his tanned, toned body. Got to be a muscleman to pull off a goofy look like that.

"They're onto us," John Ray said.

"If not, they will be soon."

"What do we do?"

"We get out of here."

John Ray stood stock still, thinking it over. "We probably got till tomorrow."

"What makes you say that?" Billy didn't like the idea that John Ray had gotten ahead of him, even for a second.

"Say the guy on the phone's calling Yip right now. They've gotta decide what to do, then send somebody here to check it out."

"They could send someone from Washington. They've got an embassy there."

"They don't have one on the West Coast?"

"No, just the one. Bennie used to call back there all the time."

"But you haven't been calling there?"

"No way. Somebody might answer, could recognize Bennie's voice."

"Right. So, even if they send somebody from D.C., we probably got till tomorrow before they get here."

"What's the difference? Let's go now."

"I think we should get some more cash first. Hit that little bank again tomorrow, get advances on all your cards."

"We've got enough to run for it."

"Yeah, except I'm about to hand over twenty grand to a guy in L.A."

"Why bother? If we're moving on, he'll never find you."

"These are the Sons of Satan we're talking about. They'd find me. Eventually."

Billy sighed. "Look, this is not my problem. Keep the money. Do whatever you have to do. But I'm leaving. I can't afford to have the Yips find me."

"Yeah? And why's that?

"Because I've been spending the prince's money, for Chrissake. What are you, thick?"

"No. Just thought there might be something more."

Billy didn't like the sly look that crossed John Ray's face.

"Something you never told me. What happened to the real prince? Where is he now?"

The chill ran through Billy again. He pulled the robe tighter around his chest.

"He took off with some chick. Went to Texas, I think. He wanted a vacation, wanted to see some longhorn steers."

"Get outta here."

"Fucking foreigners, what can I tell you?"

"And he just left you his credit cards?"

"No, I had them made up by a friend. Once you copy the account numbers, it's easy to dummy up a blank. Then it all looks legit."

"It'll look legit tomorrow, too, when we swing through some banks on our way out of town."

"They've got banks in other towns."

"Yeah, but we'd be leaving too many loose ends. Wouldn't Liza wonder where you'd gone?"

"Let her wonder. Who cares?"

"Liza gets worried, doesn't know what happened to you. She calls the hotel. They don't know where the fuck you went. Maybe she calls the cops."

"So?"

"Somebody might get curious, talk to the embassy. Before long, somebody's looking at pictures and IDs and credit card signatures, and they're after your ass."

"They're already after my ass. And yours, too."

John Ray crossed his arms over his bare chest, a portrait of resolve. "We're stayin'"

"That could've been a local call. You gonna sit up all night, waiting for Yips to kick in the door?"

"No. I've got a plan. Call Liza and that guy Lowell and see if they're free for dinner."

"And then what?"

"Then the prince will do what he always does. Throw a little party. After we down a few drinks, you'll tell them about the important business trip you gotta take. Then tomorrow, we boogie out of town."

"After we stop at some banks."

"You got it, ace."

"The Yips will come after us."

"Let 'em try. I've disappeared before. It's easier than you think. Especially if you got a big pile of money."

"My money."

John Ray smiled tightly. "*Our* money."

19

Pain stabbed Kamal in the temples. He tried to hang up the phone, but missed, and the receiver felt to the floor. Kulu shot Lombok a look and Lombok picked up the receiver and gingerly returned it to its place.

Kamal's hands went to his temples. He squeezed his head, then snaked a forefinger into each ear and shook his hands, trying to squinch some air into his ear canals. Kamal leaned his hip against the telephone table. As long as he had his weight against something solid, he'd be okay. If he tried to take a step, he'd go sprawling headlong until something—his men, furniture, the floor—caught him.

He ran his hands over his face, then tried to grin at his men. Kulu and Fong, the older two, had anxiety in their eyes. Serang looked like he was stifling a laugh.

"Fong," Kamal said, and he was surprised his voice sounded so normal. "Check out the weapons and their loads. The rest of you change into your resort clothes."

"That was not Prince Seri on the phone," Kulu surmised.

"Correct. I do not know who it was, but he was in the prince's room and he tried to tell me *he* was Prince Seri."

"You are sure it was not him?" This from Serang, the Doubting Thomas of Kamal's men. Kamal felt like smacking him with a knife hand blow.

"Of course, I am sure. You think I would not recognize the prince's voice?"

"Certainly you would. But it has been a few years. Perhaps he sounds different now."

"He did not seem to recognize Malay. Do you still think it is the prince?"

"Forgive me, Kamal." Serang gave a little bow, which made him look like a shopkeeper. "I am so surprised someone might attempt to impersonate Prince Seri."

"Perhaps there is a perfectly reasonable explanation," Kulu said.

"Perhaps," Kamal agreed. "But I am not taking any chances. We will sweep through the hotel, see if we can find the prince anywhere. If someone is impersonating him, we will catch him."

Kulu grunted and shrugged out of his coat. The others followed suit.

For them, wearing pastel polo shirts rather than the usual suit and tie probably would feel like a holiday. Kamal felt more comfortable in the standard Royal Guard uniform, but he, too, would change. Black suits gave the air of businesslike menace the Sultan preferred, but they certainly wouldn't blend with the tourists.

Serang started tucking in the tail of his pink polo shirt, but Kamal stopped him, saying, "Tails out. Cover the guns."

Serang nodded. Following that movement with his eyes, Kamal felt another wave of dizziness wash over him. He closed his eyes and waited for the vertigo to pass.

When he opened them, his men stood around him in a semi-circle. The polo shirts looked like blossoms arranged by a myopic gardener. Serang in pink. Fong in yellow. Lombok in bright peach. Fat Kulu's blue shirt barely covered his stomach. They all still wore their black pants and shiny shoes, but Kamal thought the shirts would be enough of a distraction to keep anyone from noticing.

The men jacked the slides on the Glocks and shoved them into the back of their belts.

"You are not changing?" Serang asked.

"Perhaps not," Kamal said. The thought of focusing on his shirt buttons was too much. He'd wear the same sweat-stiffened suit he'd worn over from Yip rather than risk more vertigo. "Perhaps I will deal with the hotel management. Fong, get the car."

"Ten-four," said Fong, who watched too many American police movies.

"We will park outside somewhere," Kamal said, "and keep the car at hand in case we need to follow someone. I will ride with Fong, at least until this headache passes."

Kamal pushed off the desk, took a step. His dizziness always departed as quickly and mysteriously as it arrived. He'd be okay now.

"The rest of you," he said, his voice deep with command, "will take up positions at the hotel, places where you can see much foot traffic."

Kamal opened his suitcase and dug out the padded box where he kept the radios. He passed the tiny gizmos to each of them, watched carefully as the men hooked the earphones into their right ears and ran the cords down inside their shirts to the transmitters on their belts. Kamal allowed himself to smile at the efficiency of their movements. Training pays off, as he'd told them all along.

He clipped the miniature microphone to his lapel and spoke into it in the most mumbling of Malay. In unison, the others tilted their heads to the right. They looked like a herd of gazelles alerted by a snapping twig.

"Okay, move out. Once I get Fong situated, I will go to the lobby and check the prince's registration. Operation Tiger Cub is officially under way."

Curt nods all around. The men marched toward the door, and Kamal winced at their military-stiff movements, the black pants, the loud shirts.

"And men," he said, "try not to be noticed."

20

Liza West cooled her hands against the sides of her fishbowl margarita glass. Her palms were sweating and she'd already used up the little Hotel Del cocktail napkin. It lay in a damp wad in the center of the table, an emerald eyeball staring up at her and the prince and John Ray Mooney. She was careful not to touch her crisp white dress, a sleeveless linen number with a skirt short as a cheerleader's. The dress had added another ninety-eight dollars to the amount she owed the folks at MasterCard. A drop in a very deep bucket, to be sure, but Liza intended to wear the dress more than this once if at all possible. She needed to learn to be frugal, particularly if tonight didn't go well. Hell, if tonight didn't go perfectly, she might as well go over to the Lucky Mart and choose which shopping cart she'd use when she became a bag lady.

John Ray's nasal drone had ground to a stop. He and Bennie stared at her, like they were wondering which planet she'd gone to visit.

"I'm sorry, what?"

"I said, did you work at your store today?"

What's it to you, Liza wondered. Big rube.

"No," she said lightly, "I spent the whole day primping."

"It shows, my dear." Smiling, Bennie patted her upper arm, which seemed extra tan next to the white dress. "You look spectacular tonight."

"Oh, Your Highness," she said, making with the Blanche DuBois. "You're giving me the vapors."

Even John Ray smiled at that. Liza noted that the menace evaporated whenever his face creased into that big grin. There was a human being somewhere under that sun-baked exterior.

Liza nearly hadn't recognized John Ray when she arrived at the Ocean Terrace Lounge. The new haircut and double-breasted blazer helped smooth some of his roughness. But all the new clothes in the world couldn't take away those steely eyes and hard slit of a mouth. For the life of her, she couldn't figure why Bennie would want such a man around. Maybe Bennie had taken on John Ray as some sort of charity case. Which was fine, if it meant he was feeling charitable.

"You seem terribly distracted tonight," Bennie said.

"I'm sorry. I've got a lot on my mind."

"Really?"

Liza didn't like his tone. Sounded as if he'd forgotten she had a mind. But his expression didn't leak any superiority. He seemed concerned, ready to listen.

Here goes nothing.

"We need to talk, Bennie. Think we could have a minute alone?"

The flint came back into John Ray's eyes.

"Certainly my dear," the prince said. "Will you excuse us, John Ray? Go get yourself another Jack Daniel's."

A sound rumbled low in John Ray's throat, but he left the table. He lanked over to the bar and perched on a stool. He didn't even pretend not to watch them.

"Now," Bennie said, "what's the matter, my sweet?"

Liza had fretted all day over how to say it. Just spill it, see what kind of reaction you get? Sidle up to it? Pour sugar all over it to make it more palatable? She'd finally decided to present it as a straight business proposition, a loan, a partnership. One tycoon to another. But now she felt herself falling back on batting eyelashes and a nervous smile.

"I've got a little problem with my business."

"Oh? Flabric isn't doing well?"

"It just hasn't taken off as quickly as I'd hoped. I think I need to change the name of the store, maybe remodel."

Liza got the feeling she'd lost Bennie. He kept glancing past her shoulder, as if he expected someone any second.

"Sounds like a good plan," he said.

"Yes, but it's going to be expensive. And I've already run up a lot of debts. I need a fresh infusion of money."

That brought Bennie's eyes back to her. He stared impassively for what seemed like hours before he said, "How much money?"

Liza's cheeks warmed. No need to sugar-coat it now.

"Sixty-two thousand dollars."

She had to admire Bennie's composure. He'd make a helluva poker player. Of course, sixty-two-thousand probably was pocket change to a prince. Liza was counting on him seeing it that way.

"A lot of money," he said noncommitally.

"I might be able to get by with less. But I need most of that to pay my bills. They've really stacked up during this tight spot."

Tight spot. Nicely put, Liza. Just in a bit of a tight spot, old boy. It's not like I hear the dogs of debt howling at my door.

"And you want to ask me for this money?"

Talk about cutting to the chase. Why didn't Bennie let her work up to it slower? And why does he keep looking at the door? Maybe that's where he wished he were headed.

"I thought you might help. A loan, perhaps?"

Liza felt her confidence slip. This wasn't going the way she'd hoped. She tried to prop up her smile, keep it light, but the room had begun to take on the rueful stink of refusal.

"You know, my dear, I've found in the past that romance and finance don't mix."

Here it comes, the Rejection Express, bearing down on her. She stepped out onto the tracks.

"I know what you mean, Bennie. It makes me feel cheap to hit on you for money. If there were any other way—"

Bennie patted her arm, gave her that sad, sweet smile.

"Don't torture yourself, Liza. I understand completely. My father is very wealthy. It's only natural you should come to me."

Liza's own sigh surprised her. It was like a gust of wind eroding her brave facade. Her throat constricted and her eyes felt hot, but she would not, could not, let him see her cry.

Bennie studied her face while she tried to maintain. She finally had his full attention, but she was so busy keeping tears at bay she couldn't think what to say next.

"Let me think about it," Bennie said. "A few days, okay?"

At least he hadn't said no. Not yet. She couldn't let any disappointment leak into her face. Liza made herself smile broadly, faking it like a runner-up in a beauty pageant.

"John Ray and I are going out of town for a few days," he said. "Don't frown, my dear. It's a business trip. I'd much rather be here with you, but duty calls."

"Where are you going?"

"Just over to Phoenix. We must see a man about a golf course. My father may be interested in investing in it."

Invest in me! said a voice in her head. *I'm right here. You don't need to go to Phoenix.*

"I'm so sorry you're leaving town," she said. "We've been having so much fun."

"And we'll have more fun as soon as I return, I promise you. I'll be gone three, maybe four, days at most. When I get back, we'll have another talk about your finances."

"You think you might be able to help?"

"I honestly don't know." Bennie's face went somber. "Frankly, I don't have that much lying around. It would have to come from the royal coffers, which means I must go to my father. Persuade him I've found a good investment here in Coronado."

The voice inside screamed, *Just give me the money! No investment plan, no loan. Just give it to me!*

"It's so sweet of you to even consider helping me. I wish I didn't have to ask—"

"Think nothing of it, my dear. What are friends for?"

Friends? They were more than friends, thank you very much. Liza didn't let friends hump her half the night. They were lovers, maybe even potential royal mates. Clearly, Liza hadn't made Bennie see that yet. Maybe she'd ruined that opportunity by asking for money rather than holding out for princess, but it was a chance she had to take. At least she'd made her pitch before he left town.

"I'll think about it," he said. "You'll have your answer as soon as we return."

"Thank you, Bennie. I mean that."

She leaned over to give him a grateful peck on the cheek, ignoring the inner voice that said, *Bite his nose off.*

21

Lowell Huganut felt like Captain America. He wore his standby blue blazer, but he'd gussied it up with a fresh white shirt and a new necktie. It was the tie that did it. Red silk sprinkled with blue stars. Just what he needed to pump him up.

He swung through the saloon door like Mighty Joe Young and spotted the prince in deep conversation with Liza at a corner table. It took Lowell a second to recognize John Ray at the bar. John Ray, too, wore a blue blazer, but Lowell didn't let that deflate him. Blue blazers were standard uniforms for bodyguards. John Ray had a new haircut, too, and his skin sort of glowed and Lowell wondered whether the man had spent the day working out. John Ray answered that by lighting a Marlboro and blowing the smoke toward the frowning bartender.

Lowell waved a paw at John Ray, but went no closer. His goal was the corner table where Liza graced the prince with a kiss on the cheek. No time like the present, as Mama always said.

"Good evening."

"Ah, Lowell! You're looking splendid tonight. Is that a new tie?"

Lowell blushed and mumbled.

"Come, join us! How about a Coors?"

Lowell's throat felt dry as a dune, but he shook his head and said, "Maybe later." He needed to be stone cold sober for what he planned to do.

"I was wondering," he said, turning to flash his teeth at Liza, "if I could have a minute with Bennie?"

Liza looked confused for a second, and her hand went protectively to the prince's shoulder.

"Alone?"

"Just for a minute."

"Of course, Lowell," Bennie said. "Liza can keep John Ray company. He looks lonely over there."

Liza silently gathered her drink. She trailed her fingernails across Bennie's shoulders as she passed behind him, and the sight gave Lowell an empty flutter behind his Abs of Steel.

He waited until Liza was out of earshot before he dragged out a chair across from Bennie. The table was a little wide for conspiratorial conversation, and Lowell caught himself leaning forward on his elbows, his big, gnarly hands a squirming centerpiece. He sat up straight and hid his hands in his lap. He took a deep breath, let it out slowly, as if he were about clean-and-jerk a heavy barbell. Then he said what he'd come to say, the words spilling out like bananas off a jouncing truck.

"Bennie, I've been doing a lot of thinking the last coupla days. About my life and all. Being around you's kinda opened my eyes, you know? I mean, I see possibilities. Something more than sitting around a firehouse, wishing I had a woman in my life."

Lowell ran out of steam on that one. He could practically hear beads of sweat popping out on his forehead, but he barged ahead.

"I like you, Bennie. I mean, like, man-to-man, right? I like hanging out with you. Anyway, I was thinking maybe you could hire me, you know?

Give me some kind of job to do so I could hang out with you some more and earn my keep, too. I'm no freeloader, Bennie. I want to make that clear. I always pull my own weight. But I don't know, man. I don't think I'm ready to go back to T-or-C yet. I don't know if I can face the same-old, same-old right now. Does that make any sense?"

Bennie fought valiantly to keep a smile off his face.

"Certainly, Lowell, I—"

"No, let me finish. I've been practicing this thing all day, like a hundred reps, so I'd get it just right."

Bennie nodded and clamped his lips shut.

"Okay. Last night you were telling us how you hired John Ray, right? And so, I was thinking, maybe you had some job I could do. I mean, I actually think I'd be a better bodyguard than John Ray. I've got to say that, man. I'm about twice as strong as him and people can't hurt me, you know? I have what they call a high threshold of pain. Sometimes, I look down and I'm bleeding somewhere. I maybe stepped on a nail or bumped into the corner of a file cabinet or something. I don't know. Just bleeding. And *I haven't felt a thing!*"

Bennie's eyes went round.

"I don't brag about it. People think it's weird. Or, some of them, they've got to try it out. This guy at the firehouse, Fred, he kept sticking pins in me. I'd just be standing there, minding my own business, and he'd slip up behind me and stab a pin in my butt. Can you believe that shit? I mean, I might not feel pain like everybody else, but I'm gonna notice a pin up my ass, am I right?"

Bennie nodded slowly. Lowell took comfort in that. He'd begun to wonder whether the prince was following this.

"Anyway, I kinda got off track there. Here's all I want to say: Think about a job for me. Maybe you need two bodyguards, I don't know. Maybe you need a chauffeur or somebody to lift things. I can do all of that. You just say the word. I'm supposed to fly back home tomorrow, but I can cancel the ticket in a flash."

Bennie leaned back in his chair and steepled his fingers. He appeared to study the architecture of his hands, or maybe he was peering at Lowell through his fingers, seeing how Lowell would look in a cage. Lowell had caught people doing that before.

"How did you make him stop?" Bennie asked.

"Who?"

"The man at the firehouse. With the pins."

"Fred?"

"Fred."

"I warned him several times. I told him, 'Hey, Fred, we've gotta work together here around the clock. I don't need to be watching my back all the time 'cause you think you're funny.' But he did it again anyway. Giggling jackass."

"So what happened then?"

"I kinda lost my temper and I wheeled on him."

"You punched him?"

"No, I was too angry to fight. I just grabbed him by the head."

Lowell raised his enormous hands to demonstrate. It looked like he was squeezing a basketball.

"And?"

"And, he kinda passed out. They had to give him smelling salts."

"And he never stuck you again."

"No. He didn't really stay around the fire department after that. Went a little crazy, you ask me. Moved out to this shack in the middle of the desert, sits around a campfire all night, howling at the coyotes."

Bennie clapped his tiny hands, then grasped the chair arms to lean forward and exclaim: "You squeezed the man's head so hard he went insane?"

Lowell grimaced. He hadn't planned to tell Bennie any of this. The business about Fred and the pins just slipped out. Hadn't the prince even heard the part where Lowell asked for a job?

"I'd feel terrible if I thought it was my fault he went crazy. I think there was something wrong with him all along. You gotta be a little nuts to go around sticking people with pins."

"True. Still, to grab a man by the head and put him down is no small accomplishment."

"I was mad. I didn't know what I was doing."

Bennie nodded, amusement dancing in his eyes. Lowell felt his lower lip drooping. He tucked it up, sucked off two damp spots where saliva had accumulated during his long speech. There was nothing else to say.

"I must have some use for a man of your rare talents," Bennie said.

Lowell felt the air leak out of him, and realized he'd been holding his breath. He gulped several lungfuls to make up for lost time.

"Cancel your ticket, Lowell. I'm putting you on the payroll."

Lowell bobbed his head. "What do you want me to do?"

"We'll work out the details later. First, we should celebrate."

"Oh, man, yes. I'll have that beer now."

"Let me tell you something first. Then we'll gather the others and go to dinner."

Lowell furrowed his brow, trying to look attentive.

"John Ray and I are going out of town on a business trip tomorrow. The arrangements have already been made, and I really can't change the plans to take you along."

Lowell felt his crest falling, but he nodded some more.

"Instead, I want you to stay here at the Del and keep Liza company while I'm gone. Take her to dinner, a movie, whatever. She's not happy about me leaving and she has a lot on her mind. Could you look after her?"

This was getting better and better. Lowell felt a hot bulge in his pants and he scooted closer to the table to hide it from the perceptive prince.

"Yessir. I can do that."

"Good. But there's one thing, Lowell."

"What's that?" Lowell felt suddenly guilty, and braced himself for a warning from the prince, something about keeping his mitts off Liza.

Smiling, Bennie held up a stubby, cautioning finger and ticked it back and forth with each word.

"Don't. Squeeze. Her. Head."

22

John Ray Mooney said: "The Man from G.L.A.D."

"What?" Liza turned to look at him for the first time since she'd joined him at the bar. He'd begun to worry that her stare would burn holes in Lowell's noggin.

"The Man from G.L.A.D. I've been trying to decide who you look like. With that great tan and that white hair. You're like the daughter of the Man from G.L.A.D."

"Whatever are you talking about?"

"You don't remember him? Used to be this guy in TV commercials. He was, like, a secret agent or something. Wore one of those raincoats."

"A trenchcoat?"

"Right. A trenchcoat. He'd show up at people's houses to solve their garbage bag problems. You don't remember this guy?"

"No. But I'm sure I don't look like some man in a garbage commercial."

"Sure you do."

Liza looked ready to bristle, but he didn't give her the chance.

"I watched too much TV when I was a kid," he said. "That's what's wrong with me."

"Oh, is that what it is?"

"I'm always seeing people who look like somebody on TV."

"Maybe they're actors. This is Southern California, you know."

"No, I mean just regular people. I see a guy like the bartender over there, got a shaved head and an earring, what am I thinking?"

Liza blinked at him.

"Mr. Clean, right?"

She nodded, at least pretending to follow along.

"Or, that lady over there, wearing the hat looks like a big white Frisbee?"

Liza followed his glance to where the woman sat sulking, chewing on a swizzle stick while her husband talked sports with some other fatso.

"Speedy Alka-Seltzer!"

"Who?"

"You don't remember anything. How old are you, anyhow?"

He gave her a twinkle, but wasn't sure she could discern it. His face let him down sometimes. Especially when it came to smiling. Hadn't had much practice in the last few years.

"That's a rude question."

"And the answer is?"

"None of your damn business."

"Good enough."

"Let me ask *you* a rude question instead."

"Shoot. I've got nothing to hide."

"What did you mean, watching TV is what's wrong with you? Is something really wrong with you?"

John Ray hid behind his drink for a second, letting the cold Jack Daniel's warm his insides. He drained it and rattled the ice cubes to get the bartender's attention.

"I've got a problem with instant gratification," he said. "That's what this shrink told me."

"You went to see a shrink?"

"Not voluntarily. It's a long story. The point is this shrink said I spent too much time watching TV when I was kid. It spoiled me. I want all my fun right now, all the time. I want every problem solved within thirty minutes. I want a laugh track."

"That's what the shrink said?"

John Ray shrugged. "You can't believe anything those jackasses say.

Though it would explain why I've never been able to stick it out in a long relationship."

"Never?"

"Well, there was this one woman, named Angel. That lasted a while, but it turned out wrong."

"What happened?"

"Another long story. Let's just say Angel, while she was heavenly to behold, turned out to be more like the Devil."

"You've got a lot of long stories you're holding back."

John Ray looked down at his hands, flexed his fingers. She wants to hear a story, he could tell her about how Big Odie wants to chop off a few.

"Ain't that what life is?" he said instead. "One long story?"

Liza turned away from him, looking thoughtful. Then her gaze lit on Lowell bending the prince's ear and her frown reappeared.

"So what about Lowell?" she said. "What TV character does he remind you of?"

"Magilla Gorilla."

"I don't remember him, either. And, besides, that's mean. Lowell's sweet."

John Ray chewed on that for a second. "He sure is flapping his lips."

"Yeah," she said. "I wonder what's going on. I thought Lowell was only allotted a dozen words per hour."

"He is the quiet sort, isn't he?"

"I like that in a man."

John Ray didn't care for the way she said it, but he didn't let on.

"Strong, silent type for you, huh? Then how'd you end up with Bennie? He's a talker."

"I didn't say silent, you did. I said I like quiet men. I'm not surprised you don't understand the difference."

Damn, she could be snooty. She comes around with that white hair and her short skirt and those jumbo green peepers and she looks like some mutant hooker you'd give anything to spend one night with, and then she opens her mouth and gives you the country club snub. It was unsettling.

She turned her attention back to the corner where Lowell sat with the prince, and John Ray followed, and he was surprised by what he saw. Lowell's muscles stood out in all directions and his smile was like headlights.

"Looks like good news," Liza said bitterly.

23

The Hotel Del Coronado reminded Kamal of the Royal Palace back in Bandar Surijawa, the capital of Yip. Like the palace, the hotel was built on many levels around a central garden. Its exterior was a hodgepodge of decorative shingles and spindly balcony rails, all painted a brilliant white, just like the palace. But the hotel's roof was a gaudy red only a decadent American could love, and its corner towers were steeply pitched cones that had none of the grace of the onion-shaped palace minarets. While grand in an old-fashioned way, the interior didn't have the arched doorways and cool tile floors that made the palace seem open and airy. And, of course, no tame tigers roamed among the palm trees in the garden.

Kamal prowled the hotel, hunting for Prince Seri or the stranger who'd answered Seri's phone. It wasn't as easy as he'd expected. The hotel was huge, well over four hundred rooms, and he had no idea which one the pretender occupied. He'd managed to bull his way through the front desk by phone, when he first called the prince's room, by claiming it was a Yip national emergency. But he didn't want to try such tactics in person. He and his men needed to stay undercover, so they could find Seri and take him home without the interference of the local authorities. The Sultan wanted it all handled swiftly and quietly, without drawing the attention of the voracious American media.

Hours passed without incident. Only once did anyone question why the Asians in the pastel polo shirts loitered around the hotel, talking into microphones clipped to their collars. A blue-suited security man stopped Lombok and asked questions. But Lombok, following Kamal's orders, feigned ignorance of English. He jabbered in Malay until the security man walked away, shaking his head.

As the night wore on, the men began to complain about the chill fog rolling over the coastline. They all had the thin blood of the tropics, and the short-sleeved shirts weren't enough protection from the cold and damp.

"Quiet, Kulu," Kamal said when he tired of the carping. "Your fat will keep you from freezing to death."

One of the men snorted into an open mike, but Kamal didn't think it was Kulu. The fat old bear knew better.

Kamal too felt cold and weary. Jet lag had hit him hard, and he kept being wracked by face-stretching yawns. He was close to summoning Fong on the radio and having him pull the Cadillac around, so the men could return to their hotel for some rest. But he wanted to sweep through the hotel once more first, checking the halls, the lobby, the bar.

Kamal knew the pretender the second he laid eyes on him. The resemblance to Seri was vague—the man had an insult of a nose—but the showy way he held forth at a table in the bar told Kamal this was the one who pretended to be the prince. Others sat at the table with him. A tall man whose eyes were shadows beneath his brows. A woman with white hair and a short white dress, who made Kamal think of angels. A beefy man with the face of the orangutans slowly going extinct in the jungles of Yip.

Kamal didn't enter the bar. He watched the table through narrow windows set into the swinging doors. The longer he watched, the more certain he was.

"I think I've found our prey," he said into his microphone. "Surround the bar on the ocean side of the hotel. Surveillance Mode Watchful Mantis."

That was all he had to say. He'd drilled his men so thoroughly over the past year that he knew their discipline would control matters from there. Kulu, Serang and Lombok would take positions within sight of the bar's entrances, remaining carefully invisible, until ordered to do otherwise. No matter how cold and tired they were.

Kamal cast about the narrow gallery outside the bar's interior doors until he found the perfect chair from which to watch the windows. Someone had left a copy of the San Diego Union-Tribune in the chair, and Kamal picked it up and spread it in front of him as if to read. But his eyes were on the party in the bar.

He needed proof. His men needed rest, and it made no sense to waste the night if he was wrong about the man in the bar. But how to check? Then he got an idea. He neatly folded the newspaper, rose and marched off down the hall to a house phone. He pressed zero, and asked for the bar.

"Ocean Terrace Lounge." A man's voice.

"This is the front desk," Kamal said. "Is the Prince of Yip there?"

"Just a minute."

Kamal wished he could see into the bar from where he stood.

"Hello?"

Kamal said nothing.

"Who is this?"

It was the same voice as before, Kamal was sure of it. He hung up and said into his microphone, "Someone in the bar just received a phone call."

His earphone crackled with static, followed by Serang's reedy voice.

"This is true, Kamal. A small man in a black suit. The bartender brought him a phone that had no cord."

Kamal looked up and down the empty corridor before he replied.

"This man is sitting at the center table with three others. Two large men and a woman with white hair."

"This, too, is true, Kamal," said Serang, who let a little awe creep in this voice.

"The small man is the target. He will lead us to Prince Seri."

His men muttered affirmatives, then Kamal returned to his chair and his concealing newspaper.

It wasn't long before there was movement at the table. First, the ape-man and the blonde stood and came toward the door. This surprised Kamal, who had judged the woman to be the pretender's companion. He hid behind his newspaper as they passed through the door and headed toward the lobby.

"Serang," he said into his microphone. "Follow those two."

Five minutes later, Serang reported that he'd found a hiding place in a broom closet from which he could watch the room the pair had entered. Fifteen minutes after that, the tall man rose from the pretender's table and he, too, left the bar. He walked with the unsteady feet of a drunkard. Kamal did not approve of liquor, but its consumption by others sometimes made his job easier. The man didn't even look at Kamal as he passed.

"Lombok," he said from behind his newspaper. "That one is yours."

Kamal watched the pretender, who now sat alone at the table, fiddling with his cocktail napkin.

"The tall man went into a restroom, about twenty meters from where Kamal is sitting," Lombok said into the earphones of the Yips. "I am waiting for him across the hall."

The man would not be gone long. Now was Kamal's chance to approach the pretender and perhaps remove him from the bar.

Before he could move, though, another man came into view through the narrow windows. A man with black skin and a broad mustache as white as the sandy beaches of Yip. He was dressed casually, in tan slacks and a brown shirt with a dipping yoke, like something Roy Rogers would wear. He carried a large manila envelope, and he reached out to shake the pretender's hand. He took a chair and leaned over to whisper in the smaller man's ear. Then he slid the envelope across the table. The pretender didn't touch it at first, but the black man's head bobbed as he urged him to go ahead, open it.

Then Kamal was on his feet, not even warning his men first, going through the doors into the bar. He needed to get a look at that envelope. Because, at a distance, it seemed to bear a pattern, an ink stamp in the shape of an orangutan astride a rearing tiger, the Royal Seal of the Sultanate of Yip.

24

Earl Shambley spotted the little Asian in the black suit as soon as he came through the swinging doors. For a second, Earl thought he'd made a mistake, that somehow he'd missed one of the prince's entourage. The guy was small but wiry, and the fluid way he moved made Earl think of martial arts. The Asian glanced Earl's way, but a glance was all it was, then he went to the bar, where he clambered onto a stool and sat with his feet dangling.

Whew. Earl felt like he'd dodged a bullet, though the Asian clearly had no connection to the prince. He wasn't even looking their way. Earl tried to focus on the task at hand.

Outwardly, Earl was smooth and oily as ever, a good old boy in a homeboy's skin. Inside, he felt the surging adrenaline of anticipation.

It had been just a twitch, the tiniest of leaks in the prince's impassivity, but Earl had seen it and he knew he'd won. The prince had seemed mildly surprised when Earl approached him the way he had, just walking up, shaking the man's hand, taking a seat. The twitch came when the prince saw the envelope, marked all over with royal seals and a return address that said, "Embassy of the Sultanate of Yip, Washington, D.C." The prince recovered quickly, but it was too late. Earl had seen him falter. Getting the prince to open the envelope and look inside was just icing on the cake.

"Go ahead," he said. "Nothing in there that'll bite you."

"I'm sure I'm not interested." The prince looked around the room, as if searching for a bouncer.

"I think you will be. Look, it's from your embassy."

"I see that. And it's addressed to you here in Coronado."

"Yes, it is. I called 'em up and asked 'em to send me some information on you."

"Is that so? And they did that? I'll need to speak to my father about security."

"Want me to get you a phone? You can call him right now."

"Don't be absurd. Just tell me what you want."

"I want you to open the envelope."

"Oh, very well."

Earl's mustache widened as a grin pulled at the corners of his mouth.

"See? Two whole pages, typewritten, all about your life. I see you went to USC."

"So?"

"So, go Trojans, right? You a sports fan?"

The prince shook his head, tried to look bored.

"Wait, you haven't seen the best part. Look inside. There's more."

The prince turned the envelope upside down and gave it a shake. A photograph fell to the table, face up, staring up at them.

"Now, see, here's my problem," Earl said casually. "That don't look like you."

The prince said nothing.

"I mean, it sorta looks like you. But not the nose, not the cheekbones. They're different."

The prince stared at the photo like he was looking into a coffin.

"There's a simple explanation," he said finally. "They sent you the wrong photograph. That's my brother."

"Your brother? Well, that would explain everything, wouldn't it? Except, how come it's got your name printed across the bottom like that? That is your name, ain't it?"

The prince nodded slowly. "Clearly, someone's made a mistake."

"I don't think so, pardner. I been thinking about it, see, and I came up with a different theory."

"I'm really not interested—"

"You should be, though. It's a helluva theory."

Earl glanced around to make certain no one listened, then leaned closer to the prince.

"My theory is: You're not really the prince of Yip. You're a bank robber."

"A what?"

"You heard me. I think you're planning to rob the bank where I work."

"That's ridiculous. Is that what this is about?"

"You don't have to pretend with me, friend. I know what you're up to. And I might be able to help."

The door swung open and the big redneck pushed through, looking tired and irritable. The crease between his brows deepened when he spotted Earl sitting with the prince.

"What've we got here?"

A muscle twitched in the redneck's jaw. Earl leaned back in his chair and smiled, wondering how quickly he could get to his ankle holster.

"This is Mr. Shambley," the prince muttered. "John Ray Mooney."

Earl reached out to shake John Ray's hand. It wasn't the safest position to take, reaching out like that. The big man was still standing and could swat Earl upside the head. John Ray ignored the gesture, keeping his eyes on the prince.

"What does he want?"

"You'll have to forgive my friend," the prince said. "He fancies himself to be my bodyguard. Nothing to worry about John Ray. Unless I've misunderstood, Mr. Shambley has come to us with a business proposition."

"Is that so? Are we interested?"

"I don't know yet. He was just getting started. Why don't you sit down and we'll hear him out."

John Ray grumbled, but took a chair.

"Now," the prince said, "tell me about this robbery. And make it good. Because if I don't like the plan, I think John Ray here will have to kill you."

25

Liza and Lowell rode up in the birdcage elevator, the same jolly Asian at the controls. Liza tried not to smile at the way Lowell's profile looked against the bars of the cage. Then he turned to her, tugged at his big lower lip, and said, "Want to come to my room for a quick nightcap?"

It was the surprise that did it, Liza decided as she followed Lowell down the hall. If she hadn't been so startled by his sudden boldness, she would've begged off. Besides, she had Bennie's cardkey. He expected her to be waiting in his room when he finished talking with John Ray about his business trip to Phoenix.

She needed to part well with Bennie. There still was a chance he'd return from Phoenix ready to give her the money to save Flabric. One drink with Lowell, then she'd go to Bennie's room. Keep up the front for one more night, let him get his jollies in bed. But she wasn't kidding herself. Her affair with the prince wasn't charging forward anymore. She was simply protecting herself in retreat.

Lowell stripped off his constricting blazer as soon as he entered his room. Liza admired the way his shoulders stretched the white shirt tight as he squatted before the minibar.

"Beer okay?"

"Sure."

Lowell stood with two Heinekens, twisted off the lids and handed her a cold bottle. She noticed a splash of red as she took it from him.

"Lowell, your hand is bleeding."

He stared at the jagged little cut on his palm.

"Dang. Guess those bottle caps aren't the twist-off kind. I'll get a towel."

He didn't seem particularly alarmed by the sight of his own blood as he ambled off toward the bathroom. Liza checked over her bottle to make sure it didn't have blood on it, then he returned with his fist wrapped in a white cloth.

"You want a glass?" he asked. "There's some little ones in the bathroom or I got these big plastic cups from the zoo."

"No, this is fine. I can only stay a minute. Doesn't your hand hurt?"

"Naw. I do that kind of stuff all the time."

Liza took a swig of the cold brew, and watched Lowell do the same. His lips wrapped around the bottle and he tipped it straight up, his eyes crossing slightly as he watched the liquid chug inside the green glass. Everything he did looked funny because of his simian features, some kind of circus trick, a marvelous feat someone trained him to do.

"Zoo cups, huh?" She passed close to Lowell's chest as she went over and picked one up. They were the size of Big Gulps, white plastic decorated with "San Diego Zoo" all around the rim and pictures of a panda below.

"I went to the zoo today. It was the one thing I wanted to be sure to do while I was out here."

Liza playfully tossed the cup to Lowell, trying to catch him off-guard, make him nervous. But he caught it smoothly, again giving her that sense of the unseen animal tamer.

"All their souvenirs have pandas on them, but I didn't see a panda the whole time I was there."

"No?"

"I must've taken a wrong turn or something."

"Well, it's such a big zoo. You really can't see it all in one day."

That's what people always said about the San Diego Zoo. Liza, like most local folks, hadn't been there in years.

"I tried to cover it all," he said, shrugging. "I was stepping out."

Liza could picture him swinging along the zoo's asphalt paths, startling the tourists.

"What did you like best?"

"The birds."

The answer surprised her. "Birds, really?"

"Yeah, I like those aviaries, where the birds fly free. I could stand in there for hours, watching them."

Liza imagined Lowell, standing among the rain-forest plants, gaping up at the birds, and the image caused a happy little thump inside her chest. She took another sip of beer.

"You want to sit down?"

Liza sashayed to the sofa and curled up in one end of it. Lowell looked nervously at the other end of the sofa, then pulled out a straight-back chair from a writing desk and perched on it, his big feet flat on the floor, his elbows on his knees.

"Lowell?"

"Yeah?"

"Why did you invite me to your room?"

He flushed furiously.

"Well, there were two reasons."

He seemed to get hung up there, so Liza prompted him. "And those reasons are?

His lips worked against each other.

"First—and I don't want you to take this the wrong way—I like you and I wasn't ready to go to bed yet and I just thought it might be nice to talk a minute."

Liza hid her pleasure, saying, "That's three reasons."

"Whatever. The other reason is—and I don't want you to take *this* the wrong way either—Bennie told me to keep you entertained while he goes to Phoenix."

Liza set her bottle on an end table and dropped her feet to the floor, ready to leave.

"So you're just doing your job?"

"See, you're taking it the wrong way. I just thought it would all go smoother if we got to know each other better. I know you're not happy about Bennie going out of town. And you don't seem thrilled about him hiring me and John Ray. But I like you even if you don't like me, and it looks like we'll be spending time together. I want us to be friends."

Lowell looked exhausted from stringing together so many words. Liza got the feeling the big lug had talked more tonight than he had in the past year.

Despite herself, she felt a welling-up inside at Lowell's sincerity, his simple way of asking for friendship. He might not have a lot of brains, but he clearly had a heart.

"We can be friends, Lowell. I like you just fine. I'm not too crazy about John Ray, but I like you."

Lowell grinned from ear to giant ear.

She picked up the beer, took what she knew would be her last swallow. She needed to heel it over to Bennie's room. Lowell had a certain animal magnetism beneath his boyishness. All those muscles. If she didn't leave soon, she might say or do something she'd regret.

"I've got to go, but I want to ask you something first."

Lowell still smiled, his eyes shiny and attentive behind his smudged glasses.

"What kind of name is Huganut? I've never heard it before."

The blush returned to his cheeks.

"We don't know for sure. My mother used to say she thought it came from the Huguenots. Ever heard of them?"

"Vaguely."

"They were some kind of Protestants over in France, a long time ago. Huganut kinda sounds like Huguenot. But mostly Mom just liked the idea of the family being French."

"You don't look French to me."

"Yeah. I don't see it either."

Lowell looked a little glum.

"Are there lots of Huganuts in New Mexico?"

"None that I know of. None of my relatives are named Huganut. It was my Dad's name and he died when I was little. I may be the only one."

"Really? The last of the Huganuts."

Lowell popped out of his sudden low mood, slipped her a sly grin.

"That's why I've gotta find a woman to have my children," he said. "To carry on the Huganut line."

Liza's cheeks suddenly felt warm. "I've really got to go now."

26

Downstairs at the Ocean Terrace Lounge, Billy Ho watched as John Ray opened the embassy envelope, studied the contents and recognized what they meant. Billy half-expected some explosion from John Ray. But he became motionless and his voice went cold.

"What's this about? Hush money?"

"Apparently not," Billy said.

"Naw, boys, I don't play that shit." Earl Shambley kept his voice low. "Blackmail's for losers. There's no percentage in it. I want to score big. A one-shot deal."

"What does it have to do with us?" John Ray's hand slid off the table, casually dropping into his lap, and Billy wondered whether he was wearing his new shoulder holster under his blue blazer.

"Why don't you keep your hands where I can see 'em," Earl said. "We're all friends here."

John Ray didn't move. "Funny, I don't remember making friends with you."

"Give it a little time. We're gonna be more than friends. We're gonna be partners."

"What makes you think the prince and I would be interested in your score?"

"'Cause it's the same one you been planning yourselves."

John Ray blinked, then looked over to Billy in consternation. Billy shrugged elaborately.

"Y'all don't have to pretend with me. I been watching you. I know he's not really a prince and I know you're no bodyguard. You've been casing the bank, all three of you."

Billy raised a finger for a point of information. "Three?"

"You two and your friend, that boy who looks like an ape. Where'd y'all get him anyway? Barnum and Bailey?"

Billy let that slide. "Lowell's a new addition to our team."

"Yeah? Well, he came loping into the bank today, looking all around, cashing *traveler's* checks. Tell me he wasn't casing the bank for a heist."

It's just one wonderment after another, Billy thought. Lowell, a bank robber? That's like suggesting John Ray Mooney was a ballerina.

"I saw you, too," Shambley said, pointing one of his amber-nailed fingers at John Ray. "First, that day you came in wearing a sweatsuit, then walked out again without transacting any business."

John Ray gave the slightest wince, like he'd been speared by a sharp memory.

"Then the prince here came in, making a big production."

Billy felt mildly offended. A "big production" indeed. His performance had been perfect.

"Then again today, you're in there. And your friend here is waiting in the car."

Billy glanced over to John Ray, whose glare had lost some of its ferocity to bewilderment. Billy knew exactly how he felt. Where was this man coming up with this stuff? The bank's the most convenient one to the Hotel Del. No surprise they'd all been in there at one time or another. And, for that matter, John Ray had indeed planned to rob that bank before he'd spotted an easier pigeon. But this Shambley had put together all those little accidents and come up with a Grand Conspiracy. A nimble act of fantasy, to be sure, but dead wrong.

John Ray, surprisingly, recovered quicker than Billy.

"You think we're planning a bank job."

"That's right."

"Say it's true for a minute."

True?

"Where do you fit in?"

This, of course, was the pertinent question. John Ray had made the leap quite deftly.

"We-l-l." Shambley drew the word out long enough to look around the bar. "I'd be the inside man."

"What makes you think we need one? Simple little bank like that."

Oh, quite good, John Ray.

"'Cause I know some things you don't. Like, when the bank's got the most money in it. And how to disable the alarm system."

John Ray sat back in his chair and slapped a big hand to his forehead. He massaged vigorously, as if keeping disbelief off his face had given him a cramp.

Shambley leaned back in his chair, smoothed his mustache with his thumb. Billy noticed the hand didn't tremble. Shambley looked as relaxed as a hound in the sunshine.

"Would you like a drink?" Billy asked him. The perfect host, no matter what.

"I wouldn't mind a taste of Jack Daniel's," Shambley said.

Billy glanced sideways at John Ray, who cocked an eyebrow at the mention of his brand. The corner of his mouth twitched. Billy signaled the waiter, wondering whether Earl Shambley usually drank Jack. If he'd overheard John Ray ordering that drink, and then had requested the same to establish some camaraderie with him, then Shambley was sharper than he appeared. It was just the sort of subtle gimmick Billy would use.

Billy distractedly held a palm over his own glass. He need to think now, to burrow through the mental goosedown of the martinis and sort out how to handle this new situation. Instead, he found himself thinking about a silver flask full of Jack Daniel's, the flash of the dashboard lights in the silver as the Prince of Yip tilted the flask to his lips.

He blamed the whiskey for what happened. Bennie hadn't been himself. He'd said things he never would've thought when sober. He'd threatened the one thing Billy couldn't tolerate: abandonment. You can't open the golden doors to the royal treasury, then expect to close them in the face of someone like Billy Ho.

They'd been driving through the moonless desert night in Bennie's red Mercedes, Billy at the wheel with a head full of coke to keep him awake. He hadn't been happy about Bennie's sudden plan to drive to Las Vegas. They'd already had dinner at Spago, then had stopped by a party thrown by a hard-drinking Hollywood producer around his penis-shaped swimming pool. Billy was ready to call it a night, but the prince was just getting started. He announced he wanted to see the sun rise over the casinos. They'd gamble through the weekend, he said, pick up the Vegas girls who fluttered around the neon like moths.

Which meant Billy would drive, of course. Bennie was too easily distracted to be a good driver, even when sober. The new convertible ought to at least turn four digits on the odometer before Bennie cracked it up as he had his last three cars.

Bennie jabbered beside him in his singsong English, the cocaine making him talky, the whiskey making him belligerent. It wasn't a good combination. Bennie couldn't stick with one topic long enough to make much sense, but it seemed he harbored several grievances against Billy and had chosen this moment, miles from anywhere, to list his flaws. He said he knew Billy skimmed money off the many purchases he made for the prince. He said Billy's usefulness didn't justify cheating. Plenty of others would gladly take his place.

Billy stood it in silence for a while, keeping his eyes on the road. But the longer Bennie prattled, the clearer it became that he was working up to giving Billy the boot. They'd have the weekend in Vegas, one last blowout, but he'd wake up some morning soon and the prince would be gone. In his drunken monologue, Bennie even mentioned the possibility of returning to Yip. Billy couldn't have that. It would ruin all his plans.

"I think you'd miss California," he said. "I get the feeling the women aren't so friendly back home."

"I am a prince! I can have any woman I want. And the women of Yip are very desirable, very willing, very clean. Here, I always feel they want something from me. The same way I feel about you."

"You're drunk."

"And you are insolent! This is exactly what I mean. I do not need someone to tell me when I am drunk. I know full well when I am drunk. And I do not need someone who steals from me."

"You keep calling me a thief. Do you have any proof?"

"I need none! You serve at my pleasure. And I must tell you, Billy, I am no longer pleased."

Billy saw an abandoned service station up ahead. The building was dark, a swaybacked relic, broken down by the years, the sun, the wind. The headlights caught a faded, peeling sign that said, "Gas. Water. Genuine Petrified Wood!" Billy hit the brakes and swerved onto the rutted dirt lot that separated the station from the road.

"Billy! What the hell—"

Billy threw the car into Park before the prince could recover. Then he pulled a pistol from his belt and pointed it at Bennie's face.

"You're dumping me? I don't think so."

The prince froze.

"Get out."

"Billy—"

"Get the fuck out."

The memory of his own rage made Billy cold now. He told himself he'd only meant to scare the prince. Let him cool beside the highway for a few minutes, then come back for him, see if he sang a different tune after some time alone in the empty night. But Bennie wouldn't let go of the car door once he was out. He hung on like a child, shouting and waving the silver flask around. Billy popped open his own door and stalked around the car, the pistol pointing at the prince.

"Goddamit, I said get away from the car."

"It's *my* car."

"Not anymore. You want me out of your life, we'll start right now. I'm getting in that car and leaving you here."

Bennie couldn't take it like a man, couldn't just watch the taillights disappear into the night. He had to make one last gesture, a royal mistake.

He threw the flask at Billy, right at his head. Billy flinched away, just enough, and the gunshot split the night with fire and noise. The boom echoed across the desert ridges. Bennie went flying, falling.

Billy stood beside the car a long time, the gun hot in his hand. Then he got a flashlight from the car and illuminated Bennie lying in the dust. He still breathed, but his shirt was soaked with bright blood. His eyelids fluttered when the flashlight beam settled on his face.

"Billy?" The prince's voice was a hoarse whisper. "Billy, you shot me."

Billy needed the prince to be quiet now. He needed to think.

"You shot me, Billy!"

The gun jumped in his hand and the prince said nothing more.

Billy blinked as the waiter returned to the table with drinks for John Ray and Earl Shambley. The memories distracted him from the matters at hand, but they weren't the worst of it. It was what happened next that still haunted him.

It had taken a while to work it out, leaning against the darkened car. He'd reacted to the threat of abandonment in the most absurd way. He'd killed the fatted calf rather than let it wander off on its own. If he'd waited until Bennie sobered up, he could've talked him out of it. Instead, Billy sat there with nothing but a corpse that he couldn't leave where it lay.

Well, not exactly nothing. He had the car. And in the prince's pocket was a wallet fat with cash and credit cards. Billy could become the prince, at least for a while. But first he had to make sure no one found the body.

Billy used the flashlight to search around the old service station, carefully avoiding the spot where the prince lay, his blood soaking the sand. It didn't take long to find a place, to make a plan.

An old outhouse stood behind the service station, leaning precariously toward the east. The weathered boards hung loosely on rusty nails. But the wooden seat remained and, Billy found by shining the light downward, it stood over a deep, rough-hewn pit filled with ancient black refuse.

Dragging the prince's corpse to the outhouse and hoisting it into the pit was probably the hardest thing he'd ever done. The whump of the body falling to the bottom of the pit still made him gag.

Once Billy caught his breath, he found a piece of plywood so ragged its edges were like fringe. He dragged the splintery panel behind him to the car, obliterating the bloody trail in the sand. Then he was back behind the wheel, pushing the Mercedes through the night, racing toward the sea.

Such a long, strange trip. Now, here he was, sitting in a walnut-paneled bar at the Hotel Del with two men who knew he was a fraud, listening to them calmly discuss a bank robbery. Billy suddenly felt very tired.

"See, the Navy has this little base here in Coronado, the North Island Naval Air Station?" Shambley was saying.

John Ray nodded.

"The payroll comes in once a month. Over a million bucks. It all comes through the bank where I work. The Navy wires the money to us, it's just on paper, right? But a lot of these sailors want to get their money right away, in cash. So, the bank gets an extra truckload of cash the first of the month. It's all in the vault, just waiting for somebody to take it."

"The vault?"

Billy couldn't believe John Ray was hearing the man out. What could be crazier right now than trying to knock over a bank? They needed to run before the Yips found them.

"Sure, the vault," Shambley said. "Only an idiot hits a bank and just takes what the tellers have in the cash drawers. You got to get inside the vault."

"And you could arrange that?"

"Sure. The vault's on a time-lock. It's just a matter of getting there at the right time. It's already open."

"It takes a while to load up a vault full of money."

"Yeah, it does. That's why you can't let the alarm go off."

"And you're about to tell me you can fix that, too."

"Oh, yeah."

"How?"

Earl Shambley lifted his drink, brushed its rim with his mustache, smacked his lips.

"That part's my secret, for now. If I tell y'all everything, you could cut me out."

John Ray's mouth twitched. Billy was beginning to think that was what passed for a laugh with him.

"Look, this has gone far enough," Billy said. "We appreciate your offer, Mr. Shambley, but you've made a mistake. We have no plans to commit a robbery."

Shambley's eyes looked like frozen chocolate.

"Really. We have our own little operation going here. Plus, we're leaving town. John Ray seems to have forgotten about that. Or maybe he's just leading you on."

Shambley glanced over to John Ray, and some communication seemed to move between them.

"Well, now, I'm surprised," Shambley said. "I thought a man in your position could use a quick infusion of cash."

"My position? What position would that be?"

Shambley leaned toward him, laced his big hands together on the tabletop.

"A man perpetuating a fraud. One call to the right people, and you're in a lot of trouble."

The chill hit Billy again, and it took all his will to keep them from seeing him shiver.

"Is that a threat?"

The broad mustache curled up on the ends. "I wouldn't dream of threatening a member of royalty."

Billy glanced at John Ray, expecting to find him giving Shambley the prison-yard glare. Instead, something like amusement sparkled in his pale eyes. Damn him.

The martini glass held one last swallow and Billy gulped down the vodka before he answered.

"You've certainly given us something to think about, Mr. Shambley. How about if we contact you tomorrow to tell you if we're interested?"

Now it was Shambley's turn to pause over his drink. He drained the last of it, then fished a business card from the pocket of his cowboy shirt. He handed it over.

The card was for a dry cleaning service, and for a second Billy was puzzled. Then he flipped the card and found a phone number scrawled on the back.

"Leave a message," Shambley said. "Anytime. But don't wait too long. Friday is the first of October. We miss that, we'll have to wait a whole month to try it. And don't think about leaving town until we've talked. I can always find you, wherever you go."

"Think so?"

"It's what I do best."

Shambley scraped back his chair and stood. He reached out to Billy, swallowed Billy's hand in one of his big paws. Then he turned to John Ray, who still had his right hand hidden under the table.

"Nice to meet you," Earl said, extending his hand. John Ray's hand came up from his lap—empty—and shook Shambley's.

"We'll be in touch," Billy said.

"I know you will."

27

The showplace of the Hotel Del Coronado is the Crown Room, an oval banquet hall that's fifty yards long and sixty-six feet wide. The open room is lit by large windows on the south end and by two giant chandeliers shaped like Imperial margarine crowns. What makes the room special is its domed ceiling, thirty-three feet high and paneled in warm sugar pine. The panels fit together without the use of a single nail.

Billy Ho learned all this about the room where he sat Thursday morning by reading the little history lesson on the back of the menu. The idea of tons of unsecured lumber up above made him uneasy. Sure, the Hotel Del had stood on this spot since 1888 (as the menu reported), but the way things were going lately, Billy half-expected the Crown Room to choose today to collapse.

John Ray didn't seem the least affected by the towering emptiness. All his attention was focused on the buffet, where tiered tables held trays of pastries and bowls of fruit and silver platters of sausages and potatoes and blintzes. At one end, near the wall, a goateed chef in a tall white hat worked magic with omelet pans, flipping and swirling and tossing.

John Ray hadn't given the menu a glance. Not with the bounty arrayed at what he insisted on calling the "trough." If he said that once more, Billy would stab him with his butter knife.

Billy hadn't wanted to pause for breakfast. They had things to do, packing and getting the hell out of Coronado. But John Ray had insisted and, these days, his wish was Billy's command.

God, the man was a nuisance, gawking at everything as if seeing it for the first time, stopping in front of every mirror to check out his tamed hair and his new clothes. Whistling some song sounded like it was off the *Andy Griffith Show*. How could Billy convince everyone he was a prince if he's walking around with Gomer Pyle?

Billy had slept little, and he had a scratchy-eyed headache to show for it. He'd filled the empty night with his fears and his doubts, mentally playing and replaying Earl Shambley's proposal, Bennie's death, the mysterious caller.

He'd narrowed his most urgent problems down to three: Get a quick bundle of cash, get rid of John Ray and get out of Coronado before the Sultan's people found him. Despite his misgivings, he'd begun to think Shambley's heist might be a way to solve all three.

Shambley had ferreted out his scam, but John Ray still was the only one who knew Billy's real identity. If John Ray vanished, no one else could prove Billy ever visited Coronado, much less participated in a bank robbery there. And what's a bank robbery, but some guys boosting a quick bundle? Guys with guns. Accidents happen. John Ray could be the robber who doesn't make it out alive. And he might not be the only one. Billy wouldn't mind walking away with all the money rather than just a share.

The fact that I'm even considering it, he thought, shows how desperate I've become.

John Ray returned to the table with a plate weighed down with grease: eggs, bacon, sausage, fried potatoes, buttered biscuits.

"Sure you don't want to eat something?" he asked as his plate thunked onto the table.

"Just coffee. Really." With his hangover, Billy could barely stand to look at food.

"You're the boss."

John Ray straddled the chair like he was mounting a racehouse, picked up his fork and began pushing huge portions of dripping food into his mouth. Billy looked away.

"So, John Ray," he began, "what did you think of Mr. Shambley's proposal?"

John Ray had to swallow mightily before he could answer. "He had a gun on his ankle. I think he's a cop."

A cop? Billy had never considered that possibility. The man seemed so positively criminal.

"I saw no gun."

"I didn't either until he was walking away," John Ray said. "He was sitting down when I first saw him. But I sorta sensed it as soon as I came back into the bar. Something about the way he held himself set off my radar."

Now he's got radar, Billy mused. Two days ago, John Ray didn't know what a bodyguard was. Now he's a professional. On the other hand, maybe John Ray did have some sort of primitive intuition when it came to cops. Doing time in Folsom might have that effect on a man. Last night, it hadn't even occurred to Billy that Shambley might be attempting a sting. But I was exhausted, Billy thought to bolster himself, I'd been drinking. All day, people had been flying at me with proposals and schemes. I felt like the only flower in a field full of bees.

"Guy just came out of nowhere," John Ray said between smacks and gulps. "Doesn't that make you suspicious?"

"I thought about that," Billy said. "But you recognized Shambley from the bank. What's he doing, just standing there all day, waiting for the right suckers to walk in? Seems like peculiar detective work."

John Ray shrugged. "Maybe he used to be a cop, but he's not anymore. He's got that smell about him. The way he talks, the way he carries himself. He thinks he's the hero in this movie."

"Movie?"

"Aw, that's something we used to say in L.A. You know, it's like life is a movie up there all the time. Unreal. People cast themselves in roles. They're victims, you know. Or they're players. Or they're heroes with their chests thrown out. This girlfriend I had, she'd pick people out of crowds and guess which role they were playing."

Billy knew exactly what he meant. His whole life was a performance, deceptions layered one on top the other.

"This girlfriend, was she an actress?"

"Naw, but she wanted to be. She got lots of practice, pretending with me."

"Is that a trace of bitterness I hear?"

"Up yours, Your Highness."

"What's her name? Maybe I've met her."

"I doubt it. Sounds like she didn't move in the same circles as you and the prince, though she probably would've liked to. Her name was Angel Flesch."

"I beg your pardon?"

"It was a stage name. She was a stripper."

"Really?"

"Yeah, but just like everybody else, she wanted to be on TV. She thought she could be the next Vanna White."

"And where did she end up?"

Billy noted that John Ray's scowl had returned.

"I don't know. Last I heard, she was playing the role of a lawyer's squeeze."

John Ray concentrated on mopping his plate with a piece of biscuit. The conversation had hit a dead end, and Billy tried to find some way to steer it back to Shambley's proposal.

"So, what role do you play? How have you cast your life?"

"Hard to say. I didn't much like the part I'd been given, so I've been looking for a whole new movie."

"Let's just hope this one doesn't end the way the last one did," Billy said.

"See, that's the thing. I'll decide how it ends up. I'm not just an actor in my life any more. I'm the director."

"Is that so?"

"Yep. And you, Your Highness, you're my leading man."

Billy rolled his eyes and sat back. The man was impossible.

"Well, John Ray, I hope your script includes a getaway scene."

"I been thinking about that. Maybe we're getting all excited over nothing. So far, nothing's happened. This Shambley showed up with his crazy plan, but he's not from Yip."

"Is it so crazy? If Shambley's not a cop, if his offer is legit, couldn't his plan be just the thing we need? A big shot of money before we hit the road. We could let the prince's credit cards cool for a while. Find a new place to start fresh."

"You're serious?"

"Why not? Nobody knows who I really am here, nobody but you. And I believe you said you're registered under a false name."

Billy hadn't spoken loudly, but John Ray whipped his head around to make sure the roving waiters hadn't heard. Then he slapped Billy with a stern look.

"Your Highness should maybe watch his mouth."

Billy smiled. "Don't be so nervous. I was just speculating. I'm not saying we have to do the heist. Look at you, you're sweating."

John Ray dabbed at his forehead with his napkin.

"It's hot in here, especially for a man who's having himself a decent breakfast. You seem to survive on coffee and vodka. Your blood must be like sludge."

Billy tilted his head and grinned, knowing that made him look royally amused.

"You're changing the subject, but that's all right. We can talk about it later. But first, can you signal a waiter? I think it's time for a Bloody Mary."

28

If it hadn't been for the stain, John Ray Mooney might never have spotted the Yip. He and Billy went for a stroll after breakfast, skirting the front of the Hotel Del, its white woodwork gleaming in the sunshine. Pigeons waddled along the sidewalk, and John Ray thought how much they resembled footballs. He resisted the urge to kick one. He and Billy were headed to the promenade overlooking the crashing Pacific. Billy seemed to think he'd feel human again if he could have one more Bloody Mary and a spell of sea breeze. Billy's loafers clacked on the brick sidewalk and John Ray was about to slow him up, say something like, "What's your hurry, Your Highness? That hangover still got you?" But he noticed a teardrop of grease on his new white tennis shirt and pulled up short.

"Damn."

"What?" Billy had walked on a few steps before stopping.

"Think I ruined my new shirt."

Billy came closer, examined the stain with an expert eye.

"Club soda would get that out."

"Think so?"

"Sure. Get some out of that minibar in your room."

John Ray didn't like the sudden happy glint in Billy's eyes.

"Fuck it. I'll do it later. I wouldn't want you to get lonesome for me out here."

Billy shrugged, a grin tugging at his lips.

That's when John Ray saw the Yip. The man stood beyond Billy, his back to them, watching their reflections in a tall window. John Ray's sudden halt to examine the stain forced the man up ahead to put on the brakes, too.

The man wore a black suit, and for a second John Ray thought he was the same Asian he'd noticed in the bar the night before. But this guy's hair was longer, sort of bowl-shaped, and his cheekbones were broader and flatter. He reminded John Ray of rain forest people he'd seen on the Discovery Channel, little naked men running around the jungle with blowguns.

The clincher came when the man, carefully not looking their way, lifted his hand to his face and spoke into his sleeve. He made as if to brush his nose with his hand, but John Ray saw the sun glint off the wrist microphone.

John Ray grasped Billy's elbow and said, "We're being watched."

Billy tried to look in the direction John Ray's eyes pointed. John Ray dug his thumb into the tender skin inside his arm.

"Ow!"

"Don't turn around," he said. "We're gonna nail that fucker right now."

Billy yanked his arm around until John Ray unhanded him.

"What do you intend to do?"

"I'm not sure yet. Just follow my lead."

Lombok was certain he'd been spotted. Damn Kamal. If Kamal hadn't been shouting in his ear, demanding a report, he wouldn't have used the microphone. He'd tried to cover the movement, but how convincing could that have been? He looked like a man standing around talking into his sleeve. In Malay.

Lombok turned away, as if he'd suddenly noticed the surf pounding in the distance, as the tall man and the pretender came toward him. He held his breath, waiting for a tap on the shoulder, but the men walked past, pushed their way through the doors that led into a long, curving corridor lined with shops. Lombok lusted for those stores, wanted to spend time just touching things, maybe buying gifts for his two girlfriends back in Yip. But, so far, he'd had no time to shop. Kamal kept them on full alert around the clock.

"Lombok?" Kamal in his ear again.

Lombok raised the microphone to his chin. "They just went inside. I will follow."

"Not too close," said Kamal. Lombok pictured him in some Jackie Chan pose, his fists cocked while he shouted into the microphone. "I will come from the lobby, down those stairs, and pick them up at the other end of the corridor."

Lombok plunged into the shoppers who browsed the display windows that lined the hall. The two men were nearly out of sight up ahead, walking briskly through the crowd, ignoring the paradise of merchandise.

Lombok's attention was caught briefly by a sight in one of the display cases, a wall clock shaped like a guitar-slinging Elvis Presley. The King's legs swung back and forth in a from-the-pelvis pendulum. Lombok grinned, then hurried after the men.

He rounded a curve just in time to see the pair duck into a men's room near the foot of the carpeted stairs. He hurried to the stairwell and looked up. No sign of Kamal.

Lombok knew the protocol in such situations. When your quarry disappears into a restroom, you slip inside just long enough to make sure there's no way out but the door. Once you've established they'll be there a few minutes, you beat a retreat and find some hiding place from which to watch the door. Never too close, but never a lapse that would allow them to escape.

Lombok eased open the bathroom door. The tiled wall made an L just inside, creating a privacy screen, and he peeked around it. The men weren't standing at the sinks. In the mirrors above the sinks, he could see the urinals on the opposite wall, but no one stood at them, either.

Hmm. Lombok stepped around the corner. There was no window, no way out. He should get out now, wait for them outside. But where had they gone? Both into stalls? He took a couple of steps forward, bending from the waist to look under the doors. No feet in the first. No feet in the second or third. Where had they gone?

John Ray didn't know how much longer he could hold his position. He crouched in the first stall, one foot on the rim of the toilet, one foot on the steel paper dispenser. He leaned forward, keeping his head down so it wouldn't be visible above the stall walls. The door had a coat hook attached to it, and John Ray grasped this in both hands, enough weight on the hook that he worried it might pull right off its screws and send him crashing.

He watched the narrow slit between the door and its frame, waiting for the little Yip to come searching. It had better happen soon. His legs were shaking. Plus, he worried about Billy, who waited in some similar fashion in the next stall over. Billy didn't have the patience.

The Yip came into view, bent over, just as John Ray had hoped. John Ray took a deep breath, then lunged forward, swinging his weight against the coathook, slamming the door outward into the Yip.

A satisfying thud. His feet hit the floor and he plunged after the Yip, who was turning toward him. John Ray popped him with two quick rights to the chin.

The Yip's backward progress was stopped suddenly by the tile wall. He tumbled into an odd-shaped pile on the floor.

Billy came swinging out through his door and nearly bowled over John Ray. They grabbed the Yip by the arms and dragged him into the farthest stall.

Billy went through the Yip's pockets while John Ray stripped off his narrow necktie and his belt.

"Ooo." Billy pulled a Glock out of the Yip's waistband, held it up to show John Ray.

"Give me that." John Ray snatched the gun away and shoved it into his belt.

He gagged the Yip with the necktie. The Yip's head lolled, and he wouldn't sit up straight on the toilet. John Ray pinned his hands behind him, then used the belt to strap them tight to the chrome pipes at the back of the toilet.

Billy Ho stood with the Yip's wallet in his hands, staring at something there.

"What?"

Billy said nothing.

"Hey. We gotta go."

Billy's head snapped up, as if he'd returned from someplace far away.

"Look at this." He handed over the wallet, and John Ray turned it around so he could read the ID card inside a plastic window. The card had a lot of scrollwork and a watermark of a monkey on a tiger or some such shit, but the gist centered on the words, in English: "Royal Guard of the Sultanate of Yip."

John Ray looked up at Billy, didn't like what he found in his eyes.

"Let's get moving."

29

Billy Ho took some comfort in John Ray's lupine watchfulness as he opened the door to his room. Now that they'd confirmed the Yips were in Coronado, it might be to his advantage to have John Ray at his side. Eventually, Billy must rid himself of this greedy, inconvenient man, but not until he was finished using him.

John Ray followed him into the room, backing in so he could keep his eyes on the hallway. As soon as he closed the door, Billy began to speak, wanting to strategize. But John Ray shushed him with an upraised finger. Billy watched the larger man's hand as he raised another finger and another. Slowly, silently counting. John Ray still had his other hand on the doorknob, and when he reached five, he snatched the door open and thrust his head out into the hall, trying to catch anyone following them. He shrugged at the nothing he found, and closed the door.

"May I speak now?" Billy huffed.

"Make it quick. We can't stay here long."

"Where are we going?"

"I'm not sure yet. We could take the car and run for it, but they'll call the cops as soon as they find that guy in the crapper. Once an APB's out, we're fucked in California."

"Aren't you a car thief? You could get us another car."

"You want to drive a hot car after the Yips get every cop in the state looking for you?"

"No, but I don't want to stay here."

"We're not. We just came to get your money."

"My money?"

"Mine, too. Who knows if we'll get back here for our clothes and shit? Just take what you can carry for now."

John Ray went through the connecting door to his own room. Billy gathered his cash from various hiding places in his room and stuffed it in his pockets. He didn't like the bulges the money made, but he wasn't about to leave it for the Yips.

It was still a pitiful amount, nowhere near what he'd expected to make off this scam. He'd sunk a lot into merchandise—new clothes and leather luggage and jewelry—and it made his heart sink to think of leaving the goods behind.

John Ray returned to the room and Billy noted the addition of the shoulder holster over the stained tennis shirt. The Glock barely fit under John Ray's arm, but he'd traded it for the little Raven he'd used before. Billy watched John Ray shrug into his new blue blazer, which covered the holster nicely, though it didn't exactly match his jeans.

"You have a plan?"

"Yeah."

"Might I inquire what it is?"

"I'm gonna stash you in Lowell's room."

"Wonderful idea. Lowell's such a witty conversationalist. Maybe we can spend the whole day together."

"Maybe."

Sarcasm was wasted on John Ray.

"You got your stuff?"

"Yes. I was thinking, however, that since you're carrying that Glock, maybe I should have that tiny pistol of yours."

John Ray shook his head. "You won't need a piece. You're just gonna hide. I'm the one who's gonna prowl around and see if I turn up any more of them Yips."

"Still, it might be a comfort to have a gun."

"It wouldn't make me comfortable."

"You don't trust me?"

John Ray gave him the Dirty Harry squint, holding it long enough that Billy began to feel ridiculous for asking.

"Never mind. But can I ask one more question?"

"Make it fast."

"What about the bank?"

"The bank?"

"The heist. Earl Shambley. Surely you've been thinking about it."

"Yeah, some. You?"

"It might be the only way to make a clean break from here."

"We've got some dough. Your car. Tijuana's just down the road."

"Yes, yes. All true. But wouldn't you rather cash out big?"

"Sure, but Shambley said the payroll doesn't arrive until tomorrow. You want to stay cooped up in here, waiting for those Yips to come find us?"

"No, I've thought of that. I've got a plan."

Billy, in fact, had no plan at all, not until maybe ten seconds ago. Then he'd thought of Liza, and everything clicked into place.

"We'll get Liza to go in with us."

"Liza? Miss Respectable from Coronado?"

"I know it seems unlikely, but at the moment she needs money as badly as we do. She might be willing to give us the one thing we need."

"And that is?"

"A hideout. Liza's got a house near here. A big one. The Yips would never look for us there."

John Ray scratched his chin, thinking it over. "You might have something there."

"It is a solution, isn't it? At least a temporary one."

"Maybe we don't even have to tell her about the heist. Maybe we'll just tell her the prince has a problem and needs a place to stay. She'd go for that."

"Perhaps. But we need freedom to make plans, to meet with Shambley. She might even *want* to take part."

John Ray shook his head. "A woman on a bank job?"

"Is that any stranger than having *me* along on a bank job?" Self-deprecating, Billy, but imaginative.

"You gotta point there."

Billy let John Ray stew, but nothing else seemed to be boiling up. He sighed and gave him a nudge.

"You'll do it?"

"I don't know yet. But I like the idea of moving to Liza's. Be a lot easier to watch our backs at a house."

"They won't know to look for us there."

John Ray nodded slowly, and Billy could practically see the rusty gears cranking behind his sweaty forehead.

"Okay, but first I want to get you over to Lowell's. Then I'll take a look around the hotel, see if that Yip has friends watching us. Maybe you could call Liza."

"I think she should be approached face-to-face."

"Then maybe I'll do it."

Billy instantly filled with doubt. No question, the prince could persuade Liza to do whatever they needed. But could John Ray?

"Let's see what happens," he hedged.

"Let's just fuckin' go."

30

Lowell Huganut felt slick with perspiration inside his thick sweatshirt. He'd pulled it on for the walk back to his room after his workout in the Hotel Del gym. For a guy who worked so hard to have big muscles, Lowell was shy about showing them. He was remarkably pale for someone who lived in the desert, and the sight of his huge white arms seemed to scare people. Besides, you don't go schlepping through the lobby of a place like the Hotel Del in your tank top. His mama raised him better than that.

The sweatshirt was pale blue and starchy. The front sported a silk-screen sunset, palms leaning in the foreground, the word "Coronado" scrolled below. It was the largest size they carried at Flabric, but it still chafed his armpits as he swung along.

Lowell had stopped at Flabric during his stroll around Coronado the day before. Liza hadn't been there, but he'd spent so much time roaming the aisles in search of her that he felt compelled to buy something so as not to look like a total geek.

He let himself into his room with his cardkey. The prince had said something the night before about getting Lowell a different room, one near him and John Ray, now that he was on the payroll. But nothing had happened yet. Lowell hadn't heard from the prince this morning. He wasn't sure what that meant. Did he have work to do today? Would Bennie even remember hiring him? He'd seemed pretty drunk. Lowell worried these matters to a fine point while he worked out, but came up with no answers. The only thing he'd decided was that lifting weights might count as part of his job, so he'd gone ahead.

Once back in his room, Lowell called downstairs to see if Bennie had left a message for him, something about where to report for duty. A nice girl at the front desk checked, but found no messages. Her voice had a smile in it.

He hung up, muttering. Time for a shower. Then he'd go knock on Bennie's door.

Before he'd taken two steps, somebody knocked on his own door. Startled, Lowell tripped over a chair leg and went sprawling. He picked himself up hurriedly and flung open the door.

The prince of Yip stood before him, smiling his amused smile, his hands stuffed into the pockets of his well-cut suit. John Ray crowded close behind him, shooting glances up and down the corridor.

"Good morning, Lowell," the prince said affably. "May we come in?"

"Sure." Lowell backed away to make room for them to enter. "Good morning to you. I was about to call you."

"Is that so?"

"Yeah, to see what you wanted me to do today. Do we have plans?"

The prince and John Ray shared a look. Lowell got the feeling they were up to something.

"We do have a job for you, Lowell," John Ray said somberly. "Right now. I need the prince to stay here for a little while."

Lowell couldn't imagine why the prince needed this room. He had a room of his own. But if the prince wanted it, Lowell would pack up and move out into the hall.

"I think somebody's following us," John Ray explained. "I want you to stay here with the prince and protect him. Don't let anyone through that door except me."

John Ray reached into the pocket of his blazer, pulled something out and reached it toward Lowell. Lowell, unthinking, held out his hand to receive whatever John Ray wanted him to have. When he saw a little square pistol there, he nearly leaped backward.

"I don't like guns," he said, then frowned at how breathless he sounded. "I don't need them."

"From the looks of you in that sweatshirt, I imagine that's true," John Ray said. "Kinda pumped up, ain't you?"

Billy rocked back and forth on his heels, still smiling.

"Lowell once squeezed a man's head so hard the man went insane."

John Ray's eyes widened briefly. "That true?"

"Not exactly." Lowell felt himself blushing.

"Whatever. Just keep that little peashooter handy. If somebody comes after the prince, they might not stand still long enough for you to grab 'em by the head."

Lowell nodded.

"I'm gonna have a quick look around town. See if I can spot anybody who looks wrong. Then we'll see what we do next."

Then John Ray was out the door, and Lowell stood gawking at the prince, the little pistol still in his hand.

"You want to point that another direction?"

"Sorry."

Lowell put the gun in a nightstand drawer, then perched on the edge of his bed.

"You okay there, Lowell? You look like you could use a drink."

That's what I need, Lowell thought. Something else to make my head swim.

"No? I think I'll have one, if you don't mind. I feel in need of some Vitamin C."

The prince prowled the minibar, coming up with a Stoli miniature and a skinny bottle of Donald Duck orange juice.

"Ah, perfect."

As the prince mixed his drink, Lowell's circuitry began to realign. He needed to be alert. He needed to ask the right questions and take the right actions. The first job he'd been given was to keep the prince safe in this room, and he needed to prove himself. He leaped to his feet and put the security chain on the door. Then he bounded across the room and peeked out the curtains. His room had a view of the service entrance and a parking lot. Nothing suspicious out there, just the usual employees sneaking cigarettes.

"No ice?" the prince asked as he peered into the empty ice bucket. "Pity. Oh, well, it's cold already."

He took a healthy gulp, then carried the drink over to the floral sofa near the windows. He sat carefully, then propped his feet on the coffee table.

"Might as well get comfortable, Lowell. No telling how long John Ray will take. I think he'll try to find Liza while he's out."

The mention of Liza brought Lowell away from the window.

"Liza? Why's he going to see her?"

The prince still smiled, but his eyes ran over Lowell, sizing him up.

"We may ask Liza if we can stay at her house until this blows over."

Lowell's heart thudded in his thick chest. He wanted to see Liza's house, wanted to see how she lived, whether it made her happy.

"Till what blows over?" Lowell's voice came out a confused sputter. "Who's looking for you? What's going on?"

The prince took a long time to answer.

"Lowell, now that you're one of us, I guess it's time to explain that. And a lot of other things."

"What things?"

The prince sipped his drink, smacked his lips in appreciation. Then he put his feet on the floor and set his drink on the table.

"Let me ask you a question, Lowell. Have you ever considered a life of crime?"

31

Kamal prowled the mall at the Hotel Del, looking into each shop for any sign of Lombok or the man who pretended to be the prince. The variety of goods—sunglasses, clothes, souvenirs, books, paintings, toys—was too much for the senses to absorb. How did Americans tolerate such abundance?

Between stops, he spoke into the microphone concealed at his wrist, trying to raise Lombok. Nothing.

The last shop was empty except for a teen-ager behind the counter who flashed him a nervous smile before she remembered the braces on her teeth and quickly closed her lips. He smiled and nodded automatically as he backed out the door.

The only door left was a men's room tucked behind the stairwell. Kamal approached it cautiously. The door swung open silently with his push. He paused just inside to pull the Glock from his waistband. He peeked around the privacy wall, saw no one, then stepped into the room, calling gently, "Lombok? Are you in here?"

No answer but the shuffle of feet, a soft thud.

Kamal checked the stalls. Feet under the door of the last one. He knocked, but got nothing in reply but more rustles and shuffles.

"Lombok?"

The feet stamped twice. Kamal forced open the door to find Lombok sitting on the toilet. His necktie was around his mouth and his belt pinned his hands behind him.

Kamal loosened the gag, and pent-up words spilled from Lombok.

"They ambushed me! I followed them in here to make sure there was no other exit, and there was no one. No feet under the doors. Then suddenly one of them struck me. When I awoke, I was sitting here, all tied up. My gun is missing."

Kamal unfastened the belt and freed Lombok's hands. As soon as Kamal backed away and made room, Lombok jumped to his feet and ran his hands over all his pockets.

"I still have my wallet, but it is in the wrong pocket."

Lombok pulled out the billfold and looked in the money slot, then held it open so Kamal could examine its emptiness.

"I had two hundred dollars, American."

Kamal took the wallet from Lombok's hands, turned it over, looked at Lombok's ID.

"So now they know we are here," he said. "And they are armed with your pistol."

Lombok hung his head in shame.

An hour later, Kamal and his men had determined a number of things:

One, the pretender and his rangy bodyguard were not in their rooms.

Two, the red Mercedes sat empty in the valet parking lot.

Three, the ape-man appeared to be sleeping late. A "Do Not Disturb" sign hung on his doorknob.

Four, there was no sign, anywhere in the hotel or on its grounds, of the pretender.

"We've lost them," Kamal said into his radio, admitting what the others already knew. "Kulu, stay by the pool and keep watch. The rest of you meet at the car. We will make a plan."

What that plan might be, Kamal had not a clue.

As he hurried through the lobby, he felt desperation rising within him. The pretender was his only connection to Prince Seri. The trail of credit card charges ended here at the Hotel Del. If he lost the pretender, he might never discover where Seri had gone.

Kamal went outside, tripping down the steps from inattention. People lined the broad sidewalk out front, shaded by a canopy while they waited for valets to retrieve their cars. Luggage sat in pyramids around their feet. Kamal picked his way through them.

Then a thought hit him so suddenly he froze in place, drawing stares from an elderly couple who wore matching Bermuda shorts.

Kamal might've lost the pretender, but there still were the others. The ape-man, the woman, the black man with the white mustache. Kamal had not yet learned the identity of the black man. But he knew the woman. Serang had overheard her talking on a pay phone at the hotel. She'd said her name was "Liza West." Serang heard this clearly and wrote it down to show Kamal.

If this Liza West lived in Coronado or stayed in one of the hotels, Kamal would find her. And she would lead him back to the pretender. And the pretender, eventually, would reveal Prince Seri's whereabouts. Kamal would see to that.

32

Liza West threw down her trowel and brushed the soil from her hands. It was no use. She couldn't enjoy anything. Normally, her patio garden was her sanctuary, the one quiet place that was all hers. She'd created it without the help of Sam or anyone else. But even the garden was tainted now by the constant thought she might lose it. And soon.

Everything she'd built, everything she'd gained, soon would be gone. The garden, the house, social status in Coronado, Flabric. All for a lousy sixty-two-thousand dollars.

Liza couldn't lose herself in the garden because she kept running last night's conversation with Prince Bennie through her head. It had gone all wrong. She blamed John Ray for distracting the prince just as she was ready to make her pitch. The thought nagged her that maybe she'd been distracted, too, that she'd been admiring Lowell's muscles when she should've been redoubling her efforts with Bennie.

She rose from beside the flower bed and rubbed her bare knees where the flagstones had creased them. She wore one of Sam's old white shirts with the sleeves rolled up past her elbows. The tails hung down past her cutoff jeans. The shirt, she noticed, was streaked with mud. Something else Sam had left her that she'd now ruined.

The doorbell sounded, bing-bong, and Liza cursed under her breath. Probably a bill collector. She entered the house through the French doors that connected the living room to the patio and crossed barefoot to the entryway.

She opened the door and was surprised to find John Ray standing there, a big hunk of rawhide blocking the sunlight. She leaned to one side to see around him, looking for Bennie, but John Ray said, "It's just me. Can I come in?"

Liza felt a flutter of alarm in her stomach. She frowned.

"What do you want?"

"Just to talk. I'll leave the minute you tell me to. I promise."

Liza smoothed the front of the dirty shirt.

"I'm not really dressed. Could you come back later?"

"Afraid it's now or never. It's sort of an emergency."

"Has something happened to Bennie?"

"Not yet."

What could that mean? She stepped back and let him inside.

"Come to the kitchen," she said. "I'll make coffee."

"I'm kinda in a hurry."

"Just take a second."

She turned left toward the kitchen, and a tingle on the back of her neck told her he was following. She didn't trust him for a second. The kitchen would be the best place to entertain him and keep it brief. A sunny, sterile place that bore little hint of comfort. Plus, she knew where the knives were kept.

Liza waited until John Ray settled himself onto a tall steel stool at the counter that separated the kitchen from the breakfast nook before she asked, "What's going on?"

She turned away from him while he talked, busying herself with scoops and filters and water.

"The prince is being followed. I spotted a guy rigged up like a freakin' Secret Service man—suit, radio, gun. I got rid of him, but there may be more of 'em around."

"How did you get rid of him?" Liza kept her voice calm, though her breath caught at what he might answer.

"Knocked him out. Left him tied up in a shitter."

Liza glanced at him over her shoulder. If he felt any particular way about what he'd just said—proud or remorseful or valiant—she couldn't tell. His face was the same sun-baked clay as usual.

"I want to get Billy to a safe place. I was wondering if we could stay here for a day or two."

The request ricocheted around the room without hitting Liza. She'd clung to something else.

"Did you say Billy?"

"What?"

"Just now. You said you needed to get the prince to a safe place?"

"Yeah?"

"You called him Billy, not Bennie."

"Did I?"

"Yes, you did."

"You musta heard me wrong."

"I don't think so."

John Ray scratched his chin. "Maybe I did say Billy. Until recently, I spent a lot of time around a friend named Billy."

"Billy what?"

"Huh?"

"What was your friend's last name?"

"His last name? Smith. Billy Smith. Yeah, we go way back."

"You're lying."

John Ray's eyes narrowed to two black slits.

"That's not a very friendly thing to say."

"I'm not feeling very friendly today."

Liza turned back to the coffeemaker and made a show of checking the drip while she got control of herself. What's she doing, calling this brute a liar? She should just get rid of him. Phone Bennie and tell him to stop sending his goon sniffing around.

"Where's Bennie now?"

"He's safe. I put him in Lowell's room and gave Lowell a gun for protection."

Liza was surprised by the sudden thump in her chest.

"You thought Bennie was in danger, so you turned him over to Lowell? Doesn't that put them both in danger?"

"Naw. Why would anybody think to look for the prince in Lowell's room?"

"Maybe because the two of them have spent every waking hour together for the past three days. Maybe someone saw them, you know?"

John Ray looked at the floor, thinking and sucking on an eyetooth.

"That's possible," he said finally. "But I'm not gonna be gone long. I just need to know whether you'd let the three of us spend the night here."

"Three?"

"Lowell, too."

Liza shrugged. The thought of Lowell being with them made it seem okay.

"Who are these people who are after Bennie? Do I have reason to fear them?"

John Ray squirmed on his stool. "I'm not sure. I think they're from Yip."

"People from Yip have come all the way here after him? What are they, terrorists?"

"I don't know. Really."

Liza handed him a striped mug of coffee.

"Sugar?"

"Naw. I like my coffee the way I like my women—thin and bitter."

Liza took her time putting sugar in her own mug and testing its taste. When she turned back, she was ready.

"There's a lot you're not telling me."

"Some. But I promise you, I wouldn't put you in danger. We just need a place to stay for a night while we make plans."

"What about Phoenix?"

"Phoenix?"

"You were going to Phoenix on a business trip?"

"Oh, that. Um, that's out now. We called it off because of this new problem."

"Wouldn't that be a good place to hide?"

"No, that's just what they'd expect us to do. We're gonna surprise them."

"How?"

"I don't know yet."

"This is the craziest thing I've ever heard."

John Ray nodded slowly, as if he was running through an inventory of craziness and doing comparisons.

"Yeah, it's right up there," he decided. "But these things happen."

"No, they don't. Nothing like this has ever happened to me."

"Guess you've been lucky."

"My luck seems to be running out lately."

John Ray nodded again, took a big slug of the hot coffee. He seemed unbothered that he'd just scalded his mouth.

"The prince says you're having money troubles," he said.

"He told you, did he? Why am I not surprised?"

"Don't matter. Everybody needs money. I'm trying to pay off a debt myself."

Liza set her mug on the counter. She wished she were wearing shoes, something with a heel. Even though he was propped on the stool, she still was looking up at John Ray.

"Well," she said, "you seem to be making progress. I, on the other hand, have run out of options. I thought Bennie would help, but he's too busy hiring you and Lowell to protect him from strangers with guns."

It took John Ray a long time to answer. Liza didn't like the glint in his eye.

"We're working out a way to make a bunch of money before we leave town. How would you like to get in on it?"

Liza felt her interest rising. "What would I have to do?"

"For starters, you could let us stay here a night or two. We need to keep out of sight. Beyond that, we'll have to see. I need to talk to Billy."

"You said Billy again."

John Ray sighed.

"There's a lot I need to tell you. You better pour another round of coffee. You got any whiskey we could tip into that?"

"Little early, isn't it?"

"You're gonna need it."

33

Earl Shambley parked his aged, farting Buick across the street from the address John Ray Mooney had given him over the phone. Nice neighborhood. Little round park with a flagpole in the center. Boxy homes furred with ivy and surrounded by green lawns. Even at dusk, most of the homes looked empty. The house where he was headed had some lights on downstairs, but all the curtains were closed tight.

"Looks like a good place for a conspiracy," Earl said aloud.

He felt conspicuous as he got out of the car. In all his years in Dallas, surrounded by rednecks on the police force, he'd never felt so conscious of being black as he had since he came to Coronado. Probably just loneliness. He could go days at a time when the only black faces he saw were on TV. And the African-Americans he did see, the Navy men from the base or the rich tourists who wandered into the bank, gave him only passing notice, a nod of recognition for a brother. Most of the time, Earl felt like a raisin in the middle of a big white sugar cookie.

He glanced around the neighborhood before he rang the doorbell. He'd worn quiet clothes—polyester jeans and a dark, loose shirt. Maybe it was the guns that made him feel watched. Earl had brought with him every gun he owned. He had the Beretta nine he wore to work every day on a nylon swing rig under his shirt. He had his old Dallas Police Department service revolver, a .357 Smith & Wesson with a four-inch barrel, stuck in his waistband at his back. He had the little stash pistol in his ankle holster. These people he'd thrown in with, if they tried to jump him, were in for a surprise.

The door gapped an inch and an eye peeked out before the door swung open the rest of the way. John Ray stood there half-naked, wearing only a pair of jeans. His upper body was lean and well-muscled, free of tattoos and nearly hairless. Man had a helluva tan.

"This must be the place," Earl said.

"Well, if ain't Wyatt Earp," John Ray said, creasing his face into what must've been intended as a smile. "Come on in."

John Ray stepped back to make room for him to pass. Earl could feel the man's eyes on him, counting his guns. But John Ray made no move. Just taking inventory.

"Excuse my nakedness," John Ray said. "Liza's trying to get a stain out of my shirt."

Earl didn't see the pistol sticking into the back of his jeans until John Ray turned to lead him out of the little entryway.

"You always answer the door with a gun in your belt?"

John Ray reached back, touched the butt of the pistol.

"We ran into a little trouble. Come on, everybody's in the kitchen."

John Ray hummed to himself as Earl followed. What was that tune? Sounded like the song from that kids' show, *The Little Rascals*. That some kind of Buckwheat joke? Earl fought off a scowl.

The entryway emptied into a spacious living room with low, fat furniture and French doors that looked out onto a sunset patio surrounded by flowers. To the left, a darkened stairwell and a short hall; Earl guessed both led to bedrooms and baths. John Ray turned right and Earl followed him into a kitchen so gleaming and antiseptic that it made him squint. The room was divided by a central counter. On the near side stood the kitchen appliances and a sink where a white shirt soaked. On the far side was a breakfast nook that also had French doors leading to the patio. The others were in there.

The prince sat on a chair pulled out from the dining table, his feet barely reaching the floor. He held a tall tumbler of orange juice. The ape-man perched on a stool at the counter. He had a map spread out, and Earl recognized the haphazard street layout of Coronado. The woman studied the map, too, standing very close to the ape-man, comfortable an inch away from his hot bundles of muscles. She wore jeans and a pink T-shirt with a wide neck. With her leaning over the map like that, Earl could see the lacy edges of her bra.

He forced himself to focus on the prince, who looked glum and didn't stand when Earl went over to shake his hand.

"Evening," Earl said. "What do I call you? 'Your Highness,' something like that?"

The woman loosed a harsh laugh.

"How about the Con Artist Formerly Known as the Prince?" she said.

The prince shook his head sadly. "I'm afraid we're not keeping up appearances any longer. At least not here, among *friends*."

The prince shot a look at the woman and the ape, and Earl understood the group dynamic had changed. The others had found out what he already knew—the prince was a fake. Apparently, that was enough to turn off his girlfriend, who seemed to be cozying up to Monkey Boy instead. Earl supposed she was part of the heist now, or she wouldn't be here. Not sure he liked that, especially if she had an ax to grind with the prince.

"Just call me Billy. That's my real name."

"Not exactly," John Ray said as he pulled out chairs for Earl and himself. "His name's really Guillermo Ho. Ain't that a mouthful?"

Billy smiled painfully, then took a slug of the orange juice, swallowing it so eagerly Earl figured it must be spiked.

"Just Billy will be fine. Have you met the others?"

"Haven't had the pleasure."

Billy introduced Lowell and Liza, managing to be gracious about it.

"Since some of us haven't heard your plan, maybe you could start at the beginning," Billy said.

Liza pulled a stool up to the counter, close to Lowell. Earl's audience waited hungrily, and he cleared his throat, ready to regurgitate the speech he'd composed in his head all day at the National Bank of Coronado.

"Maybe," Liza said, "you could start by telling us why the robbery has to be tomorrow. That's not much time to plan."

Earl nodded sagely, giving her the Wise Old Negro look.

"Tomorrow's the first of October. The bank gets an extra shipment of cash on the first to deal with the Navy payroll. And since the first falls on a Friday, the shipment will be even bigger. The cash sits in the vault, which they keep open during the day. Just a cage across the door, and the manager has the key."

"How do you make him open it?" Liza asked. It seemed a sincere question, but John Ray snorted.

"I'll stick a pistol in his ear."

Earl nodded and smiled, but he didn't need any bravado bullshit from John Ray. Just shut up and let me tell it.

"I been standing around that bank for six months now and I've kept my eyes open. Man gets bored, he starts making plans. I think I got it worked out pretty good."

"Let's hear it then," John Ray said.

"If you'd be quiet, maybe he'd get a chance," Billy said, and he didn't flinch at John Ray's sharp look.

"Okay." Earl wiped his damp palms on his knees. "Here's how I got it pictured."

Everyone except Billy leaned closer.

"I go to work tomorrow as usual. The first thirty minutes or so, I stand at the door, unlocking it when the tellers arrive. The bank's not open yet, see. While they're getting their coffee and getting ready for the day, I'll snip a few wires."

"Wires?" The first word from Lowell.

"To the alarms. The tellers have panic buttons under the counter, and the manager has one at his desk. Silent alarms. Somebody hits one of those buttons, the cops are there in two minutes."

Lowell winced, and the others shifted in their seats.

"But," Earl continued pleasantly, "there's a place where the wires from the panic buttons come together to go into the junction box. That's where all the fuses and stuff are, honey."

He said this last to Liza, who went steely.

"I know what it is. Honey."

"Right. Anyhow, they got no backup on that circuit. You break a window or something, and an alarm goes off, even if the whole building is without power. But these buttons, because they're inside and under the counter, they didn't set them up to go off automatically if somebody cuts the wires."

"How do you know all this?" Liza asked, and her voice hadn't softened any.

"Like I say, I've had a lot of time on my hands. So, snip-snip, and the alarms are turned off. I'll do that first thing in the morning, and then y'all can get there around eleven. That way, we're sure the Brinks truck has already arrived with the cash for the payroll."

Earl looked around the room like he was counting noses.

"Are you all going to take part?" he said, letting his gaze fall last on Liza.

"If we decide to do it at all," John Ray said.

Earl let his eyebrows rise.

"I thought you were in," he said tightly. "If you're not, what the shit am I doing here?"

"I'm sure we are," Billy said. "But we're not forcing anyone to participate.

Everyone here understands that it's okay to back out, as long as they keep quiet."

Billy might have extracted pledges of silence, but Earl knew how easily cops could make such promises crumble.

"Might I ask what role the young lady will play?"

"First of all," Billy said, "this is her house you're sitting in and she's letting the rest of us stay here until the heat's gone. That alone would entitle her to some of the take, but Liza wants a full share. She's offered to drive. She's got a nice, big, anonymous car."

The corners of Earl's mustache dipped.

"Might be easier if she drives," he said.

Billy cleared his throat. "We were discussing that very thing when you arrived. I was arguing that I should drive and that John Ray and Lowell should be the ones who go inside the bank. Look at the two of them, all those muscles, they should be able to handle it."

"Who watches their backs?"

Billy loosed an exasperated sigh. "I was saying they didn't need that. The only one with a gun in there will be you."

"I been thinking about that, too," Earl said, "and it's gonna look suspicious if I just let y'all waltz out with the money. I'm paid to be the guard, after all."

"What do you suggest?"

"I think all three of you should come inside. Billy can keep the crowd under control while you other two carry out the loot. Liza can drive."

Liza smiled.

"You boys can come in there in a hurry and get the drop on me. 'Put your gun on the floor,' that sort of shit. Don't bother with the money at the teller windows. They'll just slip you one of those exploding dye packs. Instead, hold a gun on me and force me to get the key to the cage and let you into the vault. Once we're inside, no one can see us, and I can help you load the money into garbage bags."

John Ray leaned forward, resting his elbows on his knees. He looked like a big tawny puma, ready to pounce.

"Then we haul ass," he said, "out to the car where Liza's waiting. We jump in, she drives away, it's over."

Earl's head bobbed in an easy, porch-swing nod.

"Right. I'll deal with the police and the employees afterward, maybe try to plant some faulty information. Later, we'll split up the cash. I'll be trusting y'all to wait for me here."

Earl didn't like that part of his plan. He'd considered hiring someone to keep an eye on his new partners. But that would be one more person who knew Earl robbed his own bank and he liked that even less.

"What about security cameras?" John Ray said. "They're all over the place."

"Nothing I can do about them. They're on a separate circuit and each camera has a little red light that shows it's on. The manager would notice if they were shut off."

"Then we wear disguises?"

John Ray seemed a little tickled at the notion, and Earl played along. What did he care? He was the only one who didn't have to worry about the security cameras.

"Sure. You got some ideas?"

"Yeah. I was thinking about those big sunglasses like old ladies wear. You know, they cover the whole upper half of your face."

John Ray turned to look over his shoulder at Lowell.

"They fit over eyeglasses. They won't even be able to tell you wear glasses."

Lowell nodded gamely. Earl thought the boy looked a little green around the gills.

"What about guns?" Billy said. "I think we're one short."

John Ray grinned broadly. "I think Earl probably has one he could spare you."

Earl reached behind his back, palmed out his service revolver and handed it to Billy.

"Be careful with that. It's got a lot of sentimental value."

Billy looked the gun over, tilting it this way and that in the light. "Sentimental value, but no serial number?"

Earl shrugged. "Gun works just fine without one."

Billy carefully set the pistol on the floor beside his chair. Which suited Earl fine.

"Now," he said, "we can work out the rest of the details later. I got a question first. John Ray said when I got here that you've run into trouble. I'd like to hear about that."

"We can tell you, if you want," John Ray said. "But it's got nothing to do with the heist."

Earl flexed his sore feet inside his shoes.

"We're all in this together, and I'm not much on surprises. Why don't y'all tell me all about it?"

34

A shrub tickled Kamal's neck as he lay in a flower bed near Liza West's patio. He desperately wanted to brush it away, but he didn't dare move. His hiding place was just outside the pools of light that spilled from the kitchen windows. He had a perfect view of the pretender and the others inside, but any movement might catch their eyes.

Kamal's men had the house surrounded in a formation called Surveillance Mode Dragon's Breath. Fong was parked out front. Fat Kulu and Serang hid in the shadows at either end of the house. Lombok crouched at the dark end of the patio, still steaming over the embarrassment of being beaten and bound in the men's room.

After Kamal decided the woman was the key, it hadn't taken long to find her house. She was listed in the Coronado phone book as "L. West." It was a simple matter of letting Fong steer them through the curving streets to their destination. That Fong. He had the unerring homing powers of the pink pigeons native to Yip's tangled jungles.

They watched the house through the afternoon, as the players arrived. Kulu, weighing in as the senior team member, advocated rushing the house and whisking away the pretender. But Kamal opted for patience. Sometimes, the best action is none at all.

Kamal felt his forebearance was rewarded when the black man arrived as darkness fell. He wanted them all in one place. One of them must know Seri's whereabouts.

Not long after the man entered the house, Kulu's voice crackled in Kamal's ear.

"They are all there now. Is it not time to move?"

Kamal shifted in the flower bed, moving with the slow deliberation of a three-toed sloth, and brought the microphone up to his lips.

"I see them. They are passing pistols around the kitchen."

"Pistols?"

"Several."

Lombok, trying to compensate for his earlier error, spoke up: "We need not fear their guns. Surprise is on our side."

Kamal sighed into the microphone before answering. "If shots are fired, the police will come. This would require much explanation, and the Sultan would not be pleased."

Lombok's only reply was a miffed grunt.

"We are impatient," Serang said, "because we are tired of squatting in the dirt and doing nothing."

"Remember your training," Kamal said sharply. "Discipline is the difference between success and shame."

How many times had he said that during the endless training sessions back in Yip? Kamal structured their training exercises like karate *katas*, a series of moves repeated until they could be done without thought or planning. It carved channels into their brains, so the proper response was automatic. He had no way, though, to teach them patience. Meditation helped, but even a brain emptied of thought registers the passage of time. Kamal, fortunately, had been born with the ability to wait.

Besides, Kamal had guessed right already today. He was confident the pretender and the others would leave the house sometime this evening. The American woman certainly would not let them all spend the night at her home.

"Maintain your positions," he said into the radio. "Eventually, they will come out. We must be ready."

No response for several seconds. Then Fong, waiting comfortably in the car, said, "Ten-four."

35

It was nearly nine o'clock before Billy Ho got Shambley alone. Liza and Lowell went to prepare beds upstairs. John Ray—finally—needed the bathroom. Which left Billy and Earl at the dining room table.

It was about time something went Billy's way. The day had been filled with disappointments, not the least of which had been the reactions of Liza and Lowell when they found out he wasn't really royalty. Lowell seemed saddened by the deception, but it had been a snap to talk him into joining in the heist. Billy could persuade him to jump off a bridge and Lowell wouldn't realize he'd made a mistake until he hit the water. Liza was another story. Once she knew Billy had no fortune to share with her, the Ice Queen could no longer be defrosted.

Worse than watching Liza cozy up to Lowell was seeing the way John Ray installed himself as leader. The big idiot. He'd latched onto Billy like a parasite, feeding on scraps, no initiative of his own. But once they hatched the bank robbery plan, he considered himself to be in his element. Such foolhardiness. Billy had a plan for John Ray, and getting a quiet moment with Earl Shambley was part of it.

"So," he said, his voice mellow, "if this goes right, no shots will be fired?"

"That's right," the Texan drawled. "No need for any trouble."

Billy smiled ever so slightly, an imp with an idea.

"What if I needed to shoot somebody?"

"Say what?"

Billy tilted his head toward the hall, where they'd last seen John Ray. "I've got a problem with too many people in my life."

Earl nibbled his lower lip, making his mustache twitch.

"That a fact?"

"Indeed. Perhaps you and I could work out some arrangement to lessen this load. And make our shares a little bigger."

"What you got in mind?"

"It's simple, really." Billy looked through the door to make sure John Ray wasn't creeping up on them. "Your gun's there on the floor as we go out the bank door, right? You snatch it up, follow us outside to take a careful shot. You get to be a hero."

Billy tried to read Earl's dark eyes, but they could've been freshly scrubbed blackboards for all they revealed.

"You want me to shoot your friend?"

"He's not my friend. He's my problem."

"I see."

"Problems are there to be eliminated."

"Is that what happened to the real prince?"

Sharp. Shambley clearly had been thinking about Billy's situation.

"Sometimes," Billy said, "even careful men trip over cracks in the sidewalk."

The corners of Earl's mustache curled ever so slightly.

"What about the others? If I start shooting, maybe our friend Lowell's gonna turn around and blast one at me."

"Not Lowell. He'll be too nervous. Besides, he won't have any bullets in his gun."

"He won't?"

"I'll see to it."

"I see. And afterward, when they realize we took out one of our own? That Liza seems like she already wants to kill you."

"Don't worry about them. I can handle Lowell and Liza. One way or the other."

Earl leaned back in his chair and rubbed his palms on his thighs, like a man anticipating a big dinner.

"Think we got ourselves a deal."

Billy nodded brightly, then glanced toward the hall. He gave Earl a wink and held a blunt finger to his lips.

"One thing, though," Earl said, and he wasn't grinning now. "I hope you don't get any ideas about trying to get rid of me, too, or running off with the money while I'm still covering your tracks at the bank."

Billy tried to look shocked.

"'Cause if that were to happen, you life wouldn't be worth catshit."

"Of course, my friend. I don't foresee any problems. I see us splitting the money, shaking hands and going our separate ways. Probably never see each other again."

Earl's expression softened. "No offense, pardner, but that's just the way I'd like it."

36

"I've never met a Dale Carnegie graduate before," Lowell said. "Far as I know, anyway. I didn't know it was something you talked about. Guess I thought it was like AA. You know, anonymous."

"Aw, hell, no," John Ray Mooney said brightly. "It's no secret. Something to be proud of, I think."

"Has it helped you?"

"Sure. I can talk to anybody now. I'm really a friendly person."

"But you used to be shy?" Lowell didn't bother to say "like me."

"Not shy, really. Sullen. You shoulda seen me when I was a kid. A holy fuckin' terror, I shit you not."

They walked along what John Ray thought of as *his* alley, the place where he'd hidden his bank robber gear the first time around. They needed a different license plate for Liza's car, in case somebody got a look at it outside the bank. John Ray had offered to boost a fresh car off Orange Avenue during the night, but Liza insisted she was more comfortable with her own wheels.

John Ray had figured the alley would be the perfect place to pick up a license plate, but he hadn't counted on the security lights that reared up from nearly every yard. It was bright as dawn back here.

"What made you take that correspondence course?"

"I was in Folsom, see, with nothing but time on my hands. The prison shrink, he wants to save the world. Skinny guy, looks like that 'Where's Waldo' guy. In those puzzles? Anyway, the shrink wants to practice his couch technique on us hardened criminals. I figure it's a good way to kill a couple of hours, plus you talk in his office, which means it's the only time you can relax and not worry about somebody shoving a shiv up your ass."

Lowell's big Adam's apple bobbed.

"This shrink, he says I'm anti-social, right? Probably 'cause of my childhood, which I agree was the shits. I spent all my time watching TV and avoiding my parents 'cause they were crazier than shithouse rats. The shrink thinks I need training in social skills, learn how to get along with people, so he put me onto Dale Carnegie."

"Did it help you in prison?"

"This is Folsom we're talking about, not the fuckin' Kiwanis Club. You try to 'win friends and influence people' inside, and you end up on some muscle boy's leash."

Lowell stumbled, too busy imagining prison life to watch where he was walking. John Ray grabbed at his bulging arm, helped him catch his balance.

"You all right?"

Lowell nodded, looked embarrassed.

The alley was empty and the houses were quiet. To John Ray's right, a carport opened into the alley. It sheltered a white minivan that bore a big bumper sticker that said: "JESUS IS COMING. LOOK BUSY."

"This'll do. I'll take care of it. You keep a lookout."

John Ray squatted behind the minivan with the cordless screwdriver he'd borrowed from Liza. Working mostly by feel, he began unscrewing the frame around the license plate. The Black & Decker made quick work of it, and he creaked to his feet and tucked the license plate up under his shirt, anchoring its bottom edge in his waistband.

"Okay, Boy Scout," he said to Lowell, "that's it. You've participated in your first crime. Let's get out of here."

Lowell loped up the alley, and John Ray had to step lively to keep up.

"What's your hurry, Lowell? Nobody around. Just relax."

"I'm relaxed. Don't worry about me."

They walked in silence for a while. A thought nagged at John Ray.

"Lowell? Why are you doing this?"

"What?"

"The job. Why'd you get involved?"

Lowell chewed on the question, a look of concentration on his face, like somebody worrying the pit out of an olive.

"I wanted to help. I like Bennie, I mean Billy, and Liza needs the money."

"What about you, Lowell? Don't you need money?"

"I'm still sorta getting used to the idea."

"Of being rich?"

"All of it. I mean, you think you've got your life pretty well worked out. And then something like this comes along. An opportunity, I mean. And it could change everything. It takes a while to get your brain around that. Know what I mean?"

"I've been there, buddy. Remind me to tell you sometime about a woman named Angel."

Lowell pulled up short and wheeled around, peering down the alley.

"What?"

Lowell listened and watched for a few seconds.

"I don't know, man. I keep getting the feeling we're being followed."

"Get outta here."

"No, really. It's like a tingling on the back of my neck."

"You're just nervous."

Lowell listened a moment longer, his head cocked like the RCA Victor dog.

"You're probably right. Let's just get back to Liza's."

"Sure, Lowell. Turn left up here at the street."

They emerged from the shadowy alley onto a broad sidewalk that lined the street. Ahead, the round park sat unlit.

John Ray tried to think of something else to say, some way to engage Lowell. He needed to ingratiate himself with Lowell and with Liza, too, if he could manage it. He didn't trust Earl, who'd admitted before going home for the night that he was, indeed, a retired cop. And John Ray sure as hell couldn't trust Billy. He needed somebody to watch his back tomorrow. Too many untrustworthy people waving guns around. Accidents happen, sometimes on purpose.

"You know, Lowell, I think Liza really likes you."

Lowell snorted and looked away so John Ray couldn't make out his face.

"No, really. After this is over, you should try to make something happen with her."

Lowell pushed up his glasses, ran his fingers through his tight skullcap of hair.

"Oh, man, I don't know."

"Think about it, Lowell. You and Liza rolling around in a big pile of money."

"Oh, man."

37

Lowell Huganut had been asleep nearly an hour when he was awakened by a warm hand on his shoulder. He kept his eyes closed for a time, foggily afraid the sensation was a dream and he'd interrupt. But when he fluttered open his eyes, all his dreams came true.

Liza leaned over his bed, her hand resting lightly on his shoulder. She wore a shimmering white nightgown that glowed like her hair in the velvet darkness of his borrowed room.

"Lowell? Are you awake?"

"I must be. You're talking."

"What?"

"I'm awake. What's up?"

"I need to talk. Can I get in bed with you?"

Lowell seemed to have a baseball stuck in his throat, but he managed to squeak out, "Please do."

Liza grasped the edge of the blanket that covered him, started to pull it back to crawl in beside him.

"Um, I'm not wearing any clothes."

Liza's smile added another flash of light to the darkness. "Nature boy, huh?"

"I don't have my suitcase. I usually wear pajamas."

"I'll bet you do."

Lowell's cheeks warmed.

"Well," she said, throwing back the covers, "I don't mind if you don't."

Her legs were warm silk as they brushed against his. And then she was beside him, her hand resting lightly on his washboard stomach.

"Lowell, I'm worried."

He was in shock, but he managed a silent nod.

"How did we get mixed up in this? We're not criminals, you and me. We're just regular people, right?"

Another nod. Lowell tried to will away the giant erection that had risen from his loins. Surely Liza would notice it, poking up at the blanket like a tent pole. Lowell knew she wasn't here for sex. She needed to talk. He needed to pay attention.

"How can we trust these others? Billy's a little con man and that Earl looks like he'd just as soon shoot you as eat. John Ray is fresh out of prison. What does that tell you?"

Lowell shrugged the massive shoulder where her head rested.

"Well, that he's a criminal, for sure," she said. "And, worse yet, an unsuccessful one. But I'm not here to talk about John Ray. I'm worried about you. Are you sure you want to go through with this thing tomorrow?"

He cast about for how to say it. No, he wasn't at all sure. He'd spent the whole evening feeling queasy about it. The only moments he'd enjoyed were the ones with Liza, talking over the maps, making up the guest beds together. How could he explain that was enough to persuade him to stick it out? How could he tell her he'd decided to rob a bank on the off chance that it somehow would result in Liza in his own bed?

"Aren't you?" he asked her.

"I guess so. I don't think they'd let us back out now anyway. We know all about it. If we don't go through with it, something worse could happen."

The same thought had plagued Lowell all evening.

"But I'm worried," she said. "Not so much about myself. I'll be out in the car. You're the one who'll be in danger. What if something goes wrong?"

"Nothing will go wrong," he said. "I'm very strong. I can take care of myself."

She raced her fingertips up and down his chest, sending an electric charge surging through him.

"I don't feel so strong right now," she whispered.

"You'll be fine. And if something does happen, you should just drive away. Pretend you know nothing about it."

She raised her head to look down at him, and Lowell kept his lips shut tight so his giant teeth wouldn't glow at her.

"You think I could just abandon you there?"

"It would be best," he said, and he tried to sound resolute. "You can walk away at any time."

"Are you sure? I'm afraid of John Ray and Earl. I think we can't turn our backs on them for a second."

"Don't worry about them. I'm keeping any eye on them."

"You are?"

"You bet."

"And Billy?"

"You'd better watch him. I've got my hands full with the other two."

Liza giggled and dropped her head back to the taut pillow of his pectoral muscle.

"I'll watch him," she said. "The little shit."

Lowell snorted, then wished he hadn't made that noise with her lying right there on his chest. She giggled again.

"It's nice to hear you laugh," he said.

"It's just hysteria. I swing back and forth between terror and giddiness at the thought of all that money."

Lowell grunted.

"What are you going to do with your share?" she asked, and the lilt in her voice signaled the giddiness had returned. Lowell would like to encourage that giggle, but he couldn't think of anything funny to say.

"I don't know," he admitted. "I'm sorta overwhelmed. I mean, I have my place back in T-or-C, and I guess I'll go back there while I sort out what I want to do with my life."

Liza traced a heart on his chest with her fingernail, and Lowell was sure she could feel his own heart pounding in there like a jackhammer.

"Tell me about your place."

"Oh, it's nice. Not as big as this house, but I've got it fixed up real pretty. Three bedrooms, stucco. A patio out back where you can see an arm of the lake in the distance."

"It's warm there, right? I like warm climates."

"You'd like T-or-C then. It's hotter'n blue blazes nine months out of the year."

"What about the other three months?"

"The wind blows."

"Oh. But Lowell, we're going to have so much money, we could go away on vacation those months."

"Sure," he said, and he thought he sounded remarkably calm. His brain screamed, *"WE? There's a 'we?' Did she just say 'we' could vacation together?"*

"I was thinking," she said, "after it's over, I may need to get out of town for a while. You think I could go to New Mexico with you?"

Lowell didn't trust his voice, so to buy time he wrapped a thick arm around her, gave her a squeeze.

"That would be great," he said breathlessly.

She cuddled closer against him, gave him a little pat to show he'd made her happy.

"Lowell?"

"Yeah?"

"Can I ask one more favor?"

"Sure. Anything."

"Would you kiss me?"

38

Lowell seemed a very happy monkey the next morning. Billy Ho watched Lowell and Liza breeze around the kitchen, chattering and smiling and touching. Didn't need to be Dr. Ruth to see what's happening there.

Billy leaned morosely against a wall near the French doors. The sunshine outside made Liza's flowers glow against their green backgrounds. The weather seemed all wrong for a robbery. Where was the fog when you needed it?

He figured he would be easy to spot in any weather, dressed in a red T-shirt that hung nearly to his knees. John Ray had ordered them all to wear loose T-shirts and stupid baseball caps as their disguises. Liza had supplied the shirts from her ex-husband's left-behinds, but they were all too big for Billy. John Ray wouldn't even let him tuck in the ridiculously long tails because they were supposed to hide the gun he'd be carrying. Billy could barely stand the thought of walking around in such a cheap, sloppy garment. He looked like a tourist.

John Ray sat tensely at the dining table, gulping coffee, eating Marlboros, mindlessly humming snatches of music from *The Wild Wild West*. Occasionally, he'd bark out a question, some last-minute detail, and Billy would nearly jump out of his skin. Billy would massage him with a reassuring answer, and John Ray would return to his brooding.

Worse yet, John Ray had all the guns. Billy went to sleep with Shambley's revolver under his pillow, but awoke to find nothing under there but rumpled sheet. Apparently, John Ray had sneaked into Lowell's room, too, because he'd collected the little Raven as well. All three pistols sat on the table in front of John Ray, a neat place setting of death.

"Gasoline!" John Ray barked, making the other three start. "Liza! Is that car of yours all gassed up?"

"Half a tank," Liza said, and Billy picked up her sly smile. It saddened him, thinking of all that splendid womanhood being wasted on a big lug like Lowell.

"Oughta be a full tank!" John Ray's nervousness had turned him into a Doberman.

"We're only going about eight blocks," she soothed.

"Still. Preparation's everything. Any idiot knows that."

Lowell turned from the kitchen sink, his hands dripping, and stared at John Ray like he'd never seen him before.

"It probably would be better if we didn't throw around words like 'idiot.' We're all kinda high-strung right now."

Billy thought Lowell sounded more reasonable than ever. Thank goodness someone still had his wits about him. Maybe Liza hadn't completely lost her mind, allying herself with Lowell.

Billy shifted against the wall, trying to find some relief for his tired feet. He was afraid to sit. He must remain ready. If John Ray ever left the table, Billy could palm Lowell's little gun and unload it. He didn't want Mr. Hear No Evil carrying a loaded pistol when the shooting started. After Shambley took out John Ray, Billy might put a bullet through Lowell's thick skull.

John Ray muttered about how he'd say "idiot" anytime he wanted, then he suddenly stood up. Billy felt a rush of excitement. His opportunity was coming. John Ray eyed Billy, saw something in his expression and made a point of picking up the Yip's Glock and stuffing it in his belt. Then he turned away and sauntered toward the bathroom, never looking back. Billy didn't move a muscle until John Ray turned the corner into the living room. Then he hurried over to the dining table. He paused before snatching up the gun, and glanced into the kitchen. Lowell and Liza had stopped with the dishes to watch him.

"Oh, heh-heh, just thought I'd check out these guns."

"John Ray already checked them six times," Lowell said, making Liza giggle.

"You trust him?"

Liza and Lowell looked at each other, then back at Billy, their heads turning in unison. Both shrugged, then they caught themselves and burst into laughter.

"I'm glad you're both so mentally prepared to rob a bank," Billy said.

"We're just losing our minds," Liza said, chuckling and wiping at her eyes. Lowell wrapped a giant arm around her and gave her such a squeeze that her feet lifted off the floor.

"I'm quite sure now," Billy said, "that I'm going to vomit."

The merriment didn't die from Liza's eyes.

"Spoilsport."

He frowned at her until she turned back to drying the dishes. Then he scooped up the Raven, popped the magazine out of it and, using his thumb, flicked free the bullets there. He kept his hands close in front of his body, shielding them from view. When all the bullets lay cool in his hand, he jammed the magazine back into the gun butt and set it down quickly. He pocketed the bullets, then picked up Shambley's revolver and turned back toward Liza and Lowell, making a show of checking each chamber.

"They look fine," Billy said. "Let's just hope we don't have to use them."

Lowell nodded somberly. Liza rested her hand on his inflated arm.

John Ray rounded the corner and hesitated a second when he saw Billy standing at the table with the revolver in his hands. Billy quickly set down the gun. No need for a shootout here in Liza's kitchen. Plenty of time for that later.

"About time to go do it," John Ray said. "C'mere, Lowell."

Lowell followed John Ray around the counter, drying his hands on a towel.

"I was just thinking about something," John Ray said. "Pick up that gun."

Lowell didn't seem to like the idea much, but he picked up the tiny Raven.

"See if you can put your finger on the trigger."

Lowell licked his lips and turned the gun around in his big hands. His finger barely fit through the oversized metal loop that formed the trigger guard.

"See, that's what I was thinking. That gun's too small for you. You can't go around with a gun like that. You might shoot yourself. Trade with Billy."

"What?" Billy felt a stab of pain in abdomen. Sometimes, when his best-laid plans exploded before his eyes, he got physical manifestations of it, shooting pains in his gut.

"Trade," John Ray repeated. "Give that bigger gun to Lowell."

"I like this one," Billy said. "I need a big gun. I'm in charge of crowd control."

"Those suckers in the bank won't care what caliber you're packing. That little gun will look like a cannon to them."

Billy couldn't protest further without making John Ray suspicious. He handed the revolver to Lowell, and took the Raven in exchange.

"There," he said. "Everybody happy now?"

"Happy as a pig in shit," John Ray said. "Now what say we go rob a bank?"

39

The garbage bags around Kamal softened in the warm sunshine, and their contents emitted a sweet, sickly stench. The odor reminded Kamal of the slums back in the Yip capital, Bandar Surijawa. The slums always stank of garbage and rot and human sweat. Kamal avoided going out into the city whenever possible. Better to stay at the hilltop palace, where the floors gleamed and the scent of flowers wafted through the air.

Kamal recognized that part of the stink was from his own body. He'd been on surveillance more than twenty-four hours, without sleep, with almost no food, crouching in flower beds and crawling across lawns. His black suit had muddy knees and elbows. Bits of grass littered his hair. Occasionally, he felt the telltale tickle of insects crawling on him.

When something—an ant, a spider, who knew?—chomped into his thigh, Kamal didn't cry out, didn't move. He just flexed his ironclad thigh muscle until the creature was crushed against the fabric of his pants.

Kamal didn't know how much longer he could occupy this hiding place. It wasn't the bugs or the stench that would drive him out; it was the traffic. Twice in the last hour, cars had rumbled through the alley behind Liza West's house. Both times, Kamal had gone unnoticed, burrowed as he was under a pile of black garbage bags. But he had no explanation if some homeowner did spot him there. And didn't Americans have trucks that came to their homes and took away their trash? Wouldn't that be the final indignity, to be scooped up by some mechanical monster?

Pain shot through Kamal's head, and he gritted his teeth and toughed it out. Once the pain was gone, he waited for dizziness to arrive, but he felt none. That, at least, was going better. Eventually, the pretender and his compatriots must come out of the house. When they did, Kamal couldn't afford to hesitate.

After the pretender and the two Caucasians surprised Kamal by going to bed at the woman's house the night before, he'd thought carefully about how to arrange his men. They needed to be near the house, ready to snatch the pretender, but hidden from any midnight joggers or roaming police. Kamal had opted for a modified version of Surveillance Mode Orangutan Paw, with Fong leaving the car to trade places with one man at a time, so each could get a light nap in the back seat. Everyone except Kamal, of course, who skipped his turn to sleep. He also had taken the best vantage point, the place behind the neighbor's house, where he could watch Liza West's garage. Nobody would drive away from that house without Kamal's notice.

Kulu's voice crackled in his ear.

"I saw them pass a window. It appears they are going to the garage."

Before Kulu finished his alert, the garage door began to creep open.

"I see them," Kamal said into in his wrist mike. "Fong, pick up the rest of the team. Prepare to drive up the alley."

"Check." Fong said this in English, though Kamal had warned him about such clowning.

Kamal burrowed further under the garbage bags, until only his eyes and the top of his head peeked up from the pile. The garage door was fully open now, and he saw the four of them surrounding the car. He watched the lanky man squat behind the beige Volvo and quickly remove the license plate. Then he attached another plate with a different number. Undoubtedly, it was the one Lombok and Serang had seen him steal the night before.

While the man was occupied with the switch, the others jockeyed for seat position. The woman took the wheel, which surprised Kamal, and the little pretender and the ape-man both tried for the handle of the front passenger seat door. The larger man won out, giving the pretender a jostle with his hip. The pretender seemed inordinately sad about having to sit in the back seat with his rangy friend.

Kamal noted that the men wore big sunglasses and baseball caps and loose T-shirts that easily could conceal the guns he'd seen the night before. The woman wore sunglasses and a straw hat pulled down tight over her white hair. The disguises and the license plate switch indicated they were up to something. Kamal made an on-the-spot command decision: They wouldn't try to snatch the pretender here in the alley. No, they'd follow the Volvo and see what these people were up to.

The Volvo roared backward out of the garage, wheeled halfway around, then flew off down the alley. The woman drove like Bruce Lee when he played Kato, the Green Hornet's TV sidekick. Roar, screech, swoosh.

Kamal scrambled out from under the garbage as the Volvo thumped into the side street. He shouted into his wrist mike, "Hurry, Fong!"

"Roger wilco."

40

Earl Shambley stared stonily at the bank clock, willing the second hand to tick faster. All was in readiness. The Brinks truck had arrived at ten with the extra payday cash. The wires to the panic buttons were snipped, and the wirecutters quietly stashed under some crumpled tissues in a teller's wastebasket. No one had noticed a thing.

Earl looked at the manager pushing a pencil at his desk, the loan officer talking on the phone, the tellers at their posts, licking their thumbs and counting. It had been a busy morning, but things were slower now in the usual lull before the lunchtime rush. The time was right. Where were the robbers?

It wasn't just the robbery making him edgy; it was what came after. He felt confident the heist was planned perfectly. The robbers would be in and out in under three minutes. With Earl covering for them, it was a cinch they'd get what they came for.

I'll wait until they're clear of the door, he thought, before I go after them. That'll look more natural, more heroic. Make sure the innocents in the bank are safe, then pursue the robbers and gun one of them down.

Earl was pretty sure—not a hundred percent certain, but pretty sure—he was going to shoot John Ray Mooney. He could control the others. He didn't trust them, but he could control them. But John Ray was a problem that ought to be eliminated before it got worse. Like a leak in a dam. Or termites.

The only reason Earl doubted whether he'd shoot John Ray was that he wasn't able to visualize it. Earl was a careful man, a planner, and he always tried to play things out in his head before they happened. It was as if a movie unfolded behind his eyelids.

Like the time he popped that doper. What was his name? Tommy Two-hits, everybody called him. Tommy thought he could hold out on Earl and keep more than his share of their profits from dealing Mexican smack in South Dallas. Earl knew what was happening, and he knew how to fix it. He'd visualized it beforehand—his hand coming up with the Smith & Wesson, Tommy's eyes getting wide, the quick bang-bang. It had gone just as he'd imagined. Hell, even the pattern of the blood spray on the wall of Tommy's cheap apartment was exactly as he had pictured it.

Damn. What was that boy's last name? You think you'd never forget something like that. I'm getting old, Earl thought, I can't remember shit.

And now he couldn't visualize shooting John Ray Mooney. He'd tried the technique late last night and again this morning, trying to see himself picking up his Beretta from the bank floor and stepping up behind John Ray and blowing his brains all over the clean Coronado sidewalk. But it wouldn't come. He could see himself with a gun in his hand. He could see himself walking out the doors, trailing the bank robbers. But he couldn't see himself killing John Ray. It was worrisome, because Earl was pretty sure he was going to shoot him. He'd like to know what to expect.

He checked the round clock again. It's stopped, he told himself, the clock finally has died because time no longer is passing on its face. Where were they?

Then out of the corner of his eye, he saw John Ray stroll past the doors of the bank, looking lean in a black T-shirt and jeans. Earl guessed he peeked inside to make certain everything was ready, but he couldn't tell because John Ray wore wide, black sunshades over his eyes.

Earl glanced around the bank again, but all the suckers seemed as oblivious as before. Only two customers at the teller windows, both older women. Perfect. Nobody who'd try to be a hero.

Outside, John Ray turned on his heel and walked back to the bank doors. The other two, looking ridiculous in their caps and oversized sunglasses, appeared behind him and they all came inside. John Ray reached behind his back, and Earl deliberately turned away, looking over toward Gary Warren, the bank manager, to see whether anyone would ever snap to what was coming down.

Then the steel circle of the gun barrel pressed against Earl's neck. He almost smiled.

41

Billy Ho had never felt more wretched. The worst hangover in the world, the worst beating he'd ever taken while growing up in Tijuana, couldn't measure up to the misery of walking into a bank robbery with an empty gun.

He could feel the bullets in his pocket, just waiting to return to the Raven's magazine. But he'd never gotten the chance. John Ray sat right beside him on the ride to the bank. Billy had tried to get in the front seat, where maybe Liza would be too busy driving to realize he was reloading the pistol. But Lowell had insisted on riding next to his new gal. Moron.

With John Ray watching, all Billy could do was act ready and alert. He couldn't jeopardize the heist. He needed the big payday. The Sultan would keep sending his agents to find him and to find out what happened to the real prince. The only way to escape was to go completely underground. Get a new identity, a new life, maybe a new nose. All of which cost money. Once he had the cash in hand, perhaps he could risk stiffing the others and making a run for it. But first the bank robbery had to be a success.

"Nobody move!" John Ray shouted. "This is a holdup!"

John Ray pressed the Glock against Earl Shambley's neck, and Earl raised his empty hands. John Ray pulled Earl's gun from his holster and stuck it in the back of his belt. That wasn't the way it was supposed to go! He was supposed to drop the Beretta on the floor, so Shambley could scoop it up and follow them far enough to plant a bullet between John Ray's shoulder blades.

Billy couldn't believe how badly this was going.

John Ray couldn't believe how well this was going. Smooth, baby, smooth. Got the jump on everybody in the place. Look at 'em all. Frozen. Earl's doing just what he's told, Billy's got the counter covered, Lowell's got the drop on the suits over at their desks. John Ray had to admit Lowell looked menacing with the big gun and the giant arms and the sunshade that covered up much of his monkeyness. Billy didn't look too imposing, pointing that little peashooter, but John Ray didn't worry about him. Billy might be a near-midget, but he exuded so much confidence, he was like a poster child for Dale Carnegie.

John Ray felt like a panther, light on his feet, his body tight under his clothes. This was going to be quick and easy. We'll get the money and get out here so fast, this sweat on my forehead won't even have time to get into my eyes.

"All right," he shouted. "Everybody's doing just fine. Don't move a muscle and we'll be out of here before you know it."

Billy watched John Ray. Make a show of it, you big ham. The problem with low-lifes is they don't understand subtlety.

John Ray had a wad of Earl Shambley's shirt twisted tightly in his left hand, and he gave him a push to get him moving.

"I want the key to the cage," he said, as he shoved Earl toward the manager's desk.

The manager didn't move, but his face turned very red. Billy kept an eye on him. Earl had told them the night before that the manager had a fetish for cash. Billy could perfectly understand such a fixation, but he worried it might make the manager do something foolish.

John Ray marched Earl into the vault. Lowell backed in behind, keeping his gun pointed at the bankers until he was out of sight inside the safe.

Billy Ho sighed and waved his empty gun around.

Lowell had never been inside a vault before. The giant, layered-steel door made him edgy. He wouldn't want to be shut up in the safe. That would be worse than jail. Inside, the walls were covered with safety deposit boxes, hundreds of little shiny doors. Beyond them, Earl Shambley unlocked a second cage door that opened into a larger room. The room was dominated by a rolling table in the middle that was covered with decks of money and soiled canvas Brinks bags. Holy shit. Look at that money. Wait until Liza sees that.

John Ray paused just inside the door and exhaled a low whistle. He mumbled something, sounded like, "First thing you know, Ol' Jed's a millionaire."

Lowell wondering, who's Jed?

"Get over here, Lowell," Earl hissed. "Put on your gloves."

Lowell stuck his pistol in his belt and obeyed, though the thin rubber gloves barely stretched over his giant hands.

Earl handed him a Hefty bag and Lowell fumbled with the edges, trying to open it. The slick bag and the rubber gloves were a bad combination. Why hadn't John Ray thought of that when he was so busy planning everything?

"Hold it right there," Earl said, and Lowell held the maw of the bag wide while Earl raked money off the tabletop and into the sack. The money felt like thunder hitting the bottom of the bag.

John Ray worked frenziedly on the other side of the table, chucking decks of money into another bag. Earl and Lowell loaded up a second one while John Ray finished his and then cast about the vault to see if they were missing any. Shelves held bonds and documents and a few small deposit bags, but nothing worth snatching up.

They were ready to go. Lowell couldn't wait for this to be over. He felt knotted up inside. He bent, grabbed the necks of the two bags and slowly straightened his knees, just the way they teach you in the gym. Lot of pounds there, but nicely balanced since he had one in either hand. He headed for the door, glad to be getting out of the stuffy vault. Just another minute and it would be over, and he'd be back with Liza.

Billy let his pistol's black eye roam the bank, settling on no one long enough to cause panic but keeping them all covered. He could feel the tension rising with each passing second. The blue-haired lady nearest him had begun to leak tears. Time to give them something else to think about.

"Simon says hands up!"

Half the people already had their hands above their heads, but they stretched to put them higher.

"Simon says put your hands on your head."

Eight pairs of hands slapped onto the tops of heads so quickly it sounded like applause. The old lady mashed down her blue coiffure, which looked brittle as a Brillo pad. Billy winked at her, but of course she couldn't see it because of the big shades he wore.

"Simon says stick your fingers in your ears."

They all obliged, though two of the tellers exchanged a quizzical look first.

John Ray and Lowell stormed out of the vault, John Ray swinging his gun in all directions. He carried a heavy-looking garbage bag in his free hand. Lowell carried two, both stretched tight with the heft of money. Earl Shambley followed slowly, his hands upraised. They stopped cold when they saw everyone but Billy standing stock still, fingers in their ears as if expecting an explosion.

"What the hell?" John Ray looked irritated, his brow creased above the dark glasses.

Billy smiled as he backed toward the exit. He used one hand to hold the door open and the other to keep the crowd covered with the empty gun. John Ray and Lowell hurried through the door, leaning against their loads of loot.

42

Liza West watched her mirrors. She'd lucked into a parking space half a block from the bank's doors, and she sat behind the wheel with the motor running, her eyes begging the mirrors for the sight of Lowell emerging unharmed from the National Bank of Coronado. Spending the night with him had changed things. Wrapped in his massive arms, she'd been able to forget everything—his simian face, her money woes, Billy Ho's betrayal. Everything except the bank robbery, and her feelings toward that changed, too. Throughout waiting for the appointed hour, her main worry was getting big, sweet Lowell through this unharmed.

She tried to put that out of her mind. Lowell would be fine. The whole robbery was planned to happen so quickly, they'd be pulling back into Liza's garage by the time the first cop rolled up to the bank. Just a few minutes of daring, of total concentration, and her life would change again.

She'd already popped the trunk latch under the dashboard. The trunk lid sat ajar an inch, ready for the men to fling it open and heave their bags of loot inside. Then she'd drive away, into a new existence. But first, Lowell and the others needed to get out of that bank.

Liza glanced at her watch. They'd been inside three minutes, which was as long as Earl had predicted the entire heist would take.

She looked back at the mirrors. Nothing.

A black Cadillac screeched to a halt opposite her, then roared backward to park in the mouth of an alley behind a restaurant across the street. The Cadillac's doors flew open, and four little Asian men spilled out. They all wore matching black suits. It was like a circus act, when a dozen clowns clamber out of one little auto. Liza nearly smiled, but then she saw them reaching under their coats and pulling out big black pistols.

Oh, shit.

Liza looked to the mirror again, and saw Lowell and John Ray and Billy backing out the bank door. She lay down on the Volvo's horn, producing a sustained bleat that froze the Asians. In the mirror, she saw John Ray's head whip around at the noise, his lips silently curse. Then his gun came up and spat fire.

Lowell and Billy ducked into crouches at the sudden explosion, but John Ray stood tall, his arm out from his body at a perfect right angle. His bag of money dropped to the sidewalk as he concentrated on his shooting.

The shots were so loud! They split the quiet air of Coronado with their fire and fury. Surely they could be heard at the police station, which was only eight blocks away.

The Asians fell to the pavement, though none of them looked hit, and the four of them went into another type of circus performance, rolling and tumbling and somersaulting their way toward the cover of the cars parked along the curb in front of hers.

The acrobatics were too much to follow. She looked to the mirror to see John Ray run out of bullets. He looked at the big square gun in his hand as if it had betrayed him.

Beyond him, coming through the bank door, a gun in his hand, was Earl. He raised the pistol and started firing.

Liza gunned the engine of the Volvo. She couldn't just sit here watching.

43

John Ray Mooney couldn't believe he was such a bad shot. He'd emptied the gun without nicking a Yip. Of course, he hadn't actually fired a gun in maybe a decade. Car thieves don't need guns. Hell, even bank robbers don't shoot; they just wave their guns around and holler.

"Shoot, dammit!" he yelled at the others. "Those are the Yips!"

Billy and Lowell were crouching statues, gargoyles. Lowell had dropped his bags of money and he held the big Smith & Wesson, but it was pointed at the ground. Billy had his gun up, and appeared to be taking aim at the Yips, but no bullets came out.

"What the hell are you doing? Shoot!"

John Ray still had Earl Shambley's Beretta stuffed into the back of his jeans, and he pulled it out and thumbed off the safety. Got to remember to aim this time. Makes a world of difference.

The Yips had massed behind the fender of a maroon Chrysler parked three cars beyond Liza's Volvo, but they clearly weren't staying there. John Ray could see their shiny black heads moving around, just above the hood of the big car. They were making their way to the sidewalk.

John Ray concentrated on aiming, trying to put the pistol's front sight exactly on one of the bobbing heads before pulling the trigger.

Then a gun cracked behind him and the air near his head was split by a whirring bullet. John Ray ducked and turned, bringing the Beretta around, to find Earl standing just outside the door of the bank, pointing a little revolver his way.

"What the hell are you doing?" he shouted. "You almost shot me!"

But Earl paid no attention. He was looking past John Ray's shoulder. "They're coming," he said.

John Ray wheeled to find the Yips charging toward him, spaced evenly along the sidewalk in a flying wedge. They held their guns high, and he detected no fear in their eyes. He brought up the gun and fired.

He didn't like Earl Shambley standing right behind him, firing past his ear, but he couldn't shoot in both directions at once. Lowell and Billy clearly were useless. He'd have to trust that Earl was shooting at Yips.

The Yips dodged and ducked, but they kept coming. John Ray tried to focus on the lead man, tried to remember to squeeze the trigger, not yank it. But the leader fell flat, and John Ray's bullet sailed off down the street without hitting anyone.

The leader's headlong sprawl caught the others off-guard, too. A fat Yip tripped over the fallen man and he, too, went flying, his arms cartwheeling as he tried to catch his balance. He smacked into the granite wall of the bank and went down, flat as a flounder. The leader rolled on the ground, holding his head like he'd been shot, but there wasn't any blood. What the hell was happening here?

The other two Yips pulled up, brought their guns to perfect shooting stances, and fired. The air suddenly was filled with bees, and John Ray couldn't stand it. He ducked into a squat and bounced sideways, getting behind Lowell's crouching bulk. Bullets screamed off the sidewalk around them.

"Fuck it," Earl said, and he dived back through the doors of the banks. Screams came out the open door and they reminded John Ray his first priority shouldn't be shooting Yips. Job One was getting away from here with the money.

The Yips stopped firing and approached the crouching bank robbers, their guns ready as they shouted in well-rehearsed English: "Drop your weapons. You are surrounded."

John Ray sure as hell felt surrounded, but he wasn't about to drop his gun. He peered around the great boulder that was Lowell Huganut's head, looking for his best shot. No way could he shoot both Yips before they fired back.

Then an engine roared and Liza's Volvo leapt up onto the sidewalk like a clumsy beige bear. The car's rear wheels squealed and smoked as they pushed the heavy car up over the curb. The nearest Yip shouted in alarm, but he was cut short when the Volvo's square fender whammed into him and sent him flying. The airborne Yip took out his partner as he crashed into him. They fell in a jumble of arms and legs.

"Come on!" Liza yelled out the car window.

John Ray snatched up his bag of money and, pushing Lowell ahead of him, hurried for the car.

As soon as everyone was aboard, Liza rocked the car off the sidewalk and rocketed down the street. The robbers held the big bags of money in their laps, not taking time with the trunk. As the men watched out the rear window, holding their breaths to listen for sirens, they saw the trunk lid bobbing with the motion of the car, waving bye-bye at the Yips and the National Bank of Coronado.

44

Kamal admired the way the American policeman commandeered the hospital conference room. He bulled his way past the objections of a woman in sterile eyeglasses, flopped his wide butt in a swivel chair and gestured for Kamal to sit opposite him at the table. The woman waited at the door a few seconds, frowning, but she knew she was beaten. She gently closed the door.

The detective introduced himself as R. J. Reynolds, automatically mumbling, "Yeah, yeah. Like the tobacco company. My old man loved his Camels."

Kamal had no idea what he was talking about. Camels?

Reynolds was a disheveled haystack of a man, and he seemed softly piled into the chair. He wore battered khakis and a faded blue shirt and a brown blazer that was shiny on the elbows and dotted with ancient stains. His yellow hair was matted on one side and sticking out on the other. His wide-jawed face glowed with a perpetual sunburn.

Kamal gingerly sat. The dizziness had abated, but the headache still lurked like thunderclouds on the horizon. Any sudden movement might tip the world and send the clouds of pain rushing to fill his head.

He felt betrayed by his own body, ashamed of its failure. Just when it mattered most, as he and his men were moving on the bank robbers in the form of the Attacking Cobra, Kamal's ears had stabbed him in the head and sent him reeling. He was aware of the blizzard of gunfire that followed, the screeching tires of a car. But all he could do was writhe on the sidewalk, clutching his head, until the spell passed. By the time he recovered, the police had arrived and disarmed the Royal Security unit, which wasn't difficult with all four of them sprawled on the sidewalk.

Only Fong remained free. Kamal guessed that Fong followed the robbers when he saw them escape. Kamal prayed to Allah that was the case. The pretender dared to commit a crime while posing as Prince Seri! Kamal would punish him for that, as soon as he could extricate himself from this mess.

"You know how many shell casings my men found outside the bank?" the detective asked, and Kamal carefully shook his head.

"Thirty-three."

Kamal didn't know what Reynolds wanted him to say to that. If the man had a point, he wished he would get to it soon. Kamal needed to tend to his men, get them checked out of this Western hospital with its echoing hallways and antiseptic smells. He needed to find Fong and learn where the robbers had gone. He needed to redeem himself.

"And you know what else?"

Kamal raised his eyebrows to show he was listening.

"Near as the doctors can tell, nobody was hit."

He shrugged. He hadn't decided how much English he would admit to possessing. He'd spoken no more than necessary, but the ruddy detective, like most Americans, assumed he understood every word.

"No, those injuries your men suffered, they're all blunt trauma, like you get when somebody runs over you with a car. No gunshot wounds."

"We were very fortunate," Kamal said, his voice barely more than a whisper. He knew it was true.

"Looks like none of the robbers got hit either."

Kamal shrugged again. His men were better marksmen than that. But he took all the blame. When the leader falls, the others sometimes stumble.

It anything, he was proud of Serang and Lombok. They performed perfectly up to the point where they were surprised by the woman in the big car. If he'd been on his feet, maybe he could've seen the danger and shouted "Code Orange" to warn them. Instead, Serang had a broken femur that would have him laid up for months. And both of Lombok's wrists were cracked, as if he'd tried to catch the flying Serang. Kulu, who'd gone headfirst into a solid wall, had a concussion. He now wore a huge turban of gauze wrapped tightly around his head. It was a sight Kamal would've enjoyed at any other time.

Kamal looked down at his own ruined suit, his muddy shirt. He straightened his narrow tie. The room had no mirror, which made him glad.

Americans, he knew, always let the accused make one phone call, and one call was all he needed. His team was registered with the Yip embassy in Washington and was protected by diplomatic immunity. The police couldn't hold him long. But so far, Reynolds had managed to overlook protocol. He didn't want Kamal on the phone, or talking to his men, until he was done with him.

Kamal had already told his men what they needed to know. As they were being loaded into ambulances, Kamal ordered them, in Malay, not to say a word to the police. Let him handle it. Which took its own sort of courage, really, since he felt like his head was in a vise at the time.

On the ride to the hospital, he had settled on his story. It had its flaws, but it was the best he could do on short notice.

"So, tell me," Reynolds said, "how you came to be at that bank robbery."

"It was a coincidence," Kamal said, trying to sound as matter-of-fact as the American. "My men and I are here on vacation. We were driving, looking for a restaurant, when we saw men running from the bank with guns. We took action."

"And you just happened to be packing four Glocks?"

"We always travel armed, just like your own Secret Service."

Reynolds paused to consider this, pressing his lips together and staring past Kamal's head. His square hand fished around inside his shirt pocket, came out with a little sliver of wood. As Kamal watched in amazement, the detective spread his lips and went at his teeth with the little splinter, cleaning between them. It was more than Kamal could bear to watch. Americans had such disgusting habits! The detective accomplished his excavation work, smacked his lips and hid the sliver away in his pocket.

"So you don't know who you were shooting at?"

"No, as I told you, we just happened onto them."

"Did it ever occur to you to call the police? That's the way we handle crime in this country, bud. We don't just shoot up the streets. People could've been killed. We've got bullet holes in buildings on the far side of Orange Avenue, a good hundred feet away. What were you thinking?"

Kamal gave the detective a shrug, one that communicated how little thought had gone into his actions.

"See, I don't like your version," Reynolds said impatiently. "Coincidence is no good. I don't believe in it. I'd prefer to think that maybe you were tailing those robbers, maybe looking to rip them off. Or maybe you were in on the robbery yourselves. A falling-out among thieves, you know? Though usually thieves wait until after they make their getaway before they start killing each other."

"I am sorry," Kamal said, bowing his head slightly, "but that is what happened. May I call my embassy now?"

"What's the rush?"

"They will be worried."

"How will they even know about it? You're here on vacation, right? That's what you said. They keep track of you even when you're on vacation?"

"We are always on call if the Sultan needs us."

"The Sultan, huh? I wonder what the Sultan's gonna think when he hears you're over here shooting up a resort town."

Kamal had wondered that very thing himself. The Sultan didn't like that kind of attention. He preferred exposure only on his terms, which usually included the cover of a magazine and a favorable feature article about his wealth and good works. Bank robberies and gunfights didn't fit the public relations campaign.

Only one thing would redeem him in the Sultan's eyes: Find Prince Seri. And, if he could manage it, capture the pretender and take him to Yip for punishment. Justice was swift and merciless in Yip, all based on a signal from the Sultan's hand. If the Americans, with their civil liberties and misguided notions about personal freedom, got involved, the pretender might never get his due.

Kamal would not tell the American police about the missing prince or the pretender's involvement in the robbery. For eventually he would be free of these entanglements—the hospital, the police—and he would track down the pretender the way the tiger stalks the monkey.

"May I make my phone call now?"

45

Lowell Huganut shifted on the barstool in Liza's kitchen, trying to find a position where he couldn't see his face in a mirror on the far wall. He had enough reason to be miserable right now.

Besides, he wasn't sure he knew the man in the mirror anymore. A week ago, the sight of that face would've meant something—Lowell Huganut, honest to a fault, friendly, hard-working, a quiet hero as a firefighter, former wrestling champion, Presbyterian, a man who'd cared for his ailing mother until she was planted in her grave. Now all that had changed. Now he was Lowell Huganut, bank robber. And an incompetent one at that.

He had choked. When the Yips surprised them at the bank, he'd been unable to raise his pistol and fire it. He told himself that maybe his moral upbringing prevented him from snuffing out another human life. But the ugly truth was that nothing that noble stewed inside him when the Yips came running at him. He'd been empty, without thought or emotion, watching it unfold around him.

He'd seen guys choke before, plenty of times, especially when he was wrestling. Some guy would step into the ring, and you could watch something—concentration, confidence, courage—leak out of him, leaving him an empty husk that was easily crushed. But it had never happened to Lowell. Until now.

More proof that he wasn't cut out for crime. He needed a normal life. A job, a home, a family. Not these constant surprises and anxieties. Even now that it was over, he felt shaky. It didn't help that John Ray kept yelling.

"It seems like a simple thing to me," John Ray shouted as he stalked around the kitchen. "You point the gun, you pull the trigger, a bullet comes out of the hole. Somebody says, 'Shoot!' and you're holding a gun, you shoot. Bang. Simple, right?"

Lowell had no explanation. He'd admitted that he'd choked, though the words went sour in his mouth, and you'd think that would be enough. You'd think John Ray could calm down now. The money was hidden in the crawl space under Liza's bedroom, stuffed through a nearly invisible trapdoor in the floor of her closet. All they had to do was wait out the police alert, then slip away. But John Ray couldn't leave it alone. Things hadn't gone according to plan, and he wanted someone to blame.

Liza stayed busy making coffee after they hid the money and changed back into their regular clothes, but now she sat opposite Billy Ho at the dining table, staring into the dark liquid in her mug. She'd avoided eye contact with Lowell since they arrived at the house, and he assumed she was ashamed of him. Which only made him feel worse.

The only thing he really wanted out of all this, he'd decided, was Liza West. It still seemed a dream to him, this sudden connection with her. When she came to his room and so gently awakened him, it had taken a while to separate his dreams from his new reality. Only afterward, when he still gasped from exertion, did he know it was real. Because he never, ever, had dreams that good.

Her misgivings about the robbery had offered him an out, and he hadn't taken it. He'd thought the robbery was what she really wanted, and giving Liza what she wanted seemed a meaningful way to spend his life. So Lowell went along with the heist—monkey see, monkey do—and he choked. Right in front of her.

"What about you?" John Ray turned on Billy, demanding an answer. "Why didn't you shoot?"

"I tried. The gun wouldn't fire."

"Aw, now that's bullshit. I checked that gun out myself."

Billy lifted a shoulder to indicate it was beyond explanation.

"It doesn't matter now," he said. "We made it. Why don't you chill out?"

"Chill out? I'll tell you why I won't chill out. I nearly got my head blown off out there today. And I didn't get any help from you."

"We got the money, didn't we?"

"No thanks to you. All you did was wave your gun around and play games with the bank tellers. When it got to be nut-cutting time, you and Lowell went south on me."

Liza lifted her gaze and leveled it at John Ray.

"Earl shot at them," she said. "It didn't seem to make a difference."

John Ray wheeled on Billy again.

"And what about that? That wasn't part of the plan. Where'd Earl get that little gun?"

Billy's eyes narrowed. "It wasn't part of the plan for you to keep his gun, either. I'm not surprised he had a backup. Probably a good thing, too. He distracted the Yips long enough for us to get away."

"He almost shot off my ear!"

"He wasn't shooting at you. He was shooting at the Yips."

"How do you know?"

"He was a lot closer to you. He could've hit you if he tried. Hell, I could've shot you from that close, and I'm terrible with guns."

"Can't prove it by me. I can't tell you even know how to shoot one."

"I told you. The gun wouldn't fire."

"I've had about enough of that."

John Ray stormed past Lowell and snatched up the little Raven from the countertop where they'd left the guns handy.

Liza spoke sharply: "Don't you shoot that gun in my house."

"I'm not gonna shoot it."

John Ray shook the clip free from the pistol and peered inside.

"It's empty," he said, and surprise seemed to take the bluster out of him.

Liza looked right at Lowell and their eyes met for the first time since the robbery. He shook his head slightly to show her he hadn't unloaded the gun.

"How the hell could that happen?" John Ray's voice was low and dangerous. "I checked this gun myself. Somebody unloaded this gun before we left for the bank."

"That would explain why it wouldn't shoot," Billy said.

"Why would somebody *do* that?"

"Don't look at me," Billy said. "I certainly didn't want to go into a hold-up with an empty gun."

John Ray turned to Lowell, who tried not to wince at the ex-con's cold stare.

"Lowell, you had this gun this morning. Did you take the bullets out?"

"I didn't do it."

"You had it first. Then I made you and Billy trade guns. Somehow, this gun turned up empty. How do you explain that?"

Lowell felt the trembling fingertips of panic creeping up his back. He hadn't done anything wrong. Why did he feel so guilty? But wait. He *had* done something wrong. He'd robbed a bank. Stealing went against everything he'd been brought up to believe, yet he'd done it. Maybe this is what it feels like to go crazy. You do stuff you never thought you'd do, then have no memory of it. Hell, maybe I emptied the gun and don't remember.

"I don't know what happened." That much he could say with conviction.

"Now, Lowell," and John Ray really was patronizing now, like he was coaxing a four-year-old out of a tree, "did you maybe take out the bullets to look at them or play with them or something? Maybe you forgot to put them back."

"Leave him alone!" Liza stood at the table, leaned across it to shout at John Ray. "He didn't do anything! Why can't you just let him alone?"

John Ray locked eyes with Liza for a long time. But he blinked first, and Lowell felt pride well up within him. It was a shame Liza had to defend him like that, but he was more impressed than mortified. She was a woman who could stand her ground. She was exactly what Lowell needed to complete his life.

"All right," John Ray said quietly. "I'll drop it. For now. But I'm keeping my eye on you, every one of you, until we split up that money tonight."

John Ray set down the Raven and picked up the Smith & Wesson. He stepped around the counter and marched off toward the other end of the house.

"And," he said over his shoulder, "there better not be any more mistakes."

46

John Ray Mooney slid open the bathroom window and let the sea air wash over his face. The little window looked out onto a side yard and didn't offer much of a view, but John Ray could see a slice of the empty street that encircled the park. All was quiet, the only movement a gull worrying the nourishment out of some pilfered trash.

Good thing this window's so small, he thought, or I might crawl out and go screaming down the street.

He was pretty sure he was going insane. He'd seen it often enough in others to recognize the symptoms. Hell, it ran in his family. Just a matter of time before he cracked, too. He felt hot inside, like his engine was overheating. The heat came spewing out as wild accusations. He could see the others thought he'd gone nuts.

But, dammit, the gun *was* empty. That was no hallucination. He'd checked that gun, he was sure of it. Why would somebody empty a gun? Without bullets, it's a conversation piece.

And another thing. Billy could play the innocent all he wanted, but John Ray felt sure Earl's first bullet was meant for him. Those two had cooked up a plan. Probably figured that if they took him out of the picture, they could steamroll Liza and Lowell. John Ray thought they were maybe half right. Lowell would roll over like a puppy, but Liza wouldn't be manipulated. In some ways, Liza was more dangerous than any of the others. Because she kept her cool. The others were busy conspiring and scheming. Liza always watched. Look how she'd handled things at the bank robbery. She waited until the time was right, then slammed into the Yips with her car. John Ray thought he could take a lesson from her.

And what about the Yips? How had they shown up at the bank when they did? Have they been following us all along? Were they watching the house now? The ones at the bank had been left in scattered heaps, thanks to Liza, but were there more out there? He peeked out the window, saw nothing, took several deep breaths of the fresh air.

He heard a motorcycle sputter in the distance, and it reminded him that, out there somewhere, roaring around on their Harleys in search of him, were the Sons of Satan. John Ray wondered briefly what Big Odie used to snip off fingers—knife, hatchet, pruning shears?—but quickly changed that line of thinking. He had plenty to face right here in Coronado.

He needed to calm down. Much more of this stress, and he'd make mistakes, maybe get caught. Before he knew it, he'd wake up back at Folsom, maybe back in his old cell, with Georgie Zook still talking.

Georgie had it all wrong. Bank robbery's easy. Any jackass can charge in there and wave a gun around. It's afterward you have to worry about. Greed is too powerful a force. You've got five people—by definition, a gang of thieves—sitting on a pile of money. Somebody's going to make a move, try to take more than their share. Now was when John Ray needed to calmly dominate. He needed to be sane. Because now was the dangerous part.

47

"My ex-husband had sort of a luggage fetish," Liza West said hours later, as she and Lowell peered into the oversized closet where suitcases shared space with dusty tennis rackets and stray chairs. "There's this Korean guy, runs a liquor store over on Orange Avenue. His family owns luggage factories all over Asia, and he always cut Sam sweet deals on more bags."

Lowell waded into the closet and started pulling softside duffels from their shelves.

"You probably can find five that are the same size," Liza said. "I don't know exactly what Sam took with him, but he left plenty behind."

Getting the luggage ready was the last piece of business before they split up the money. Liza figured luggage would look less suspicious than having a stream of people leaving her house carrying Hefty bags. Not that it mattered much. It was nearly midnight, and her quiet neighborhood was fast asleep.

Lowell, reaching high for the top shelf, grunted as he tugged against a suitcase that was hung on something. The bag came loose with an unmistakable rip, and he blushed deeply. He's so cute, Liza mused, such a boy.

A certain boyishness was exactly what she needed. She'd had it with slick characters like Billy Ho or scary men like John Ray Mooney or stiffly oblivious types like Sam West. Give her someone like Lowell, someone without hidden agendas. A willing boy with a body like a brick shithouse.

"Lot of stuff here," he said, as he cast about for another bag.

"Sam liked to buy things. Only way he could justify working eighty hours a week."

Lowell shook his head. "Sounds like a man who had a problem relaxing."

"Exactly right. You ever have that problem?"

"Never. I sleep like a log. Or, at least, I always have before."

"Think you'll have insomnia now?"

"I don't know. I'm so keyed up right now, I might never sleep again."

"It's the coffee."

"I didn't have any coffee. I've been drinking water."

"Not good."

"I just want this to be over."

"It won't be much longer, Lowell. Then you and I are leaving town together. Right?"

"You still want to go with me?"

"Sure. I've been thinking of nothing else."

Lowell blinked rapidly, and she thought for a second he might burst into tears.

"I didn't know how you'd feel after seeing me freeze up at the bank. All day, I've been wondering how you . . ."

Lowell turned away from her, focusing on the bags piled on the floor. Liza wrapped her arms around his big shoulders and stood on tiptoe to kiss him on the ear.

"It could happen to anybody. Let's just forget it."

"I'm not sure I can. Nothing like that's ever happened to me before."

"And it won't happen again. We're not going to be robbing any more banks."

He turned within her arms until he was facing her, inches apart.

"You promise? 'Cause, Liza, I don't think I can take it again. It's just not me, you know? I'm not used to that kind of excitement."

"Me, either, sugar. I run a sweatshirt shop, remember? I don't see us as Bonnie and Clyde. I think we take our money and live simply for a while. Forget all this happened."

Lowell hugged her so hard Liza couldn't breathe.

"You're making me very happy," he grunted into her ear.

"You're breaking my back."

"Sorry." He released her and turned away, bending over the black suitcases.

"Wait," she said. "I just thought of something. Pull that box out from under there. It's full of clothes from the store. We can use them to cover the money, in case a cop or somebody wants to look inside the bags."

"Good idea." He hoisted the box, turned and handed it to Liza, who nearly fell under its sudden weight. Boys, she remembered, don't know their own strength.

Lowell gathered up the suitcases in his long arms and backed out of the walk-in closet, closing the door with his foot. Liza felt him behind her as she lugged the box to her bedroom. She threw a little extra hip action into her walk for his viewing pleasure. Boys like to be teased, too.

She dropped the box beside her bed, and made way for Lowell to dump his load of bags. Then they fell into each others' arms for a long kiss.

"It'll all be over soon," she said. "Then we'll go to your house and start over."

"I can't wait."

"But we've got to be careful. Things are very tense. You know that, right?"

"Oh, man, do I ever."

"Something bad can happen if we don't stay on our toes."

"Right."

"Follow my lead, all right? I'll try to keep the rest of them from killing each other until this is over."

"What about after we split up the money?"

"I've been thinking about that. I think we get out of here. As soon as the others go their own ways, we'll walk over to the Hotel Del. You've still got a room there, right?"

"Yeah. We never got a chance to check out."

"I think we haul our bags over there, cuddle up together till morning. Then we'll rent a car to drive to New Mexico."

"We could fly."

"I don't think you want to go through airport security with a bag full of money."

"Oh. Right. A car, then. But not your car."

"The police might be watching for it. They may already be tracing beige Volvos."

"We could say the car was stolen, then returned."

"I'd prefer not to say anything at all. Let's just get out of here without attracting attention to ourselves."

"Right."

"But keep your eyes open. If one of these guys tries to pull something, you'll need to pounce on him."

Lowell enthusiastically bobbed his head.

"And Lowell?"

"Yeah?"

"I think I'm falling for you."

Lowell hugged her fiercely. Boys like to hear that sort of thing. And Liza, to her own surprise, enjoyed saying it.

Then the doorbell rang.

48

Earl Shambley felt himself slumping as he pushed the doorbell button. He took a deep breath and threw back his shoulders. A long fucking day. And it wasn't over yet.

It had been eight o'clock before Earl got home to his tiny apartment. He'd spent the afternoon with FBI automatons and local cops who cut him no slack at all, even though he was a retired officer himself. The Coronado PD detective on the case, fucker named R.J. Reynolds, made it clear he suspected Earl. Earl had made it too easy for the robbers to get inside the vault. Chasing them outside and shooting made Earl look a little better, but he hadn't hit anybody, had he? And the Yips claimed he was shooting at them. Reynolds tried all the tricks to cause Earl to slip up, but Earl had seen them all before, had been on the other side of the table plenty of times. He managed to stay one step ahead the whole time.

Earl hadn't counted on R.J. Reynolds, exactly. He'd figured anyone making a career as a cop in Coronado wouldn't be a hard-charger. But Reynolds seemed to possess a certain wiliness under that rumpled exterior, and Earl took care that he wasn't followed when he went home to his apartment. He had a sandwich, soaked his aching feet, and sat in the dark for two hours before going to Liza West's house.

Waiting in darkness gave him plenty of time to analyze what had gone wrong at the robbery. John Ray had kept Earl's gun, which hadn't been in the plan, but Earl had been prepared for that. The little ankle gun should've been enough to do the job, but he was distracted by the Yips, who came springing up from behind a parked car like a volley of little cannonballs. The shot had gone just wide, and Earl didn't get a second chance. When the Yips opened fire, he'd seen the need to go indoors. Better to save his own ass than to put a bullet in John Ray. Plenty of time for that later.

The door swung open and John Ray swung up the Smith & Wesson and planted the muzzle between Earl's eyebrows.

"Tell me one reason why I shouldn't shoot you right now."

Earl froze. He'd been afraid something like this would happen. He'd arrived unarmed, and that was a bad decision. Reynolds had kept the ankle gun as evidence, and every other gun he owned was already in the hands of his partners.

"It would make a lot of noise," he said, barely moving his lips.

"Tell me right now you didn't try to shoot me today outside the bank."

Earl's mustache twitched. "I didn't try to shoot you today outside the bank."

"The bullet went right past my fuckin' ear."

"You moved. I was trying to shoot those little chinks."

"I didn't see you hit any of them."

"Same to you."

John Ray breathed deeply. He took the gun from Earl's head, lowered until it pointed at his chest.

"Fuckin' cop."

"Ex-cop."

"You make one wrong move—one—and I'll shoot a hole in you. Make you a fuckin' doughnut. You got that?"

"Got it."

"Now get in here and close the door. You're attracting attention."

"Me? You're the one playing Billy the Kid."

Earl shut the door behind him as John Ray backed out of the entry-way. Billy and Liza and Lowell stood in a clump in the kitchen doorway, watching it all. Billy met Earl's eyes and shook his head, as if to say, "I told you John Ray would be trouble."

Earl fell in with the others as they marched down the hall and into a bedroom. The sight of the money stacked on the bed took some of the wind out of him. Lordy, look at that. And it's all mine.

John Ray planted himself in the doorway, the pistol dangling in his hand, and kept an eye on Earl while Billy and Liza counted the money. Earl didn't look at John Ray. He didn't want to set him off again. Besides, nothing he could do about him right now. But there may be time yet to eliminate his partners and walk away with the whole haul.

Liza and Lowell loosed a little cheer when Billy announced the million-dollar mark. When he finally stopped counting, at $1.26 million, nobody said a thing. They all stood looking at the stacks of money, doing the math.

"That's two-hundred-fifty-two-thousand apiece," Billy said. "Split five ways."

"So what are you waiting for?" John Ray said. "Split it up."

"What am I? Your accountant?"

"Then get out of the way and let Liza do it."

"I'll do it," Billy said. "Why don't you and Earl make us some drinks?"

"Why don't you just split up the money while I'm watching? Then you can make your own drink."

"Why are you so nervous?" Billy asked. "We'll get our shares and get out of here before the Yips track us down. And the cops have no clue who we are, do they Earl?"

Earl shook his head smugly. "They don't know their ass from a hole in the ground."

"See? If you'd just relax, John Ray, you might even enjoy the moment."

"I'll relax when I've got you people and this place in my rear-view mirror."

They all understood that feeling, and no one argued. Billy deftly separated the loot into five equal portions, then Liza began loading the bags. Earl watched her for a second, but the sight of her tight ass bent over like that was too distracting, and he looked away.

"What's that big box?" he asked.

"Shirts," she said. "Inventory left over from my store. I thought I'd put one in each bag to cover up the money."

"In case somebody pokes around in there, huh? Good idea."

"How about that drink now?" Billy asked.

"You fellas go ahead," Liza said. "I'll finish up."

John Ray hesitated, then said, "All right," and waved the rest of them toward the kitchen with the pistol.

"Why do you have to keep pointing that gun at us?" Billy said irritably.

"Just trying to stay alive."

49

Kamal didn't know what kind of tree he was climbing. Something native to America, a leafy monster that stretched arms in all directions. One branch reached very near a second-story window of Liza West's house. From the ground, he'd seen the window was slightly ajar, just enough to let in a breeze. Climbing the tree's evenly spaced branches was easy, but he wasn't looking forward to shinnying all the way out that limb to the window.

Normally, swinging from a branch into a second-story window wouldn't cause him to hesitate. It was just the sort of stunt Jackie Chan would do, and if it was good enough for Jackie, it certainly was good enough for Kamal. But his head throbbed and he was fatigued from two days of nonstop alert. When he stretched out on the branch, he might just fall asleep.

Instead, he slithered along it like a boa, bending his elbows and knees to push-pull himself toward the window. The branch bent under his weight, ready to dump him on the ground like an overripe coconut.

He knew Kulu was somewhere in the darkness below, just waiting to see him fall. That would give the fat old bear something to recount back at the palace.

The window had a wooden sill, maybe two inches wide, and no screen. That was all Kamal needed to know. He grasp the branch tightly and let his legs swing free. He walked hand over hand the last few feet to the side of the house. Reaching with his feet, he found the sill and carefully shifted his weight onto his toes.

The hard part was letting go of the branch. He needed to open the window the rest of the way, but he couldn't use his hands without risking a fall. Then he got an idea that was pure Jackie. Kamal hooked the toes of his right foot under the window and pulled upward. The window stuck briefly, then slid up noiselessly. He hooked his heels inside the sill and dropped to a sitting position, still holding onto the dipping branch. Then he let go and tumbled inside. He hit the carpeted floor a little harder than he liked, then rolled to his feet, quick as a cat.

Kamal was in a dark bedroom nearly empty of furniture or decoration. Just a mussed bed and a half-empty bookcase against one wall. The door was closed. He stood very still, listening, but no one downstairs sounded the alarm over the thump he'd made.

He allowed himself a smile. Now he hoped Kulu had been watching.

He pulled his gun and thumbed off the safety. Finally, his patience was paying off. Even without Serang and Lombok—who remained hospitalized overnight for observation—Kamal had the bank robbers right where he wanted them.

He risked speaking into his wrist microphone.

"I'm inside, going downstairs. Get ready at the doors. Operation Rhino's Milk."

Kamal tiptoed to the door and peeked out. The hall was empty. He slipped through the door, happy to see the hall was thickly carpeted. He reached the stairway, and even the stairs were carpeted. Americans. He silently descended the stairs, his pistol poised, moving toward the loud voices of the fools who'd wronged him.

50

Billy Ho, the perfect host, had the drinks ready by the time Liza joined them in the kitchen. He raised his martini to toast their success, and the others hoisted their glasses, too. Except for John Ray, who seemed determined to rain on the party. He stood with his hips leaning against the kitchen sink, his arms crossed, the big pistol dangling from his hand.

"It's been a true pleasure working with all of you," Billy said. "And I hope to never see you again."

Liza laughed and Lowell snorted. They all tipped up their drinks, and that eased the tension even more.

If anyone had reason to be tense, it was Billy. He was the one the Yips were after. If any Yips survived Liza's assault with the Volvo, they were somewhere in Coronado, hunting him. Yet he was surprisingly calm. The money sitting in the bedroom helped a great deal.

It wasn't millions and he'd have to be judicious in how he spent it. He'd like to make away with the entire haul, but that was looking less and less likely. Earl had his chance to take out John Ray outside the bank, and he'd blown it. He didn't seem inclined to try again. The other two, the starry-eyed lovers, probably could be bamboozled, but Billy wondered whether it was worth the effort. Let them have their shares. Everybody walks away a winner. Of course, if a last-minute opportunity presented itself . . .

He tipped up the stemmed glass again and watched the level of the cold vodka drop. Ahh. Hell, let them keep their shares. Billy had enough money to keep himself in martinis for years. And, really, what more did a man need?

They all stood facing him, in deference to his role as toastmaster, so only Billy saw the dark shape descending the stairs.

"Oh shit," he said. "Oh dear."

Then the Yip in the filthy black suit was in the kitchen with them, his pistol pointing at John Ray, who leaned helplessly against the kitchen counter. An easy shot, even for the little Yip who'd thrown himself to the sidewalk earlier in the day. John Ray didn't even try. He unwrapped his fingers from the Smith & Wesson and let it drop to the floor. Billy flinched, expecting the gun to go off, but it made only a dull thud on the linoleum.

"Good," the Yip said. "Now everyone stand very still."

He lifted his wrist to his lips and spoke quickly into it in a singsong language. Billy recognized the language and the voice. This was the man who'd called his hotel room in search of the prince. And that, he reflected, was when everything had gone wrong. He'd fooled himself into thinking it would all be fine. He'd even insisted on hanging around long enough for a parting drink. But his success had been a mirage. The shit still flew toward the proverbial fan, and Billy still stood squarely in the way.

The French doors in the breakfast nook flew open, and a fat Yip with bandages wrapped around his head burst in, pointing his gun at everyone before settling on Billy. There was a moment of silence while everyone's eyes danced about, sending messages and issuing stern warnings. Then someone knocked at the front door.

The head Yip spoke to the fat one and the fat man hustled around the counter to the entryway. They all listened to him unlock the door and exchange words with someone there. When he returned, another gun-toting Yip, this one cleaner and unbandaged, trailed behind him. Billy thinking: They're like dandelions in a lawn, these pesky Yips. They keep springing up everywhere.

The Yips spread out around the room, forming a triangle. All three kept their guns pointed at the bank robbers, who stood in a clump, still holding their cocktails.

"Okay," the Yip leader said. "We will all hold still while we have a little talk."

Nobody said a thing.

"My name is Kamal. I am the leader of the Royal Guard of the Sultanate of Yip. I am here in search of Prince Seri Hassan Bandapanang bin Mohammed. Where is he?"

All eyes shifted to Billy. His skin prickled. There was no good answer to the question. He'd been so busy avoiding this moment, he hadn't bothered to invent a lie.

"Well?" Kamal demanded.

"I don't know," Billy said calmly. "I wish I did."

"You were staying in the hotel under his name."

"I work for him. Hasn't he written home about me?"

Kamal's eyes narrowed.

"He told me to meet him at the hotel," Billy said. "He gave me a couple of his credit cards, told me to enjoy myself and wait for him here. We've been living in L.A., but he wanted to get away for a while. So I came ahead and got everything set up with the hotel people. But Bennie—that's what we call him over here—never showed up."

It all sounded perfectly plausible, which helped Billy sell it, but Kamal wasn't buying.

"The people at the hotel told me *you* were Prince Seri."

Billy tried to look alarmed. "They must've misunderstood. I clearly told the front desk I worked *for* him, not that I *was* him."

"I do not believe this story."

"I'm terribly sorry, but it's the truth."

"I do not think so."

Billy shrugged. "What can I tell you?"

"The truth."

Billy set his martini glass on the counter. He might need his hands free, though what he planned to do with them, he had no idea. Billy was no fighter. But his feet remembered what it was like to be chased. They'd carried him out of more than one scrape on the back streets of Tijuana. Given the slightest opening, he was sprinting for the door. Better to take the chance than to stand around, trying to talk his way out of trouble.

Kamal barked something in his native tongue and the fat man bulled his way into the cluster of robbers and grabbed Billy by the elbow.

"Come with me," he said in a hoarse baritone. Then he yanked him toward the living room.

"The rest of you move, too," Kamal said. "Slowly."

In the living room, the third Yip lined up all the robbers except Billy against a wall, and ordered them to clasp their hands together behind their necks. They all obeyed, though he was sending them furious mental signals to do something to save him.

"Lie down on the sofa, please," the fat man said.

"Me?" Billy didn't like the sound of this. Why would they want him to lie down?

"Face down."

"Hard for me talk that way. Shouldn't we be figuring out a plan to find the prince?"

"Shut up. Lie down."

He did as he was told, stretching out on the beige sofa, his arms tight against his body.

The man reached over and pressed the gun barrel to the back of his head, and Billy's bladder suddenly felt very full. Then the fat man pivoted and lowered his wide butt onto Billy's back.

"Hey! Get off me."

"Be still."

"I can't breathe."

"Too bad."

The fat man shifted his weight, trying to find a more comfortable position. Billy's spine felt as if it would snap. His lungs were flattened.

Kamal squatted before him, their noses inches apart.

"Where is Prince Seri?"

"I told you," he gasped. "I don't know."

"Not good enough. Kulu, are you comfortable?"

The fat man grunted happily.

Billy needed to get some oxygen to his brain. He needed to think up an answer that would satisfy these Yips. But nothing came to mind but the pain in his back, the burning in his lungs. And the truth certainly wouldn't do.

"Where is Prince Seri?"

"I don't know."

Kamal rolled his eyes and sighed. "Fong, come join Kulu on the sofa."

"Roger."

"Wait!" Billy said. "Okay, I'll talk. Just get Jumbo off me first."

"No. Talk first. Then he gets off."

"I can't breathe."

"I do not care."

Billy grimaced against the pain. Think. Think.

"Where is Prince Seri?"

"He's dead."

Kamal sucked in his breath sharply, and Billy envied him that pleasure. Kamal seemed stricken by the news, but he caught himself and put his stoic face back on.

"What happened?"

"An accident."

"What kind of accident?"

"Please get this brute off me."

"What kind of accident? A car, a plane?"

"A gun."

Kamal stood and backed away. "Get up, Kulu."

The fat man gave Billy an extra squish before getting to his feet. Billy took ragged breaths and creaked to a sitting position.

"You killed him, did you not?" Kamal demanded. "You killed him and then took his credit cards and pretended to be him."

"It was an accident."

"You do not accidentally shoot royalty. That is assassination."

"I swear, it wasn't my fault. He was playing with a gun and he was drunk. I told him to put it away—"

"You are lying."

"Come on, give me a chance here. I'm trying to tell you what happened."

"You are trying to make fools of us. You don't understand you are in deep trouble. We are the Royal Guard, the best-trained security force in all of Asia. We could spend days torturing you without repeating any torture once. We can be very creative."

"You can't do that," Billy said, and he seemed to have recaptured his indignation as well as his breath. "This is America."

"This?" Kamal gestured around the room. "This is a den of thieves. There are no rules here. Now, do you tell me exactly what happened to Prince Seri or do I ask Kulu to take a seat?"

51

Earl Shambley had been in scrapes before, but nothing ever as bad as this. Billy was talking a mile a minute, sitting cross-legged on the floor while the rest of them stood against the wall like targets in a shooting gallery. Worse yet, Billy couldn't seem to get his story straight. The Yips were losing patience. Seemed the Yips have special ceremonies for their dead royalty, and this guy Kamal was determined to return home with the corpse. This was a major sticking point for Billy. He'd already admitted killing the prince, though he insisted it was an accident. Why wouldn't he tell them where he put the body?

"Quit dancing around it," Earl said. "Tell 'em. The rest of us might get out of here alive."

"Fuck you."

"Both of you shut up now." Kamal stepped forward and placed his gun barrel against Billy's head. Billy tried to duck away, but he was trapped there, his head bent over as if in prayer.

"The Sultan will allow me to execute you," Kamal said, and his voice was murderously low. "I can do it in Yip, or I can do it now. The Sultan will not care."

"I've told you everything I know."

"Where is Prince Seri's body? I will either return to Yip with his body in a coffin, or it will be your body in there."

"It's out in the desert."

"Where?"

"I don't know exactly. I'm not even sure I could find it again. It was dark."

"Where?"

"At some old service station or something. After the gun went off, I got scared. I thought the police would blame me. So I dragged his body behind this building and, um, buried it."

"Buried it? You dug a hole in the ground?"

"There was a hole there already."

"A hole? For what?"

Billy pressed his lips tightly together and closed his eyes. Kamal yanked the slide on his pistol, sending a round flying through the air, putting a fresh one in its place. The sound was like the cracking of a dam, and Billy's words gushed forth.

"It was an outhouse, okay? There was an outhouse there and I dumped his body down the hole."

Liza gasped, a sharp intake of breath that got the two backup Yips pointing pistols at her. Earl tried to lean away from her, in case they were so jumpy they pulled the triggers.

"What is this, an outhouse?"

"You know, a shitter," Billy said. "An outdoor bathroom."

"You put the prince's body down a toilet?"

"It was an accident. A mistake."

"It will be the last mistake you ever make."

"I doubt it."

Earl couldn't get comfortable. Everyone else got to lean against flat wall, but the room's one painting—a wide oil of a vase of flowers—hung behind Earl and the heavy frame dug into his shoulder blades. He had an idea about that painting.

"Get up," Kamal said, and Billy struggled to his feet. Kamal kept just enough distance to prevent Billy from making any kind of move. Not that he seemed so inclined. He looked as miserable as a steer at a slaughterhouse.

"Come with me. I am calling the police. Where is the phone?"

"In the kitchen," Liza offered, which got guns pointed at her again.

"Watch the rest of them," Kamal ordered. "We will hold them until the police arrive. But this one goes back to Yip with us."

Earl watched Kamal march Billy to the counter where they'd left their cocktails. That little celebration seemed a long time ago. The telephone sat on the counter not far from the drinks, but Billy pulled up short, standing between the phone and Kamal.

"May I please finish my drink? It might be the last one I'll get for a while."

"It will be your last, ever. We do not indulge in the filthiness of drink in Yip."

"Your loss."

Billy grasped the glass and turned to face Kamal while he tipped up the martini. He smacked his lips and sighed with delight when the vodka was gone. Then he smashed the fragile glass into Kamal's face.

Earl saw Kamal's head snap back and blood spurt out in a narrow fountain. Billy snatched up a ring of keys from the countertop and raked them across Kamal's forehead before the security man could recover. Then Billy was running toward the garage.

The other Yips cried out in alarm, but Kamal shouted, "Stay where you are. Watch them. I will get him."

He wiped his bloody face with his sleeve and took off after Billy.

As soon as Kamal went through the door to the garage, Earl unclasped his hands from behind his neck and grabbed the painting's gilt frame. Then, in a fluid movement, he lifted it off its hanger and swung it down over his head, crashing it over Kulu's turbaned head. Glass sprayed everywhere. Kulu went down like he'd been struck by lightning. The other Yip yelled and wheeled, but Lowell was ready. He brought both fists down hard on top of the Yip's head. The little man crumpled. Damn, thought Earl. Most men hit somebody on the skull like that, it'd break their hands. Lowell didn't seem the slightest bit pained.

Earl snatched up Kulu's fallen pistol from the floor, but watching Lowell had stalled him a second and John Ray already had the other Yip's gun in his hand. They stood facing each other for a tense moment, eyes searching.

"Let's get out of here," Liza said.

"She's right," Earl said quickly. "Get the money. We'll take my car."

52

Billy Ho was behind the wheel of Liza's Volvo by the time Kamal crashed through the door into the garage. Billy already had hit the garage door button; the door crawled ever so slowly upward. He threw the car into reverse. Tires screamed on the concrete floor as the Volvo lurched backward. The garage door hadn't risen quite far enough, and the car's roof scraped loudly as the car roared backward into the alley.

He spun the wheel, making the car slew around crazily as he backed up the alley. He cut his eyes from his mirrors to the front of the car and there was Kamal, chasing after him, blood all over his face, his gun held high. Billy slammed the brakes and shifted the car to Drive. He stomped the gas.

Kamal's eyes widened as the car zoomed at him, but he didn't hesitate. He nimbly leaped and landed on all fours on the hood. He found a handhold near the base of the windshield and, with the other hand, tried to bring the gun around to put an end to Billy's flight. Shit. Billy yanked the steering wheel back and forth, knocking over trash cans with the Volvo, raking Kamal with overhanging tree branches. Still the Yip hung on.

The tires shrieked as the heavy car swung onto the street that encircled the round park with the flagpole. The park gave Billy an idea. He twisted the wheel sharply, deliberately steering into the high curb that surrounded the park. The Volvo banged to a stop so suddenly that his head smacked the top of the steering wheel.

Kamal flew. One second he was a hood ornament. The next, he was twenty feet away, rolling in the grass. Billy held one hand to his forehead and threw the car into reverse with the other.

Jesus Christ. Kamal was rolling to his feet. Shouldn't he be dead? Shouldn't he at least be too dazed to keep chasing me?

The Volvo backed up with a decided limp, and Billy knew he was in trouble. He'd blown the left front tire when he hit the curb. He could feel the bump-thump as the car lunged forward. He stomped the gas anyway, urging the car around the street that ringed the park. But the noise grew louder and he smelled burning rubber.

Shit. Shit. Shit.

He peered into the half-light of the park, trying to see Kamal. He spotted the Yip's white shirt. Kamal limped hurriedly across the park, trying to cut off the car. No surprise. The man just kept on coming. He was the Energizer Bunny of cops.

Billy felt hope slipping away. If only the tire hadn't blown. If only he'd taken off earlier, instead of waiting for Shambley's midnight visit. If only he'd never gotten mixed up with the fucking Prince of Yip. If only . . .

Kamal had the angle on him. He leaped into the street sixty feet ahead of the staggering car, aimed his gun at Billy. His foot hit the brake of its own accord.

"Get out of the car!"

Billy opened the door.

"Keep your hands high!"

Once Billy was standing next to the car, wincing against the scorched smell of the destroyed tire, Kamal grabbed him and spun him around. He held Billy bent over the fender, his pistol poking between his shoulder blades, while he fished handcuffs out of his pockets.

Lights came on in windows of the nearest houses. Maybe someone would see them out here, wrestling around by the crippled car, and call the cops. The American cops. Billy would rather try his luck with the Coronado police or the FBI than with the Yips. At least the Americans hadn't already heard all his lies.

Kamal yanked him upright.

"We must hurry," he said, and limped away, dragging Billy behind him.

53

"We could steal a boat," John Ray Mooney said, his voice filled with sudden inspiration.

"Don't be crazy," Earl said from behind the wheel of the rumbling Buick. "What do you know about boats?"

"Don't call me crazy."

"When was the last time you drove a boat? They got boats in Folsom?"

"Maybe it's been a while, but I know this much. You don't 'drive' a boat. You steer it. So stuff that up your ass."

"They keep these boats locked up. You know how to hot-wire a boat?"

"Why are you so dead-set against a boat?"

Silence settled over the car. The point was moot now anyway. They'd left the last of the boatyards behind as Earl sped south on the highway that followed the Silver Strand. Only a handful of high-rise condominiums stood south of the Hotel Del Coronado, and the Buick had gone just a mile or two before they were beyond the town's lights, ripping along a dark highway with the bay to the left and the ocean to the right. The windows were down, letting out the smoke from John Ray's cigarette.

"I can't swim," Earl said. Even though John Ray had been looking right at him, he hadn't seen Earl's lips move in the light from the dashboard. It was almost like telepathy, something out of *The Twilight Zone.*

"You can't swim?" John Ray wasn't even sure the other two, cuddling in the back seat, had heard. "I thought you were in the Navy."

"I was, but I didn't have to swim. I was Shore Patrol."

"Still, they make you learn to swim. I saw it on the History Channel."

"I faked it."

"How do you fake swimming? You either swim or you sink."

"I sink," Lowell said from the back seat.

"What?"

"I can't swim, either. I sink like a stone."

John Ray felt like shooting them all. They were driving him crazy. Especially Earl. If Earl weren't steering the car, John Ray might pop him right now.

"I wasn't talking about swimming anyway," he said. "I was talking about a boat."

"One thing leads to another," Earl said. "Especially with you at the wheel."

"At the *helm.* What the hell kinda Navy man are you, anyhow?"

"I told you. I stayed on the shore, making sure Commie frogmen didn't attack from the sea. My whole tour of duty consisted of walking on the beach."

John Ray mulled that for a moment. "Right now, that doesn't sound so bad."

"Bunch of beach right over there. You want to get out and walk?"

John Ray *really* felt like shooting Earl. He tossed out his Marlboro butt in a spray of sparks.

"Why don't you two be quiet?" Liza said. "I'm nervous enough thinking we might hit a roadblock any second. I don't need all this bickering."

John Ray thought she sounded like his mother, who bracketed every request with a description of whatever mental attack she was having that day: "I'm just a nervous wreck today, Baby. You've got to be quiet and let Mama rest."

The prison shrink told John Ray that hadn't been a healthy environment for a boy with anti-social tendencies. The shrink said John Ray tended to over-analyze himself and everyone else, searching for symptoms. Now here he was, doing it again. Thinking about insanity all the time was driving him crazy.

"Ain't gonna be any roadblocks," Earl said. "If we've made it this far, we're clear all the way into the city."

"And just how do you figure that?" John Ray asked.

"Call it an educated guess."

"That's what I want my ass dangling by. Your guesses."

"You got a better idea, pardner?"

"I've been saying it. We could get a boat."

They all groaned.

54

The Dew Drop Inn in Chula Vista was a dump by anyone's standards, but it was a welcome sight to Earl Shambley. The cinderblock motel sat in a puddle of asphalt between a rental warehouse and a neon-lit beer joint that should've had last call by now. A row of Harleys was parked in front of the bar, and the sight made John Ray whip his head around. What was that about? Man was jumpy as a frog on a griddle.

As if there were any further need to call attention to the seediness of the block, Horace Feathers had strung concertina wire around the top of the fence that surrounded his motel parking lot. Horace wasn't really the anxious sort, though people got that impression. He had a nerve disorder that made him twitch his head constantly. He looked like he was being startled by loud noises or trying to yank a kink out of his neck.

Earl knew the whole Feathers clan back in Dallas. Small-time hoods and drug dealers. He'd regularly arrested Horace and his seven brothers, sometimes the whole bunch at once. The crimes usually were so petty, and the Feathers so pathetically stupid in court, sighing judges usually let them go with time served. But the Feathers boys kept Earl's arrest numbers up, which kept his bosses off his back and gave him time for profitable sidelines.

Horace had been the first of the brothers to drop out of crime. He was just too easy to identity. All a victim had to say was, "The guy was twitching like a rooster," and Earl would be on his way to the rambling old house where Mama Feathers and her boys lived.

To hear the brothers tell it, they'd all chipped in to create a grub stake for Horace's new life. He'd moved west, searching for opportunities, and stumbled onto the motel in Chula Vista while driving around lost. He'd gotten a great deal on it because nobody else wanted to invest in this neighborhood.

Earl steered the Buick into the parking lot and stopped in front of the tollbooth-sized lobby. The Buick's engine knocked and gasped when he turned off the ignition, and he made a mental note: First purchase to make with that bank loot is a new ride. He needed to ditch the dying Buick anyway. Maybe he'd unload it on Horace Feathers.

"Wait here," he said to the others. He made a point of pocketing the keys.

John Ray Mooney lit a cigarette, his hard eyes on Earl. Liza yawned. Lowell looked like he'd been whacked by a two-by-four, jaw hanging slack and eyes glazed.

A bell on the lobby door jangled as Earl entered. Horace Feathers sat in a ratty armchair behind the front desk, watching a flickering little TV. Canned laughter rose from the television as Horace rose from his chair, his head jerking around like he was in a swarm of bugs only he could see.

"Earl?"

"Horace. What's up?"

"Nothing, nothing. Just keeping my head above water."

Earl imagined how much splashing that would cause.

"Listen, Horace. I'm kinda in a hurry here. I got some people out in the car. We need a room. You got any vacancies?"

Horace laughed merrily.

"Man, that's 'bout all I have got. You can have any room in the place except Number Three. Some whore working in there."

"Give me a room in the back."

Horace handed him a form to fill out, but Earl said, "I'll pay cash in the morning. And I need a car. Just a loaner for a few hours around sunup. I'll pay cash for that, too."

The motel owner managed to look dubious before something surprised him and his head whipped around.

"I might have one you could use. Kind of a junker, but it'd get you around. How much?"

"How's two hundred dollars sound?"

Horace agreed so quickly that Earl wished he'd only offered one hundred. Horace handed over some keys from beneath the counter.

"It's that gray Ford across the way there."

Earl peered across the parking lot at the car, which sported a dull finish of gray primer.

"That car hot?"

"No, man. It's mine. Registration's in the glove box."

"All right. I'll get it back to you by ten o'clock."

"My wife'll be here then. Leave the keys with her."

Earl shook Horace's hand.

"Thanks, brother. Appreciate it."

"No problem, Earl."

Earl turned and jingled through the door. No problem now, mother-fucker. Maybe big problems later when you got cops crawling all over this place, investigating three corpses in the rearmost room. Earl knew Horace would keep his mouth shut. And, by then, Earl and Horace's Ford would be far away, buying a new existence.

Earl felt John Ray's suspicious eyes on him as he walked around the Buick and climbed behind the wheel.

"Got us a room in the back," he said. "We can get some rest, figure out what we're gonna do next."

55

Liza West dumped her bag of loot on the bed with the others, certain nobody would be using the bed to rest. They were all long past tired, running on nervous energy.

John Ray paced the cramped room, measuring its dimensions with his long strides. Probably something he picked up in prison. Lowell still seemed thunderstruck. Earl worried her most. He stood just inside the door, looking like a man at an all-you-can-eat buffet.

Liza wished she had one of the guns they'd left back at her house. Not that she knew the first thing about shooting one, but it might help her peace of mind. John Ray and Earl both were packing the black pistols they'd taken off the Yips, and she feared someone would be shot before this long, terrible night ended.

"First thing we do," said Earl, "is split up Billy's share."

Something rose in Liza's throat. Splitting up the money meant opening the suitcases. She didn't want that. Not right now, when they all walked the razor's edge of panic.

"Split up his share?" she said quickly, trying to sound upset. It wasn't hard. "That's not fair, is it? How do we know he didn't get away?"

"Even if he did," Earl said, "he won't know how to find us. I don't know about you, but I plan to disappear pretty damned quick."

"I think we should try to find out," she said. "Maybe we can find him in a day or two."

"I'm not waiting around here that long."

"What about you, John Ray?" she said. "What do you think?"

"Billy Ho is the last thing on my mind right now."

"But maybe he got away."

"Maybe so. Who cares? Little shit's been lying to all of us since Day One. It's not our fault he's got the Yips after him. He almost got us all caught."

"Lowell?" She turned to her new beau, her eyes pleading, but he was no help. His huge brow knit in concentration, but it was clear he couldn't form an answer.

"It just doesn't seem fair," Liza said, crossing her arms over her chest.

"Aw, hell, let's not stand around here jawing all night," John Ray said. He stepped to the bed, leaned over the bags and began to unzip one.

Liza forced herself to look away, to look over at Earl with one last appeal. He was reaching behind his back, up under his shirt, and Liza knew what was coming next. She screamed, loud and long, a horror-movie scream that nearly peeled paint off the walls.

John Ray reacted. Without straightening from his position over the bed, he pivoted and lunged, just as Earl cleared his belt with the pistol and tried to bring it around.

The two men slammed against the door and fell into a writhing heap. John Ray managed to get hold of Earl's gun hand, and the black gun whipped back and forth as they struggled, threatening to spray the room with death.

"Lowell! Get down!"

Liza ducked behind the bed, peeking out while the men wrestled on the floor. John Ray was on top, trying to pry the gun from Earl's hand. Earl's other hand was pinned between their bodies, but he pulled it free and made a fist. The short punch caught John Ray in the ear, snapping his head sideways and forcing out an angry bellow. He shifted his weight and snapped one knee forward, trying to catch Earl between the legs.

Liza screamed as the gun went off, blowing a hole in the ceiling. White dust drifted down from the sheetrock and settled on the struggling men like quick snow.

Lowell took a step forward, ready to separate them, but she shouted, "Don't do it, Lowell! Stay back."

He made a sad, apologetic face as he said, "I can't. I've got to stop them."

John Ray adjusted his grip on the gun hand, getting hold of Earl's wrist and twisting it backward. He outmuscled the older man, and Earl's eyes got very wide as the gun barrel pointed back toward his face.

Lowell grabbed John Ray by the shoulder and tried to pull him off Earl while reaching for the pistol with his other hand. He grasped the barrel and pulled, trying to point it toward the ceiling, trying to twist it away from the others.

John Ray got his free hand on the gun and pushed with both hands, trying to keep the gun pointed at Earl. But Lowell was stronger, and the barrel began to climb, a centimeter at a time. Earl's mustache twitched as he grinned, began to relax.

Then the gun erupted and Earl's head exploded in a red mist.

Lowell threw his hands up and jumped back. Liza screamed. John Ray rolled off the bloodied man, gasping, his long face spattered with red.

"Shit," he said as he rolled up onto his knees.

Liza straightened from her hiding place and rushed to Lowell.

"Are you hurt?"

"I don't think so. I never can tell."

Her heart in her throat, Liza quickly looked him over, ran her hands over his chest. He was dotted with Earl's blood, but didn't seem to be leaking any of his own. She grabbed his big hands, turned them over to check the palms.

"You've got a big burn here."

"I do? Oh, that's a burn all right. Don't worry about it. It doesn't hurt."

Liza hugged him, then turned around to see what the pistol had wrought.

"Oh, my God."

The bullet had hit Earl in the left eye, leaving a bloody hole. The other eye was wide, staring at nothing. Blood poured from the back of his head, soaking the orange shag carpet.

John Ray, still on his knees, looked up at Lowell.

"Now look what you did."

"Me?"

"I had him. I was about to get the gun away from him. If you hadn't jumped in, he wouldn't be shot."

"I didn't mean—"

"Don't accuse him!" Liza screeched. "It's not his fault. You were the one who tackled him."

"And if I hadn't? Think you'd be alive right now?"

She felt a sob welling up within her and tried to fight it back.

John Ray shook his head. "Now what the hell we gonna do?"

Liza felt Lowell's strong arms wrap around her, felt him gently tug as he tried to turn her away from the sight of Earl's corpse. That's the fireman in him, she thought. Soothing the eyewitnesses, comforting the victims. She tried to push him away. She didn't want to be consoled. She wanted to get out of here.

John Ray got to his feet and pulled his own pistol free from his waistband.

"No," she said. "Don't."

"Settle down. I don't want to shoot you. Hell, I didn't want to shoot *him*."

He pointed at Earl, but Liza didn't look. What a mess.

"I'm just gonna take my money and get the fuck outta here," John Ray said.

He squatted next to Earl's body and felt the dead man's pockets while he kept the gun pointed at them.

"Earl made a mistake. Mistakes are costly. I hope you two can see that."

"We're not gonna do anything," Lowell said, and Liza knew that much was true.

John Ray found what he was looking for: Earl's car keys.

"There's another set of keys here. I think Earl got them from the motel guy. I saw him hand Earl something. Says 'Ford' on them. Probably to a car in the parking lot."

John Ray pitched the keys to Lowell, who loosened his hold on Liza to snatch them from the air.

"I'm taking Earl's car," John Ray said.

"I take it," Liza managed, "that we're parting company."

"The cops'll be here any minute. You can bet somebody reported those shots, even in this neighborhood. You better get the hell out of here and fast."

Liza pushed Lowell's arms away and took a step toward John Ray. The pistol swung round to greet her.

"What about the money?"

"Keep your shares. I've got more than I can carry here anyway."

John Ray grabbed up two bags with shoulder straps and slung one over each shoulder. He picked up another with his free hand. The pistol never strayed from their direction.

"I'm outta here."

He backed out the door, unsteady under the weight of all that money. The door banged shut behind him and Liza could hear his shoes clomping away. Then they heard the Buick's door slam.

"Should we go after him?" Lowell asked.

"Are you crazy? We're lucky he didn't shoot us already. We go out that door, we're dead for sure."

"We can't stay here."

"I know. Zip up that bag. I'll get the gun."

Liza heard the Buick's engine shudder to life outside the window. She crouched next to Earl's body, trying not to look at his bloody face, fighting down the bile that rose in her throat. His hand still gripped the pistol, and Liza had to peel his thick fingers away one at a time to get it free. She rubbed the gun on the carpet to get the blood off. Then she wobbled to her feet and turned to Lowell.

"Give me those keys."

Lowell handed them over, then picked up a bag in either hand.

"All right," she said. "Let's make a run for it."

56

Lowell stumbled out of the motel room behind Liza, marveling at her take-charge cool. She checked the parking lot, holding the pistol by her hip, then marched up the sidewalk toward the lobby.

The motel manager had come outside. He was a skinny black man whose head jerked to some unheard rhythm. Liza brought the gun up to point at his face. The manager spoke with surprising calm, considering he was shaking like he was on fire.

"You shoot Earl?"

"Not us," Liza said quickly.

"But somebody shot him?"

"He's dead."

"I figured. People been trying to pop that motherfucker for thirty years. When it finally happens, it has to be at *my* place of business."

She held up the keyring John Ray had given them.

"You know these keys?"

"Sure. I loaned 'em to Earl."

"They go to that car over there?"

The man hesitated, then said, "Yeah."

"Good. We're borrowing it."

"Earl said he'd give me two hundred bucks for it."

"Take it up with Earl."

The man blinked and twitched.

"Go back inside," Liza said. "And keep your hands on the counter."

The man gulped and followed orders, his head snapping back and forth like somebody trying to cross a busy street.

"You drive," she told Lowell. "I'll watch him."

Lowell tossed the bags in the trunk, got behind the wheel and cranked up the Ford. He backed it in a half-circle so Liza's door would be next to her. She jumped in, shouted, "Go!"

He roared around the back streets of Chula Vista for ten minutes before he spotted a sign that led to Interstate 5. He followed it north through Downtown San Diego, past the turnoff for the zoo, and switched to eastbound I-8. He and Liza said nothing as he drove. She sat very still, holding the pistol in her lap.

They were clear of the city before she sighed and put the pistol in the glove compartment. She slid across the seat to sit close to him. He put his beefy arm around her and she let her head fall back on it and closed her eyes. It wasn't long before Lowell's arm began to cramp, but he remained still. He'd saw off the arm and give it to Liza if he thought that was what she wanted.

Lowell imagined her waking beside him just as they pulled up to his home in T-or-C. He hoped Liza like the town. He hoped she liked the house. He hoped she continue to love him, even after the excitement and the fear were long past. They could make a happy life together. He couldn't wait for her to see it.

He just wished he'd had a chance to peel the plastic wrap off all his furniture first.

57

Kamal knew he and his men looked ridiculous, but it still was rude for the Americans to stare. The Yips hobbled through the airport in their ruined suits, drawing the attention of the crowds waiting for Saturday morning flights. Kamal and Fong led the team, each holding one of Billy Ho's elbows. Fong had big purple bruises on his forehead. Kulu walked close behind, looking like a swami in his turban of gauze. Serang and Lombok brought up the rear, one on crutches, the other with both arms in slings. Kamal knew he looked a sight himself, cuts and dried blood forming a road map on his face. Of all of them, only the pretender still seemed dapper and unscathed. But he was the one wearing handcuffs.

After Kamal fetched Lombok and Serang from the hospital, he'd considered just dumping the rental car and letting the Sultan's accountants settle up later. But the responsible thing to do was to turn it in, even though it meant marching through the main terminal.

Kamal really wished he'd dumped the car once he saw Omar Medulla Muhammed behind the counter.

"Yo, Jackie Chan, my man! Hoo, man, what happened to y'all? Looks like you been shot at and missed and shit at and hit."

It took Kamal a moment to sort that out, then he nodded wearily.

"That is exactly what happened."

"Get outta here, man. What's up, really? You guys look like you been to war."

Kamal shook his head and felt a tremor inside his ears. He wasn't looking forward to seventeen hours in a pressurized cabin, even if meant he might finally get some sleep.

"We just want to return the car. It is undamaged."

"Okay," Omar said, flashing his teeth. "That's cool."

He took the rental agreement Kamal handed him, but he still eyed the men.

"Why's that little dude got on handcuffs?"

"He is a very bad man."

"Don't look bad to me. Looks like a half-pint."

"I assure you, he is a full gallon of trouble."

"Say what?"

"Never mind. Just show me where to sign."

"Okay, Jackie, I'm punching it up here, man. Don't get your shorts in a knot."

I would like to tie your neck in a knot, Kamal thought. He watched as Omar's hands danced over the computer keyboard, but his mind drifted elsewhere. Soon it will be over. Soon I will be back in Yip where I belong. Very bad news to deliver to the Sultan, but at least I caught Prince Seri's killer.

Seri. He'd scarcely thought about his old friend in hours. He'd been too busy capturing Billy Ho, rounding up his men, getting to the airport. Now he had a long flight ahead, one that would be filled with sad thoughts of Seri.

"Okay, that's it, Jackie. Just sign right here."

Kamal picked up a pen and signed the form with a scrawl. The name he wrote was "Guillermo Ho." Let Omar explain that to his employers.

Kamal glanced back over his shoulder to make sure his men were in the formation of the Raging Stork. All was in order, despite the crutches and bandages. He gave them a quick nod, and they began the long trek to the plane.

58

Billy Ho looked down on the bay and the house-dotted hills of San Diego from the window of the royal jet. The higher the plane rose, the lower his spirits sank.

He sat by himself in a leather seat near the rear of the twelve-passenger plane. The seats swiveled, and the Yips all had pivoted on their own seats so they faced him as the jet soared out over open ocean. Five sets of unblinking, bloodshot eyes, daring him to make the wrong move.

He'd been so close! A fortune within his grasp. But the Yips ruined it for him. He'd lost everything in Coronado, all he'd worked for. The Armani suits, the Bruno Magli shoes and the red Mercedes all sat at the Hotel Del, waiting for somebody to wake up and realize he'd gone for good. By that time, he might very well be dead.

"Hey," he said to Kamal, who sat across the aisle.

"Yes?"

"I think I just remembered where the prince's body is. I mean, I think we could find it if we drove out that highway."

"Too late."

"No, really. Why don't we turn the plane around and go get it? Maybe the Sultan would go easier on me if we came back with the prince's body."

"No. We will send another team to recover the body."

"But I could take you right there!"

"You are going to Yip before anything else goes wrong."

"What could go wrong? We all go for a little drive in the desert—"

"Shut up now, please."

"Come on, give me a break here. You've got me cold, even though it *was* an accident. Maybe the Sultan would give me a lighter sentence if we—"

"There is no lighter sentence for killing royalty. If the Sultan decides you're guilty—and he will, I'll see to that—there is only one sentence under Yip law."

Billy gulped before he asked, "What is it?"

"Death, of course. But a slow death, one dictated by centuries of Yip history."

Billy glanced around at the others. The fat one was grinning.

"What is it?"

"The *Karangtabumi.*"

"The what?"

Kamal fingered the cuts on his forehead before answering. "I think it would translate to 'deep shit.'"

"What the hell are you talking about?"

"The Karang is the foulest place in the capital. For hundreds of years, ditches and drainpipes carried sewage downhill. It pools there, the lowest point in the city. It smells horrible and is full of dangerous germs, but it was all my people had. Without plumbing, you must depend on gravity."

"What's all this got to do with me?"

"We do not use the Karang anymore, of course," Kamal continued, and he sounded like he was leading a tour group. "With his riches, the Sultan built modern sewage plants as a gift to the people. But the Karang remains as a reminder of ancient law, a reminder of what happens to those who might slay the Royal Family."

"I don't get it. What does a sewer have to do with the law?"

The fat man laughed heartily until Kamal silenced him with a look.

"Under Yip law, an assassin is placed in a cage made of bamboo. The cage is on the end of a long pole. Executioners throw their weight onto the pole to raise the cage, then rotate it so the cage hangs over the Karang. Then they lower it into the shit."

Billy felt a sharp pain in his stomach. "And when this happens, when you lower the guy into this Karang, he's still alive?"

Kamal nodded somberly, but his eyes glittered.

"At first."

59

John Ray knew he was still strung-out because he was humming the theme to *Dragnet*. Earl's death had hit him hard. He didn't consider the shooting his fault—the son of a bitch had asked for it—but still his hands trembled and his eyelid twitched.

After he left the Dew Drop Inn, John Ray drove around Chula Vista for an hour, watching for police cruisers in his mirrors, formulating a plan. The first order of business was to wash Earl's blood off his face and shirt. Then he'd light out for Mexico.

He swung into an all-night truck stop alongside the interstate. He parked behind a darkened cattle truck and sat with his lights out for several minutes, making sure no one watched. Then he got out of the Buick and moved the bags of money to its big trunk. As much as he'd been through to get that money, he wasn't taking a chance that some opportunistic hoodlum might walk away with it.

His spattered black T-shirt was a lost cause, he recognized as he walked toward the convenience store that was built into the well-lit truck stop. He stripped off the shirt and stuffed it into a trash can, under some soiled newspapers, before he reached the door. The night air was brisk on his bare chest, but he paused a second to discard something else. He still had Billy Ho's wallet in his pocket, and that was a damning piece of evidence if ever there was one. He removed the thick pack of money from the wallet and stuffed it in his pocket. The rest—the eelskin wallet, the false IDs, the precious credit cards—went in the trash.

A gum-smacking woman behind the counter cocked an eyebrow at the sight of the shirtless man entering, but she said nothing. If she noticed the dots of dried blood on his face, she didn't let on. Probably nothing she hadn't seen before.

A couple of fat-ass truckers looked through a display of music cassettes, but the store otherwise was empty. John Ray went directly to the back wall, which was lined by a rack of souvenir T-shirts. He picked out a "Large" with a screaming Harley eagle on the front and took it to the cash register.

The beefy cashier shifted her gum to the other side of her face.

"Getting your clothes on the run, huh?"

"Spilled something all over the shirt I was wearing."

"Mm-hm." Uninterested. Heard it all before.

Next to the cash register was a stack of little rectangular boxes, each about the size of a pack of cigarettes, decorated with bright renderings of sports cars. John Ray noticed the one on top of the pyramid was a black Porsche Targa, just like the one he'd stolen from Dirk Brande, the car that had started his long journey through Folsom, to Coronado and, finally, to this truck stop where he stood bare-chested and bloodied, the bank haul waiting.

"Gimme a pack of Marlboros," John Ray said, "and I'll take this, too."

He picked the Porsche off the stack and set it on the counter next to the T-shirt.

"A gift?" she asked.

"Yeah."

"Boys love anything with wheels."

"Yeah."

The counter woman fetched the cigarettes and rang up the sale. She didn't bat an eye at the wad of money John Ray levered out of his pocket to pay her.

Outside, he yanked the tags off the shirt and slipped it over his head. Nowhere near as nice as the clothes Billy Ho had picked for him, but it would do the job until he could get into Mexico. He washed up in the men's room and then walked to the Buick. He lit a cigarette and climbed behind the wheel, tossing the toy car on the seat beside him.

He was on I-5, ripping along nicely, when the motorcycles appeared in his rear-view mirror. A dozen of them, in staggered formation, roaring up to his bumper, then swinging wide to pass. Bikers flashed by in a predawn blur of denim and leather and thunder. John Ray nearly drove off the shoulder as he fumbled under the seat for his pistol.

Jesus. Just when you think you've made it, here comes Big Odie after your fingers. But the motorcycles rumbled on until their taillights disappeared over a hill. He sighed and fell back in his seat. That wasn't Big Odie. Some other biker gang, tearing around the Southern California night, drunk and happy.

He wiped the sweat from his forehead. Christ, that'll wake you up. He wondered whether he'd have this reaction to motorcycle noise the rest of his life. He needed to get that money shipped off to Big Odie. Maybe then he'd be able to relax.

It was near dawn by the time he reached the border. He found that leaving the United States is a snap. No guards, nothing. Just drive up to the border crossing into Tijuana and rumble on across. The U.S. border authorities were concerned with traffic moving the other direction, trying to keep illegal goods and illegal drugs and illegal aliens from entering the good old U.S. of A. Nobody cared if you left.

On the other side of the border, though, traffic snarled at little lighted kiosks labeled "*ADUANA*." John Ray didn't speak Spanish, but he guessed that meant "Customs" or something like that. He could see ahead to where swarthy men in tan uniforms leaned into driver's faces to ask questions and check papers. Two cars ahead, a sunburned gringo in a Chevy Cavalier had been ordered out of his car to open the trunk. The officer peered inside briefly, then gave the florid motorist a freeing nod. The man bustled back behind the wheel and drove into Mexico.

The officer waved through the next car, but held up a hand as John Ray approached.

"*Buenos dias*," he said as he leaned over to peer into the car. "Welcome to Mexico. Would you please open the trunk?"

John Ray stiffened, but there was nothing he could do but cooperate. Not like he could swing the car around and try to shoot his way back into the United States. If that were possible, the wetbacks would've started doing it long ago. Anything to get across the border into Paradise.

He unfolded from behind the wheel and walked to the back of the Buick. The officer followed blithely, just doing his job.

Dammit, why does this little shit have to get curious now? John Ray had earned a vacation, but no one would let him rest.

He unlocked the trunk and let the lid rise. The Buick was in lousy condition, but naturally the light inside the trunk worked just fine. The officer peered at the three matching duffels.

"So much luggage. You must be planning a long stay."

"Not really. Coupla days. I don't like doing laundry."

The Mexican nodded, smiling, not listening.

"You would not mind if I opened the bags?"

"Go right ahead."

John Ray kept his hand on the trunk lid as the officer leaned inside and opened the U-shaped zipper of the nearest bag. Maybe he could slam the lid on the officer's head, shove him in there with the money, then drive away. Maybe no one would notice.

The officer lifted back the flap of the suitcase to reveal—a blue sweatshirt.

Oh, thank Jesus for Liza West. John Ray had forgotten her plan for concealing the money, but now he was overwhelmed with gratitude.

He tensed as the Mexican reached inside, grasped the sweatshirt and lifted it aside. Another sweatshirt, this one white, was folded neatly under it. The officer gave him a sidelong glance, checking for nervousness, but

John Ray gave him back impassive. The Mexican dropped the shirt back into the bag and politely zipped it closed.

"Okay, you may go," he said as he straightened up.

"That's it?"

"Yes. Thank you."

"Thank you!"

John Ray fought off the urge to hug the little man. He closed the trunk and returned to the driver's seat. As he put the key in the ignition, the Mexican called out from the doorway of his booth.

"*Senor?*"

John Ray's heart leaped. "Yes?"

"Enjoy your stay in Mexico."

He couldn't force up another word. He waved good-bye and drove into Tijuana.

John Ray had no idea where he was going. Away, that was all. Into Mexico, where it was less likely he'd be hunted and more likely he could buy his way out of any trouble. And where no one wanted to make a necklace out of his fingers.

He'd send Big Odie his money with no return address. Maybe once it was in hand, the biker chieftain would forget about retribution. John Ray had plans for the toy car, too. He'd mail it to Angel Flesch with a little note inside hinting at how he'd made a fortune. Let her wonder about that while she stroked her lawyer's toupee and waited for Hef to return her calls. Getting rich would be his revenge.

John Ray made his plans and tried to relax. He'd made good his escape. Close call there at the border. If that Mexican officer had dug any deeper under those shirts, he'd have found the banded decks of money stacked in there.

He hit the brakes suddenly, causing tires to squeal behind him. He took no notice. He had only this on his mind: How can there be so much room for sweatshirts if those bags are full of money?

He gunned the Buick into an alley, checked his mirrors and stopped. He doused the headlights and threw open the door, which swung with a bang into the nearest wall. He squeezed out and sidled to the rear of the car and unlocked the trunk.

John Ray unzipped the same bag the customs officer had searched, grabbed the sweatshirts and yanked them out of the way. The money was stacked neatly beneath. Whew.

"Okay," he said aloud. "Everything's all right."

He looked in the other two bags and found the same arrangement.

Money's still there, but it looked light. He looked around the alley to make sure no one watched. Somebody sees this much money here in Mexico, his life wouldn't be worth spit.

He leaned into the trunk and quickly counted decks of money in the first bag. Light. Way light. Maybe a hundred grand, a little less. And the others had about the same.

He zipped up the bags and slammed the trunk shut. His hands shook as he climbed behind the wheel and cranked up the Buick.

It was Liza. It must've been. He and the others left her alone with the money when they went off to the kitchen so Billy fucking Ho could mix the drinks. She'd put less than half the money in the suitcases. Nobody had noticed. They'd all been too busy watching their backs and escaping the Yips.

She'd made fools of them all. John Ray felt the hot bubble of rage swell within him, but there was nowhere to direct it except to whip the Buick through a vicious turn onto a shop-lined street, headed south.

He consoled himself with the thought that it was still a big pile of money, enough to set up a new life in Mexico, even after he mailed the twenty grand to Big Odie. He'd buy a little business of some kind, selling T-shirts to tourists, something like that. No more crime, no more craziness. He could get himself a house, a satellite dish out back to pick up Nick at Nite. Maybe even find a Mexican woman who expected the simple life, not furs and champagne and Hollywood parties.

The sun was up now, and the slanting light seemed filled with promise. John Ray hummed the theme from the *The Flintstones* while he lit a cigarette and rolled down the window to let the smoke escape.

He stopped for a red light. A toothless old man out for his morning constitutional shuffled across the street in front of the Buick, his back stooped and a Panama hat jaunty on his head. He gave John Ray a wary nod.

"*Buenos dias*," he called.

John Ray waved and shouted back, "Yabba-dabba-doo."

60

Liza West leaned her head against Lowell's muscular arm, letting him think she was asleep. She needed the quiet. She needed to think.

It all had happened so quickly. One day she straps on her high heels and goes down to the Hotel Del to meet her prince. A few days later, she's on the run in a hot car with a trunk full of stolen money, a gun in the glove compartment and a new lover at the wheel. And she's headed for New Mexico, a place she'd never thought to visit.

They could lie low there. Quietly put some of the cash in local banks, never enough at once to raise questions. Liza would need to write some checks pretty soon. Lot of unfinished business left behind in Coronado.

Once she was certain the police weren't onto her and Lowell, she could call a lawyer or a broker and get Flabric liquidated. She'd pay off whatever debts remained after the stock was sold off and the lease broken. Just get rid of it all.

She'd keep the house, though. Because underneath the trapdoor in the floor of her closet, half a million dollars sat wrapped up in a bedspread.

Liza had taken such a risk to get the money, she'd take no chances it would be discovered or stolen. She'd call somebody to make sure the house was locked up tight, the burglar alarm activated. Later, she'd go back for the money. Much later, though. Once she was sure there was no chance of getting caught.

She'd acted on impulse. She'd packed the bags mostly full while the men gathered in the kitchen. Then she realized the money wouldn't all fit in the five bags. She started to call to Lowell for more suitcases, but she caught herself. She stared down at the stacks of fresh bills for a long time. Then she leaped into action, moving the suitcases and wrapping up the rest of the money in the bedspread. It had been all she could do to drag the heavy sack of cash off the bed. The money made an alarming thump when it hit the floor, but the men had been laughing at some crack Billy made, and no one noticed a thing.

From there, it was easy to drag the money over to the closet and stuff it down the trapdoor. She put a new spread on the bed. Then she folded sweatshirts into the suitcases and zipped them up before strolling to the kitchen for their congratulatory cocktail.

She'd nearly been discovered at the motel, when John Ray began opening duffels to split up Billy's share. But Earl Shambley unknowingly helped her out, choosing that moment to go for his gun. Another minute, and she might've been the one bleeding to death on the ugly carpet.

The police no doubt had found Earl's body by now. That twitchy manager probably described Liza and Lowell and the car to the cops. Plus, Billy had escaped in her Volvo. If he was caught somewhere, the car would raise questions.

A lot remained unresolved. But she would figure a way to sew up the loose ends. She could invent a story to cover her disappearance. She'd think of something.

Once it was over, once she was sure she'd gotten away with it, she could relax. Stop being the practical one, the problem solver, the survivor. She might even let herself fall in love with Lowell. After all the years of striving and conniving, wouldn't that be the perfect reward? She no longer would pander to men. She'd let one take care of her.

Liza stirred from her thoughts as Lowell's big arm turned under her head. Poor baby. Probably stiff from being my pillow so long. She opened her eyes and sat up, stretching like a cat and overemphasizing a genuine yawn for Lowell's benefit. He dragged his arm out from behind her and dropped it into his lap.

"A good nap?"

"Yes. I feel much better."

Liza looked around. The land beside the highway was tan sand dotted with broomweed and shaggy Joshua trees.

"We're in the desert," she said.

"Yup. Afraid it all looks pretty much like this, all the way to T-or-C. No more ocean, no more palm trees."

"I don't mind. I was ready for a change."

"I've been thinking about that. Everybody thinks California is Paradise. They see it on TV and all. People come here from all over to make their fortunes. And here we are, driving away from it."

"But we've already made our fortune, Lowell. It's in the trunk, remember?"

"Yeah, but—"

"Let me tell you something, Lowell. California's nice, sure, but for everyone who hits it big, there's about a million who go nowhere. They end up living in the suburbs, going to work every day, watching TV. Just like people do anywhere else. Does that sound like paradise?"

Lowell's shelf of a brow furrowed. "But if you've got money, it's the place to be, right? Isn't that the American Dream? Get rich and live in California?"

"'The American Dream?' Boy, you've been thinking hard about this, haven't you?"

Lowell shrugged. "You were asleep. I needed something to keep me awake."

"You want me to drive awhile?"

"Naw, I'm fine. I was just worrying that you wouldn't be happy anywhere else. I could see a person getting spoiled by California. The Land of Plenty and all that."

"It's a land of dreamers and fools. A paradise for people who are kidding themselves. I won't miss it."

"T-or-C might seem pretty boring."

"Boring sounds good right now. I could use peace and quiet. If we need to amuse ourselves, we can always count our money."

Lowell hooted and threw his arm around her shoulders.

"That's right," he said. "We've got everything we need. Money and love."

"And that, my sweet man, is my definition of paradise."